HOLMES

VOLUME 1

Six short stories inspired by the works
of Sir Arthur Conan Doyle

MELVYN SMALL

Published in paperback in 2015 by Sixth Element Publishing
on behalf of Melvyn Small

First Edition

Sixth Element Publishing
Arthur Robinson House
13-14 The Green
Billingham TS23 1EU
Tel: 01642 360253
www.6epublishing.net

ISBN 978-1-908299-81-9

British Library Cataloguing in Publication Data. A catalogue record for this book is available from the British Library.

Printed in Great Britain.

Edited and proofread by:
Michael Richardson
Michael Streets
Richard Walker

www.melsmall.com

For the People's Republic of Teesside

Foreword

There I was, signing books in a glamorous location – WHSmiths in Stockton-on-Tees, I think it was, because I hang out at all the finest literary purveyors, me. And this fella came up and started asking me about how I go about writing books. I don't have much in the way of advice other than, "err... I sit down and I do it," which he took away like the golden nugget of wisdom it clearly is.

The next time I saw him, he'd produced all of these stories, like he was a proper writer. I was very impressed.

What he's achieved on these pages is both original and clever and somehow, typically Teessidey. What does that actually mean? If you're part of the Teesside tribe, you'll already know. If you're not, you'll have to read these stories to find out. But safe to say, they contain a lot of dry wit, dark humour and general arsiness.

Of course Sherlock Holmes wasn't a Teessider... or was he? With an inquiring mind, a refusal to bow to anyone, a life surrounded by crime and a penchant for strong drugs, that sounds very bloody Teessidey to me.

So pour yourself a big drink, settle down and find out just what Sherlock is doing hanging around the Boro.

Yeah, it turned out Mel really was a proper writer and a damn good writer too, as you're about to find out.

John Nicholson
Author of the Nick Guymer Mysteries
www.johnnicholsonwriter.com

VOLUME 1

A SCANDAL IN BORO

1

My first encounters with Holmes were that of doctor-patient. He had been found guilty of a litany of offences, from computer crime to drug abuse, and in sentencing, the judge had ordered him to attend addiction counselling sessions at my practice in Middlesbrough. These sessions with Holmes were actually amongst the easiest I'd ever given. He ceded any excuse for his various crimes and was fully prepared to atone in whatever way needed. His response to the therapy was considered, almost robotic in nature. He followed exactly where I led him, excepting the times where he seemed to get there before I did. If I were being honest, I found therapy in the sessions myself. The counselling of convicted criminals is not an activity I normally relish, and is something I only undertake out of a sense of duty to those poor souls less fortunate than myself. In the eyes of the law they were criminals, however in my view, in more cases than not, they were themselves the victims of sometimes horrendous circumstance.

I found the sessions with Holmes compelling. Indeed I often looked forward to them, firmly believing he and I were achieving some success in his reclamation. I can tell you, it was only sometime later that I realised the Holmes I encountered during those first few months, was obscured by disguise. He played the patient I wanted him to be, and he played him well. In retrospect, if anyone was under examination during that period, it was I.

Holmes was a strange creature of many contradictions. A little shorter than myself at about five feet eight inches, he had dark, often unkempt hair and would alternate between periods of being clean shaven and sporting scruffy stubble. He spoke in a very street, Teesside vernacular; however this failed to obscure an obvious intelligence. Whereas it's sometimes usual for people to attempt to be more articulate than their natural inclination, with Holmes the reverse was true.

The street vernacular also extended to his dress, his wardrobe having a distressed style and quality about it, with his favoured garment being a leather-yoked donkey jacket, invariably slung over the obligatory hoodie. Other than that it was jeans, a variety of training shoes and plain black, or sometimes grey, tee shirts.

When he finished his treatment and left, for what I thought was the last time I would see him, I missed him. Odd really, as I normally greeted the end of such programmes with relief. We moved in very different circles and it appeared unlikely our paths would cross again. It's funny but I missed him slouching into my surgery and taking up that peculiar seating position in the chair I have set out for my patients. He would observe a strange ritual each time he entered the office. First he would gain my visual acknowledgement that it was okay to hang his jacket on the coat hook. He would then place his hand on the back of the chair, requesting a further confirmation before sitting. Then he would sit, tight against the right-hand-side of the chair with his elbow gripping the chair arm. His eyes would survey the room, paying particular attention to the medical books stacked on my many bookshelves. Finally, he would fix me square in the eye and say, "What have you got for me this week, Doc?"

I saw him around town a lot following the conclusion of the sessions. He could often be found sitting in the window of one of the micro pubs on Baker Street or, of a morning, the Baker Street Kitchen on the corner with Albert Road. Always alone, he would gaze from the window, observing the passers-by intently as they struggled against the biting wind that stole in from over the

North Sea. I was tempted to join him on occasion, however I felt it inappropriate with him an ex-patient of mine, particularly a court-referred one.

I loved that area of the world, at the time just coming into its own. Historically a residential area of pre-war red brick terraced housing, the years had allowed it to descend into dereliction. Baker Street, and its parallel twin Bedford Street, connect two of the main roads of Middlesbrough. On one side there's Albert Road, an office-lined route to the university, with its estate agents, solicitors and so on. On the other, Linthorpe Road, a once busy shopping street that still retained some of its bustle.

The rejuvenation of the area served as testimony to the entrepreneurial spirit of the town. Elsewhere shops stood empty or were closing, however in our little Bohemia something new was created every month.

This rebirth had nothing to do with development corporations and government quangos, but rather local people willing to take a chance. The result was an eclectic mix of fashion boutiques, beauty parlours, tattoo studios, cafes and two excellent little pubs.

It was hard to think of a more appropriate environment for Holmes to inhabit. In the previous weeks, I'd been entertained by his curious view on matters, however I'd consigned my fascinating interactions with this strange animal to history.

Then one day I had a visit from two fairly robust American gentlemen. Rather unceremoniously they barged their way into my office before flashing identification cards, which quite frankly could have said anything. Introducing themselves as Agents Smith and Jones of the Federal Bureau of Investigation, they said they needed my help in a matter of national importance.

They asked me if I knew Sherlock Holmes, their pronunciation terrible and made worse by the sounding of the silent L in Holmes. I confirmed he had been a patient of mine, but that doctor-patient confidentiality prevented me from discussing him with them.

"We just need to find him, sir," said Smith.

"May I ask why?" I queried.

"As we said, sir, it's a matter of national importance."

"Whose nation?"

"Both our nations," snarled Jones.

"Well, gentlemen, he should be easy enough to track down. I see him around town most days."

"We don't know what he looks like."

"You don't have a photograph?"

"No, there isn't one," said Smith.

"The guy's like a ghost," appended Jones.

"Okay, gentleman," I conceded, "as it's a matter of 'national importance', for both our nations, I may be able to help. I have a copy of his mugshot on file."

With that, I located his record on my computer and pulled up the image I had stored. It wasn't him. In place of the photograph provided by the courts was an image of Juninho, a former player of the local football team, Middlesbrough FC.

"I'm sorry, gentlemen," I said, somewhat confused, "I seem to be having a few issues with my files."

"Just like I said, a ghost," repeated Jones.

Given that it was mid-afternoon, I figured the most likely location of Holmes would be a pub on Baker Street. As I led Smith and Jones through the streets, Smith explained how he expected some resistance from Holmes and that it would be helpful if I could speak to him first and get him "on side".

As we reached the first pub, Jones pulled me back and suggested he and Smith go in ahead. He asked me what drink people would normally order and I recommended a pint of the Engineer's Thumb, if it were still on tap.

I waited five or six minutes before following my newfound American friends into the bar. Fortuitously, Holmes was sitting in his usual place, the perfect vantage point for engaging in his favourite pastime of watching the world go by.

I walked up to the table where he was sitting and, figuring a light-hearted approach prudent, casually greeted him. "Hello, Sherlock."

"Hi, Doc. What's up?"

"Nothing really, I just thought I'd check on how you were doing."

"I'm good," he replied, "just sitting here watching the wheels turn."

"Are you still clean?" I queried, attempting some pretence.

"As clean as a baby's whistle," responded Holmes, the mixed metaphor somehow seeming to work.

I placed my hand on the back of one of the free chairs, raising my eyebrows to gain his acknowledgement to join him. He nodded in confirmation.

"I was wondering if you were ever gonna join me for a beer," he said before calling out to the barmaid, "Mary, a pint of the Engineer's Digit for my good friend the doctor."

"You have me down as an ale drinker?" I asked.

"Show me your right hand," replied Holmes. "See that curve in the resting position of your index finger? In lager drinkers, the curve is a little bit more pronounced due to it being served about six degrees lower in temperature."

"Really?" I exclaimed.

"No," he responded, in the deadpan delivery he'd used all through our counselling sessions, "they don't sell lager and everything else they've got on tap at the minute tastes like piss."

"Would you like me to bar you, Sherley?" threatened Mary, as she collected glasses from a nearby table.

Holmes scraped his chair around such that he sat square on to me. "It's nice to see you again, Doc, but did you really need to bring Bert and Ernie with you?"

"What do you mean?" I replied, feigning innocence.

"Those two suits at the bar. They're Bill. Looking at the creases in the backs of their jackets, I reckon they've been driving four, five hours, so up from London maybe, and the bitumen on their shoes must have been picked up from outside your gaff. It's the only place in town where any roadworks are going on at the minute. Also, the one on the right has a snag in his left trouser leg. He's been sitting in that crappy old chair you made me sit in. Oooh and those shoes. They ain't English shitkickers. They're American rozzers, aren't they? FBI? What the fuck are FBI gadgies doing in the Boro?"

"They need your help, Holmes. A matter of national importance they say." I gestured for them to join us.

Holmes rocked forward in his chair, suggesting he was interested. The two agents left their drinks on the bar and made their way to our table. Smith took a seat at the table whereas Jones sat slightly behind him, sitting the wrong way around on the chair, with his arms lain across the backrest. Holmes took umbrage to this and breathed some comment on how everything with Americans was a cliché. "Even the way they fucking sit."

Smith largely ignored this and began. "Mister Holmes, we need to make use of your, shall we say, peculiar talents to locate a media file."

"What talents are them, then?" queried Holmes.

"Your hacking talents," snarled Jones to the visible annoyance of Smith.

Holmes sat back in his chair. "I'm afraid I can't help you. The conditions of my parole forbid me from even owning a computer, let alone resuming my hobby as an ethical hacker."

"Don't worry. We can square that," assured Smith.

"Can you really, Gee Man? I'm not sure you or Toto here has realised, but this sure ain't Kansas."

"We have the full support of Scotland Yard."

Holmes pursed his lips and took in a breath to make a whistling sound. In a mock cockney accent, he retorted, "Oooh, Scotland Yard, governor."

Smith resumed, his tone taking on a more serious timbre. "Look, Holmes…"

"It's Mister Holmes."

"I've read your record and it makes for terrible reading."

"The grammar, you mean? That's not my fault, the coppers round here can't string two sentences together."

"No. I mean the computer crime, the drug abuse, the breaking and entering, the robbery. Do you want me to go on?"

"I was never convicted of robbery," appealed Holmes. "Well, apart from that one time, and that was fully justifiable. Probably less of a crime than the grammar in that file."

"That's hardly relevant," snapped Smith, struggling to maintain his composure.

"Here's the thing," continued Holmes, "they're only the crimes I was convicted of. There's quite a few not even in there. As a younger man, I was known to ride my bike on the path."

During his counselling sessions, Holmes had demonstrated a respectful reverence to the police. Given the contempt he was now showing for some serious law enforcement agents, I was starting to realise just how far I'd been taken for a ride. It was becoming apparent that, for all those weeks, Holmes had been pretty much telling me what he thought I wanted to hear. At the time, he had conceded that he'd "fought the law and the law had edged it", however I was by now of the opinion that he was struggling to find much grace in defeat.

"So this file," said Holmes, "I'm assuming it's scandalous in some way?"

"It is of a sensitive nature," confirmed Smith.

"A sex tape then? Who is it? Has Bonking Billy been at it again?"

"It has nothing to do with former President Clinton," snapped Agent Jones, who had remained silent for a while.

"Suffice to say," interjected Smith, "the contents of this file have the potential to unseat a rather important politician. If this were to happen, the impact could lead to destabilisation within both our governments."

At that point, the discussions were interrupted by a slightly-built woman with dark tangled hair crashing through the door of the pub.

"Sherlock," she screamed, "some bastard's done the shop."

Holmes sprang up from his chair and grabbed the woman by the shoulders to calm her. "It's okay, Martha, I'll sort it," he reassured her, before making for the door with her following closely.

Agent Smith called after him. "Hey, Holmes, we're in the middle of something here."

"Don't worry," he responded, "I'll be back," gesturing to Smith with a nod and reassuring point of the finger. "Hey, it's not him, is it? Arnie?"

2

Holmes and the woman, followed by myself and the two FBI agents, surged down Baker Street to a small fashion boutique at the opposite end. The boutique, called Hud Couture, had visible damage to the door, and the stock, largely consisting of what appeared to be antique second-hand clothing, was strewn across the floor in some disarray.

Holmes signalled to us all to wait outside and moved to make his way through the shop doorway. Before entering, he spun round and introduced us. "Doc, Martha Hudson. Martha, Doctor Watson."

The distressed Martha nodded an acknowledgement, which I returned. Holmes resumed his passage into the shop before spinning around again to address the two FBI agents, who had both drawn their handguns. "For fuck's sake, fellas, put your catapults away," he sighed with a tone of indignation.

Holmes entered the boutique, stopping just inside the doorway. Standing with his feet together and his hands in his jacket pockets, his eyes darted from side to side, occasionally accompanied by jerks of his neck. He scanned the room with a focused intensity, surveying not only the obvious areas of disruption but also areas of the shop that appeared untouched. He then became fixated by a pile of till receipts scattered on the floor near the counter. His intensity now replaced by exasperation, he walked over to the receipts and rummaged around in them, flicking them with the backs of his fingers before selecting one.

He returned to the doorway where Martha was standing, observing his actions.

"See that, Marth? Size six Nike Air Max 90," he said, presenting her with the receipt which had collected a footprint.

"That could be anyone, Sherley?" she queried.

"It could," said Holmes, "but these are snide. These buggers made their way to the People's Republic of Teesside from Hong Kong via e-fucking-whatdoyoucallit, I reckon. It's Bradley. I'll twat the little shite. You straighten up the shop. I've got a visit to make."

He then turned to address the FBI agents, who had by now holstered their weapons. "Oy, Butch, Sundance, back in the pub, hey? We don't need you two fuckers shooting up the place. I can handle this."

Holmes set off back up Baker Street in the opposite direction taking a hurried walk. On reaching the end of the road, he turned right down Linthorpe Road, heading towards the town. I followed, attempting to maintain a walk, however, given the speed he was moving, I occasionally needed to break into a jog to keep up with him. On reaching the bend in the road where Linthorpe Road turns into Grange Road and the pedestrianised shopping street starts, he gestured for me to wait and approached some hooded teenagers standing by the McDonald's. Following a short conversation, he beckoned me to follow him and we set off down the pedestrianised area alongside the Cleveland Centre shopping mall.

A hundred or so yards later, he ducked into Nobles Amusements. I made to follow him, but was almost knocked off my feet when a youth shot out of the arcade and back up the road in the direction from which we had just come. The youth, who appeared no older than fourteen years of age and around five foot four tall, was clearly our fugitive, Bradley.

Holmes re-emerged from the arcade with a look on his face that was half resignation and half self-disgust. He grimaced and set off after Bradley in a slowish yomp of a run which wasn't much faster than his previous walking speed. Bradley, who had left the arcade at some speed, was already out of sight by this point, however, Holmes seemed able to follow him as if on rails. We dived down alleyways behind the red-bricked terraced houses, scaled garden walls, always at the same plodding pace. Several times, we seemed to double back on ourselves and cover the same ground. Bradley wasn't apparently trying to get anywhere but away. Not once was he ever in our view.

Given my lack of confidence that Holmes was actually on the right trail, and that I had long since passed the point of exhaustion, I was on the verge of leaving Holmes to it when suddenly he skidded to a halt.

"Bradley," he shouted, "stand up, you little shite."

The youth rose slowly, emerging from behind a low garden wall, head bowed. Holmes grabbed him by the scruff of the neck, pulling him roughly over the wall. In the same motion, he drove his fist into the boy's abdomen.

"Holmes!" I exclaimed.

Holmes scowled at me and released him, letting him drop to the pavement.

"Did you really have to assault him like that?"

"When in Rome," he growled, "speak fucking Roman. It's the only language scroats like this understand. He'll thank me for it one day."

"No, I won't," responded the boy.

At this, Holmes shifted his feet, feinting to strike him again. Bradley, who was still sprawled in somewhat of a pile on the pavement, wrapped his arms across the top of his head to protect himself from a blow that never arrived.

After a short glare, Holmes stepped back, appearing to regain some composure as I tended to the boy to assess his condition.

"Take a look at him, Doc, and see if he'll live."

"I'm a psychologist, not a physician," I snapped back at him over my shoulder.

"Then show him some splodges of ink then," he sneered, his tone now settling from anger to regret.

A quick examination of Bradley suggested he was nothing more than winded. Once he had recovered his breath, Holmes frogmarched him back to Martha's. On occasions, Bradley slowed the pace in order to delay the fate awaiting him at our destination, however Holmes soon readjusted the velocity with a shove between the youth's shoulder blades. The steady progress of our return was only interrupted once when Holmes left me to look after our charge while he ducked inside the Sainsbury's Local on Linthorpe Road. It was clear that Bradley saw this as an opportunity to escape, however I managed to communicate the futility of any such bid with no more than an expression.

As we made our way back to Baker Street, I asked Holmes how he'd managed to locate Bradley in such a way.

Vermin like Bradley, he explained, have rat runs. Bradley in particular had about six, some of which intertwined. That Bradley knew his pursuer was Holmes ruled out Bradley's more favoured, and so well known routes, and the direction he set off in, scratched a couple more, the result being that only two or maybe three options remained. From then, explained Holmes, it was just a case of getting inside Bradley's head and emulating his decision-making. That was the simple bit, said Holmes, as Bradley's head wasn't a "particularly sophisticated decisioning engine". Clearly he'd made the wrong decision when he stole from Martha.

Holmes expanded by explaining how he thought 'people' to be generally predictable. They followed the same patterns, craved the comfort of routine and invariably repeated the same mistakes. "The wheels turn," he said, "but nothing much really changes. They still bump along on the same flat spots."

On our arrival back at the boutique, Holmes pushed Bradley through the door. The boy stood quite still, head bowed, in the middle of the store. Martha, who was still replacing and straightening the stock, made her way rapidly over to Bradley and cuffed him around the back of the neck. Her blow didn't contain any real malice or indeed any apparent force. However, though it was more for effect, in trying to avoid it, Bradley once again found himself on the floor.

"You do not shit on your own doorstep," she screamed, leaning over him and pointing. Holmes took hold of her by the upper arm and eased her away from the prostate youth.

"It's okay, Martha," he said. "Young Bradley and I have already had that conversation."

Bradley climbed back to his feet, his head cowered. With his eyes fixed to the carpet, he mumbled an apology to Martha.

"Right," said Martha, "where's me money?"

Bradley put his hands in both pockets of his hoodie and pulled out handfuls of crumpled banknotes. Martha nodded her head towards the counter and the youth slunk over to deliver his haul to the counter surface, attempting to straighten the notes in the process.

"How much is missing?" asked Martha, her tone beginning to soften.

"About fifty," responded the youth.

Martha sighed. "Right, you're gonna clean this shop from top to bottom. I'll decide when you've done fifty-quid's worth. Got that, Zero Hours?"

"Yes, Martha," replied Bradley, seemingly buoyed by the leniency of his sentence.

"Missus Hudson," she exclaimed.

"Yes, Missus Hudson," chimed the boy.

His relief was short-lived.

"Then," continued Martha, "you're gonna take some black bags down to the Bottle in front of MIMA and clean up any shit that scum like you have left lying around there."

"I'm not doing that, like," he protested.

Martha flashed a look of inevitability.

"Okay," he conceded, realising his appeal futile.

3

When we returned to the pub, Agents Smith and Jones were sitting at the table Holmes and I had occupied earlier, their drinks still showing little sign of consumption. The only thing that had apparently changed was that Jones now had an aluminium briefcase on the floor next to his chair. Given their earlier demonstration of arms, the thought struck me that the case may be the container for a high-powered sniper rifle or similar.

Holmes sat between them and pulled a bottle of Budweiser from each of his jacket pockets, placing one in front of each American.

"What were you saying, gentlemen? You need the assistance of my unique computing talents to protect the reputation of both our nations from some shocking scandal? You know, the ones gained through the course of my ethical hacking pursuits."

Smith shaped to respond but was interrupted by Holmes. "I'm hungry. Come on boys, let's go grab a parmo. Mary's Scotch eggs have been on the bar since the owld queen was in hot pants and I'm starving."

If you haven't had the pleasure of a parmo before, or a parmesan to give it its full name, it is a delicacy somewhat peculiar to the takeaways and restaurants of Teesside. It consists of a deep-fried breaded chicken or pork cutlet, topped with a white béchamel sauce and cheese. Each serving contains enough calories to retire several supermodels. There are rumours of a vegetarian version, however I myself have never come across such a thing, and assume this something of an urban myth.

Holmes swept out of the pub and back along Baker Street to its junction with Linthorpe Road, where he flagged a black cab.

"Cafe Central Park, pal," he instructed the driver.

It was a short journey, of perhaps only five minutes, elongated by an uncomfortable silence as Holmes and I sat facing forward with the two agents sitting opposite us in the suicide seats. Not that Holmes appeared particularly aware of any awkwardness, as he stared vacantly out the side window.

On reaching the restaurant, Holmes waved over the waiter. "Alright, Charlie, how's it going, my mate? Four Chicken Parmos, a Peroni each for me and the good Doctor, and a couple of Budweisers for Chandler and Joey here."

"I'll have a Peroni," said Smith.

"Me too," added Jones.

"Okay," said Holmes, "four Peronis it is, then. I hope you fellas are on expenses, we're drinking like bloody lottery winners."

Holmes then turned his attention to Jones' aluminium briefcase. "If you don't mind me asking, Butch, what's in the suitcase? Has your mam packed you some sandwiches and a yoghurt?"

Agent Jones placed the case on the table and clicked open the latches. He then took out an Apple laptop, closed the lid and laid the laptop on top of it.

"This is for you. Temporarily. It contains the FBI's most advanced hacking software. All you require to locate the file we need is located in this box."

Holmes picked up the laptop and smelled it before rubbing the lid against the side of his face. "Oooh baby, I've missed you," he mumbled in a mock-seductive tone. "What's that? You've missed me too? No, don't," he said before emitting a sexually suggestive giggle.

Smith and Jones gauged each other's opinion on this behaviour, each with a wary look of worry. Holmes then flipped open the laptop screen and drummed his fingers impatiently on the area under the keyboard whilst it ran through its start-up routine.

"What details do you have of the file?" asked Holmes.

Smith passed him a scrap of paper.

"Timestamp and file size. That might do it. No promises but give us a bell in, say twenty-four hours and I'll tell you how we're getting along."

"We're sticking with you," snarled Jones. "That file is sensitive. We can't have you making a copy."

"No, you're not," replied Holmes. "If you want this file, you're gonna have to leave me to it. That's non-negotiable. Doc, can you give one of the guys your digits? I'm not allowed a phone."

Jones looked to Smith who nodded his acceptance.

"You see," elaborated Holmes, "a phone is essentially a little computer and I'm banned from using computers. Did you know the iPhone 6 has more processing power than the whole of, well, the iPhone 5? It's something to do with a gadgie called Moore. Alan, maybe?"

"Okay," said Smith, "we need to find a decent hotel."

"Good luck with that," retorted Holmes before rising from his chair.

Jones opened up the briefcase and offered it to Holmes.

"I don't need the box," said Holmes. "You keep it for your sandwiches. Do you have sandwiches in America?" He then tucked the laptop under his arm, told the Americans to enjoy their food and left, with me following in close tow.

We set off back to Baker Street on foot. A few hundred yards down Linthorpe Road, Holmes stopped to help an old lady lift her shopping trolley bag on to the bus. When he rejoined me, the laptop was gone.

"Where's the laptop, Sherlock?"

"Good question, Doc. I seem to have misplaced it. Never mind, the software it had on it was shit. Would have taken me about fifty years to rewrite. And besides, I don't think the Fun Boy Two would have let us out of their sight so easily if their shiny new laptop didn't contain a shiny new tracking device. No worries, Doc, we have a plan A."

4

On our return to Baker Street, Holmes walked past Hud Couture, where I assumed he was heading, and pulled out a key to unlock the next door.

"This is my place, Doc. Chez Sherlock, Home de Holmes, 22 Baker Street, Flat 1B. Well, it's Martha's really but she lets me stay here and in return I look after the shop from time to time. Oh, I also sleep with her occasionally just to keep the rent down, but don't tell her I told you that."

"You should make an honest woman of her," I replied, not really believing him.

He turned to face me. "Doc, Martha's hung up on her ex. At the end, there's always someone left standing at the station, and unfortunately for Martha, in this case, it's her."

Flat 1B was a mess. Unlike anything you'll have ever seen. There were numerous bookcases jam-packed with books and newspapers piled from floor to ceiling.

"You have a lot of books, Sherlock," I called to Holmes who was rummaging around in another room.

"Yeah, Doc," he shouted. "I really must get round to reading a few of them sometime."

Holmes reappeared with a laptop computer. He opened it up and pointed the screen in my direction as it started to boot up.

"Plan A?" I asked.

"Plan A," he confirmed. Once the laptop had started up, Holmes began tapping furiously on the keyboard. Slumped on an old settee, his industry was apparent. Occasionally there was a sigh and the odd groan but the prominent sound was the rapid percussion of his fingers on the keys. While he worked, I wandered around the flat. I was trying not to interrupt but occasionally boredom got the better of me.

"I never knew you lived here, Holmes."

"Yep," he replied. "I have done for ages. Landlords tend not to like renting to convicted criminals, even if they are mostly innocent."

"Can I ask you something?"

"Of course, Doc."

"Did you interfere with the files I had on you on the PC in my surgery?"

"No, Doc, that would have been a violation of my probation which would have sent me back to Holme House or behind some equally unappealing iron bars. Of course," he continued, "they would have had to catch me first."

"You were caught before," I reminded him.

"I allowed that to happen, Doc, so I could meet you."

I was rapidly forming the opinion that my conversations with Holmes would invariably peter out in the same manner.

I ducked inside the kitchen which was filled with numerous glass flasks that would be more at place in a chemistry lab.

"Holmes, your kitchen looks like a meth lab."

"Don't worry, Doc," he said frustratedly, "I'm not cooking gear. I was just looking into giving that Eston Blooming-bloke a run for his money. Right, that's that."

I re-entered the room to find him reclined back on the settee with his legs crossed. The laptop was whirring away, perched on a pile of books.

"You've found the file?" I asked.

"No," he said, "but the game is now afoot. Well, eleven and a half inches at least. I've created what you might call a virus, a friendly virus, a bit like those good bacteria in the advert. This is now winging its way around the internet looking for our file."

"How long will it take?"

"A while," he replied. "We're trying to find a turd in a shitstorm."

"So what now?"

"The pub. My little nano twats can do their thing, while we party like it's nineteen ninety-eight."

As we made our way back to the Twisted Lip, a worrying thought struck me. I had stood by and watched someone create an internet virus. Does that make me an accessory?

"Holmes," I queried, "this virus? Is creating something like that entirely legal?"

"Entirely legal?" he puzzled. "No, Doc, I would say it's entirely il-fucking-legal. Don't worry though, it's only really an issue if you get caught. Here's the thing, nine times out of ten you only go to prison if you are caught."

Whilst in the pub, I got an angry call from Smith. Jones and he had spent the last couple of hours trailing the number 4 bus the seventeen or so miles to Loftus.

"Ask them if they enjoyed their parmos," called Holmes as I did my best to placate Smith.

We returned to Flat 1B around three or four hours later a little worse for wear.

"Hi Sherl, where have you been?" called Martha. "Just to let you know, I've hidden your stash again."

"She means porn not drugs, my dear Doctor Watson," Holmes

called out in a voice louder than I needed and loud enough for Martha also to hear. "I'm not allowed a computer so I've had to go a bit retro when it comes to porn," he continued at the same volume. "Martha doesn't like me looking at other women naked. Even ones with staples through their belly buttons. She'd much rather put on a show herself."

"You wish," shouted Martha in response.

We climbed to the top of the stairs to find the laptop still whirring away and Martha sitting on the settee Holmes was using earlier. She appeared to be adjusting her clothing but stopped as I entered the room. Holmes slumped on the settee beside her.

"A cuppa tea, Doc? It doesn't look like those little nano fuckers have turned up anything just yet."

Given the intimate positioning Holmes assumed next to Martha on the settee, I made my excuses and suggested we meet back in there the following afternoon.

5

After working through a number of particularly dull patients, I returned to the flat at three the next day to find Holmes sitting on the settee eating cereal. He glanced up to welcome me, however his focus was firmly on the laptop still working away.

"Breakfast?" I asked.

"Lunch," he responded.

"Cereal?"

"Easy to cook."

"Heston Blumenthal must be boarding up his windows as we speak."

Holmes scowled a look of confusion at me. For once, it appeared I had come out of an exchange slightly ahead.

As Holmes remained transfixed on the laptop, I kicked around the flat looking for some distraction. There must have been over a thousand books piled here and jammed there. There were books on an eclectic range of subjects: Greek history, physiology, project management, the Great War, witchcraft and even the husbandry of earthworms. One book I noticed of particular relevance to myself concerned the subject of cognitive dissonance. The word 'bollocks' was written across its cover in thick black pen.

"How confident are you that you will actually find this file?" I asked.

"Pretty confident," mumbled Holmes, still transfixed on the apparently meaningless output of the laptop screen.

"So you have your doubts, then?"

"No," he responded curiously, "a doubt is just faith in disappointment."

"Oscar Wilde?" I queried.

"The Bluetones," he clarified.

I sat down on the other end of the settee feeling at a bit of a loose end. Among the numerous books, there was nothing that struck me as useful in providing entertainment or diversion. In fact, the whole flat seemed noticeably void of pleasure or leisure, save for an acoustic guitar propped up by the fireplace.

Given the age and distress of the settee, it was surprisingly comfortable. The hypnotic whirring of the computer and the eventual cessation of Holmes' tumultuous cereal consumption had the combined effect of allowing me to drift into a shallow slumber.

I was jolted out of my doze by the ringing of my phone. It was Smith. Sounding somewhat angry and irate, he asked if we'd made any progress. I referred the question to Holmes. Holmes glanced up from his laptop which was now sitting on his knee.

"Tell him to fuck off," came the response.

"Holmes says he's making good progress and is expecting a breakthrough very soon," I recast. "Smith says you have twenty-four hours."

Holmes' frustration level now seemed to be reaching parity with that of Smith.

"Tell him to stop twisting my fucking melons, man. I've got the whole of the fucking filthanet to search. I'm boiling the ocean here, not a fucking egg," he sneered.

I translated. "He says things are going very well but he is going to need a little more time."

"Twenty-four hours," ordered Smith.

I relayed this to Holmes.

"Tell him to fuck off," came the response.

"He says he's taken that on board and he'll do his best," I replied, before returning to Holmes. "Smith says he understood you to be some sort of expert and if he finds out you're stringing him along, he won't rest until 'you're in a very small prison cell for a very long time'."

"Tell him to still fuck off. In fact, tell him to fuck further off."

"He thanks you for the feedback, Agent Smith, and says we'll get in touch as soon as we have a breakthrough."

I ended the call and looked to Holmes. His mood had transitioned from one of frustration to one of pensiveness.

"No luck?" I asked.

"No luck, no," he responded, "but I've found the file. The pisser is it's only up the road. Looks like some big gaff on Wynyard. I was hoping for a bit of a jolly on Bert and Ernie's corporate Amex."

Holmes explained how he had narrowed the location at which the file was downloaded to a street in Wynyard. He said a quick trip up there and he would be able to determine the exact house from the name of the router that was used. I complimented him on how clever I thought that was, but was firmly rebuked.

"Not really," he said. "All I've done is cobble together other people's ideas. That's pretty much all I ever do. There's a big difference between knowledge and intelligence. The universities are full of people with knowledge, but few of them are able to apply it with any intelligence. Take a working single mother with a couple of jobs and a couple of kids to look after. Someone who's constantly having to adapt to balance both her time and her money. That's where you'll find the real intelligence. I couldn't do that."

Holmes then provided me with some instructions. I was to go and get some old boots or training shoes, footwear befitting of a tradesman, and meet him down in Martha's in about an hour.

Meanwhile he had a "few bits and bobs" to arrange. I queried the legality of what he had planned and he assured me that what he had in mind wasn't illegal, and perhaps as much as ninety-five percent legal. He then quelled my concern by pointing out we were working for "the man".

I bade my goodbye and made my way down the stairs of the flat and along Baker Street, before then heading against the wind blowing down Albert Road, opposite to the direction to my travel back to the surgery.

It doesn't actually rain that much in Middlesbrough, precipitation heading over from the west tending to get tipped out over the Pennines en route and leaving the area in somewhat of a rain shadow. It would perhaps be idyllic, if it were not for the super-chilled wind burning in from over the North Sea in the other direction.

There's a spot in town where Albert Road crosses Corporation Road, near where the Madison Night Club or Claggy Mat used to be. I'm sure that on some occasions that spot is the windiest place on the planet. I've known it so bad on some days that people trying to cross the junction diagonally have been gusted to an unintended destination.

My plan on reaching the surgery was to grab my old squash shoes from the sports bag I'd thrown in the makeshift storeroom. As I hurried my way there, I suddenly felt a grab on my arm and a thud to my left shoulder. Before I could comprehend what was happening, my face was jammed into the masonry of a building wall.

I recognised the voice immediately.

"Hello, Doctor." It was Agent Jones talking in his most menacing whisper.

Smith took over. "You see, Doctor, Agent Jones and myself are getting a little frustrated at the apparent lack of progress Holmes is making. All the evidence is suggesting that the scruffy little hobo is jerking us off. We need you to take us to him in order that we can restate our objective. We need that file and we need it yesterday."

With my face pressed against the wall, I could see along the street. Holmes was running towards us at some pace. I froze, my lack of a response causing Jones to pull me away from the wall before crashing me back into it. As he did, Holmes skidded in taking out both Smith and Jones by the ankles, the three of us ending up in a pile of arms and legs. We regained our cognisance and clambered to our feet to find Holmes sitting with his back against the base of a signpost, a pistol in each hand trained on Smith and Jones respectively. The two agents hurriedly checked inside their jackets. Somehow, in the manoeuvre that had sent us crashing to the ground, Holmes had relieved them of their firearms.

He addressed them in a calm and deliberate tone. "Be very careful where you take this. Remember this is an away match for you. The people around here are really friendly, but there are some of them who can be persuaded to dislike outsiders. Especially you, Jones, no fucker likes the Welsh."

Jones looked more puzzled than concerned.

"You'll have the file in twenty-four hours. So you two prize pricks go and synchronise your watches, or do whatever the fuck you do, because if I set eyes on you before this time tomorrow, this shit will end quicker than the ninety-seven cup final. Capeesh?"

After a short pause to consider his options, Smith nodded and Holmes directed his attention to Jones. "Ca-fucking-peesh?"

Jones looked to Smith before responding with a sharp nod.

Holmes and I strode away up Albert Road. After about ten to fifteen yards, Holmes took the recently acquired sidearms from his coat pockets and, under the pretence he was fastening a shoelace, dropped them down a drainage gully.

"Who taught you that move?" I asked.

"Graeme Souness," he responded.

I stood in Hud Couture, squash trainers in hand, failing miserably to make small talk with Martha. Martha effused a raw sexuality, the result being I tended to feel a little uncomfortable in her presence, especially when there were only the two of us there. Although perhaps jaded a little by life, she had an underlying beauty and the confidence that goes with it. Her eyes were knowing and captivating, and made you feel that many of her thoughts were well-retained.

Aware of my nervousness, she exploited her effect still further, stalking round me panther-like. In an attempt to break the moment, I turned to rummage through the clothing hanging on a nearby rack.

"We also have those in a ten if you are interested," she purred.

I jumped back and stuttered something, my face flushing on realising I was thumbing through a selection of women's party dresses.

Our brief pasodoble was curtailed by the sound of a van bouncing up Baker Street. We both stepped to the window to see Holmes at the wheel of a British Gas van which he kangarooed to a halt just short of the shop.

"That man really needs a driving lesson," muttered Martha before turning away.

"Hi-Tec Squash," commented Holmes as he entered the shop. "Classics. I used to have a pair of those when they were still made by Inter." Turning to Martha, he asked her if she'd got the gear he'd told her about earlier.

"I sell high class couture," snapped Martha. "I haven't a clue what the well-dressed gas fitter is wearing this season."

"We don't have time to dance, babe," replied Holmes. "Those two good ole boys tried to remodel Albert Road with the Doc's face earlier."

Martha exhaled a short nasal sigh before retrieving a pile of blue clothing from below the counter. Holmes split the pile, threw half of it in my direction and started to change into the remainder in the middle of the shop.

"Come on, Doc, don't be shy," he said, gesturing for me to follow suit.

Martha leaned against the side of the counter, watching us both change. "It's usually me taking my clothes off for the doctor," she pouted, "not the other way around. Oh Doc, do you not iron your boxers?"

As we left the shop, Holmes handed me the keys to the van suggesting it might be better if I did the driving. As I drove us to Wynyard, Holmes explained my role in the escapade. He would identify the house using the signal from the router, then it would be my job to sneak around the back and spray a substance called mercaptan in an open window, mercaptan being the foul smelling substance they put in the otherwise odourless natural gas in order that leaks can be detected.

While I was engaged in this nefarious task, Holmes' self-assignment was the seemingly more simple and less risky activity of knocking door to door on the houses opposite. Holmes assured me that this was where the real skill lay.

As we approached our destination, Holmes asked me if he could borrow my phone to identify the router signal. I started to pass it to him and then, remembering I needed to unlock the screen, I attempted to withdraw it. Before I had chance, Holmes slid it from my grasp, flashing me a headshake of disappointment. He then angled the phone slightly such that the light reflected across its screen before tapping in my PIN number.

"There hasn't been a PIN number invented that can stop me," he muttered.

We trundled the van slowly up the road until Holmes signalled for me to stop.

"This'll do, Doc," he said, tapping his knuckles on the windscreen.

I pulled over the van, parking it two wheels on the kerb.

"Right, Doc, if my estimate, based on the information provided by your hopelessly out of date smartphone, is correct, the treasure we seek is in that there house. Number Eleven. Do you remember your instructions?"

"Yes," I muttered, as feelings of trepidation and excitement jostled for position inside me. Holmes stared back at me seemingly nonplussed by my agitated state.

I picked up the can of mercaptan and shaped to exit the van. Holmes grabbed my shoulder and gave it a gentle tug.

"Hang on, my mate," he said. "Let me go bang on a few doors, create a bit of a diversion." With that, he jumped from the passenger seat and grabbed a canvas tool bag from the rear of the van. Returning to the side of the van where I was sitting, he gestured for me to wind down the window. As I did, he whispered through the opening, his lips half pursed, "If there's a big bastard of a hound round there, run like fuck. At least, that's what I would do. I'm happy enough for you to improvise that bit."

I watched him through the wing mirror as he made for a house about twenty yards away, on the same side of the street as we'd parked. The tension fizzed through me such that I couldn't move my legs. The act I was about to engage in seemed incredibly trivial, but the trepidation I felt was palpable. There I was, a grown man frozen to the seat with my heart racing like a sewing machine. I looked at the clock on the dash. It was a minute past the hour. I felt I needed to wait until at least ten past.

I'm not actually sure what time the clock reached. I don't even recall making a deliberate decision to initiate my task. It was quite involuntary. I jumped down from the seat, my knees buckling slightly as I hit the pavement, and then headed up the road in the opposite direction to Holmes. After four or five houses, I crossed over and made my way back down the other side of the street.

On reaching Number Eleven, now from the opposite end of the street to which the van was parked, I hopped across the lawn and down the side of the house. I was certain that my flagitious activity had been observed. Fortunately, the worry of possible discovery distracted me from previous concerns regarding a snarling guard dog.

I slipped around the back of the house, fortuitously discovering an open window. My heart was pounding so hard I imagined it audible. "Calm down," I told myself in a whisper. This was hardly the most criminal of activities, and yet I was beside myself.

Sitting below the window, and therefore out of sight from any occupants, I started to empty the contents of the mercaptan can in through the open window. In order to limit the noise of the gas evacuating the can, I kept the nozzle only half pressed. It seemed to take an absolute age to get to the point where the can was starting to feel empty.

I slipped back down the side of the house and made my way back to the street. As I rounded the corner of the building, I saw Holmes by the van talking to a young woman. She was dressed in a navy blue vest with light grey cycling shorts, and appeared to be discussing the house I'd just reappeared from behind. From what I could tell from Holmes' body language, he was trying to reassure her. As I got nearer, I was taken by the intensity of her beauty. She was slim and athletic with beautiful flowing dark hair and hypnotic deep brown eyes.

As I approached to address them, Holmes spoke to me. "John, this is Missus Adler, she has smelt some gas. Probably the leak one of the neighbours reported. We need to get in there and investigate."

"Miss Adler," the woman corrected. "Irene," she said, holding her hand out for me to shake.

"Usual drill," said Holmes.

"Okay," I responded, not having the faintest clue what the 'usual drill' was.

I think that was the first of the very few times Holmes referred to me by my Christian name. I wasn't sure how he even knew it.

Holmes turned to Irene, suggesting it would be safer if she stayed behind the van. He then handed me the tool bag and we set off towards the house.

7

In the months I had spent as Holmes' psychotherapist, and in the day or so since the beginning of this little excursion, I don't think I had ever once seen Holmes smile. However, as soon as he entered Adler's house, his face sparkled, a strange knowing smirk drawing itself across his face.

"This is not her place, Doc. She's squatting. The little minx is living rent-free in one of the nicest gaffs on Teesside. Ah," he exuded, "that's better than warm undies. Straight off the radiator."

I couldn't let this new mood pass without comment. "Sherlock, I've never seen you so ebullient."

"I don't know what that means, Doc, but you might be right. Okay, you start upstairs."

"What are we looking for?" I asked. "Something the file might be stored on?"

"Nothing really," replied Holmes, "I just want a mooch around, maybe have a look in her knicker drawer. I just need to get to understand her. You start upstairs. Open a few windows and let the smell of gas out."

As I moved to climb the staircase, Holmes called me back. "The file won't be in here. In a panic scenario, like the one you've just created, people will grab the things most important to them. Given that this file is so interesting to the feds, it must be pretty high up on her list of priorities too. I think it's safe to assume she has whatever the file is stored on with her now."

I rooted around upstairs, opening windows and avoiding the temptation to "look in her knicker drawer". It was a very nice house. What an estate agent might call 'beautifully presented'. I could now see what Holmes meant. I'm not sure I would have noticed it had he not pointed it out, but the decor just didn't seem in keeping with someone of Irene's age and attire.

I returned to the ground floor to find Holmes standing motionless in the kitchen.

"Can you pass me something metal out the tool bag?" he asked.

"Anything in particular?" I queried.

"Nah, it doesn't matter."

I handed him an adjustable spanner and he walked over to the water boiler and rattled the spanner around its casing and up inside its workings. "Might as well make it look as if we've done some work."

As we made our exit, we came across Irene making her way back into the house.

"Hi, Miss Adler," said Holmes. "We've located the issue and made a repair. A connection had worked itself loose in your boiler. It's a common problem. When was the last time the boiler was serviced?"

"Erm, I'm not sure," stuttered Irene.

"Okay," replied Holmes, "you should have no further issues, but I would strongly recommend you look into one of our service plans. There are details on the website."

"Okay," she agreed, "I'll have a look."

Turning to me, Holmes gestured towards where the van was parked. "Can you saddle up the horses, John? I just want to have a word with Miss Adler here."

A few minutes later, he re-joined me in the van, issuing me with instructions as he climbed into his seat beside me. "Okay, Doc, I need you to get in touch with Detective Inspector Lestrade of Cleveland Police. Ring 999. That should get him."

"I know him," I interrupted.

"Even better," replied Holmes. "Explain all this guff about the yanks and national security, yada, yada, and that we need his help in getting the file back. We need him around Irene's place early doors tomorrow, say six o'clock, with a couple of dozen pairs of shiny boots and an accompanying set of rozzers."

I commented that I was a little surprised that Holmes was reaching out for the help of the police.

"Yeah, I know," sighed Holmes. "Normally I wouldn't set fire to Lestrade to warm frostbite off me bollocks, but we need his help. I think this Irene bird's gonna be a bit lively. We need to block the escape routes. Tell him if he's a good boy, I'll let him arrest me later. He likes that."

Confused, I asked him if he therefore knew where the file was.

"I'm not sure yet," he said. "I'll find that out tonight."

Confused still further, I asked him what was happening tonight.

"I'm going out," he grinned, "on a date, with Irene, that pretty young thing you've just tried to gas."

"How did that happen? Surely a woman of that class was not seduced by a scruffy gas fitter?"

Holmes feigned some indignation. "Scruffy?" he retorted.

"I was going for a cheeky confessions of a gas fitter type thing. Anyway, I think it's little to do with my powers of seduction and more to do with us being rumbled. It must have been your shoes that tipped her off, Doc. She wants to find out more about us too."

"My shoes," I protested. "Two hours ago you thought they were the bee's knees."

"Yep," said Holmes. "Clearly I was dazzled by your retro chic, however the lovely Irene wasn't so easily deceived, ya trendy get."

On our arrival back in Middlesbrough, we parked the van in the Bedford Street car park, opposite O'Connell's Irish bar. I did suggest we returned the van to the gas board, however Holmes said it would probably be better if we left them to find it. As a consequence, I wondered how strong a defence of ignorance was in the case of taking a vehicle without the owner's consent. In the space of a day, I reckoned I'd broken the law at least three times.

Holmes jumped down from the van and cantered down Bedford Street. He then rounded into Baker Street where he ducked into Martha's boutique. I followed hot on his heels, wanting to distance myself from the van.

Martha was busy rearranging the stock as Holmes crashed through the door. Her look was a cocktail of annoyance and confusion.

"What the…" she winced, before being interrupted by Holmes.

"Martha, I need some gear. Top half navy blue, bottom half grey, light."

"Should be easy enough," she responded. "Would you like me to revisit your inside leg measurement, or hasn't it changed in a while?" She made her way over to the male side of the shop and started pulling articles of clothing from the shelves and hangers. As she did, I mentioned that Holmes had a date. I think that was probably a mistake as her response of "every old sock finds an old boot" was one of obvious annoyance.

Holmes grabbed a deerstalker from the hat stand in the corner. Placing it on his head, he asked, "Is this me?"

"Yes," glared Martha, "if the look you're after is bit of a twat."

"You sell 'em," he retorted, somewhat crestfallen, before placing the hat back on the stand.

I must say, once Martha had finished her work Holmes was quite presentable. Despite her consternation, Martha had transformed a scruffy gas fitter into a half-presentable gent. Holmes surveyed her work in a full-length mirror to the rear of one of the changing cubicles.

"Not bad, Mart," he said, "that should do the trick. Right, I need some kip. I'm reckoning on having a long sleepless night ahead of me."

"He'll be back by half seven," she sneered as he breezed out of the shop.

I nodded a nervous apologetic smile to Martha before following him out of the door. Figuring a face to face discussion with Lestrade was more likely to bear fruit than an unannounced telephone call, I made my way to the police station.

8

Holmes stumbled back into 1B at around one-thirty in the morning. I had crashed on his comfortable settee in order to ensure I was there in time for the early start the next day.

"Whoa, that woman can drink," he muttered as he slumped face down on his bed. "That's my deductive reasoning muscles buggered."

"How did it go?" I asked.

"Okay," he responded, clearly drifting out of consciousness.

Concerned his inebriation would cause him to forget anything he had learned, I pressed him further. "Did you find out what you wanted?"

"Yup," he mumbled, "she's definitely a lesbian."

"The file, Holmes, the file. Do you know where it is?"

"Yep, Doc. I'll show you in the morning."

"Holmes, tell me now."

That was the last I got out of him.

Sometime after, Holmes relayed the story of the evening to me. As he did, he was perhaps the most effusive I'd ever seen him. It was perhaps the last time he referred to Irene without provocation and almost certainly the last time, in sound mind, he referred to her using her name.

Holmes had taken Irene to Southfield Road, a street of several loud bars just a short walk from Baker Street. He described the conversation with Irene as a "deadly tango" cut with suggestion and innuendo.

From what I could gather, Irene had assaulted his every sense, including his sense of superiority. Although Holmes was very self-effacing, you knew there was a certain confidence bubbling around under his guarded facade. Dressed in a figure-hugging emerald green dress, and looking even more radiant than she had earlier in her civvies, she'd hung on his every word, constantly directing the conversation back to Holmes. The result of this was that Holmes came away knowing little more about Irene than he had going in.

There was no doubting Irene's physical beauty, I can provide you my personal testament to that, however from what Holmes said, she had a method of heightening her allure yet further. She would gaze into his eyes with this flirtatious underlook, taking care not to hold her stare too long. When she spoke, she dropped the tone of her voice a semitone to give it a more seductive timbre. Then there was the touch. She stood close. Closer than the acceptable norm for those of such short acquaintance. This had two effects: it meant there was a preponderance of seemingly innocent accidental contact, whilst also allowing her expensive scent to operate at its optimum range. Poor Holmes, how could he, how could any man, resist such an onslaught?

When Holmes originally mentioned the injury to his deductive muscle, I'd presumed he meant it dulled by the alcohol. Following his description of that evening, I can do nothing but presume he meant Irene had rendered it impotent. Indeed he later described Irene as a "book nailed shut". Irene Adler was to Sherlock Holmes as kryptonite is to Superman.

You would think I would be intrigued by this woman, both as a man and as a psychologist. After Holmes had replayed his vignette, I came to fear her.

9

Lestrade arrived at five-thirty the next morning, with a procession of six police vehicles in tow. I leaned around the bedroom door to find Holmes lying on the bed fully dressed. He had however changed out of the clothes from the previous night.

"Is that the taxi, Doc?" he asked, his gravelly mumble suggesting he was struggling with the previous night's excess.

"Yes," I replied, "Lestrade seems to have brought the cavalry with him."

"Right, okay," said Holmes, struggling to extricate himself from his slumber, "I'm sleeping in the back."

We wandered out into the crisp morning air to be greeted by an annoyed-looking Lestrade.

"Hey Lestrade, fist bump," said Holmes, holding out his knuckle.

Lestrade stood motionless, his annoyance elevated.

"No fist bump," appended Holmes. He then glanced at him a stare of mock disappointment, shrugged and rolled into the nearest police car.

As we approached Number Eleven, it was obvious that Irene had absconded. I can't really explain it. The place just had an air of desertion. Oddly, Holmes sensed it without even peering from the car window. He perked up from his position slumped in the corner of the car's back seat and sprang open the door, alighting the car before the wheels had quite finished rolling. He then slid around the rear of the car and made his way up to the driveway.

On reaching the door, he poked out a finger and prodded it. Unlocked and unlatched, it swung open. He then made his way into the house trailed by myself and Lestrade. All the evidence confirmed that Irene was gone, with various items left scattered across the floor in her apparent haste. We entered the lounge to find a digital photo frame set central on the mantelpiece. It was displaying a series of still pictures of Irene cobbled together to form a crude animation of her waving. At the end of the sequence were the words, "Goodbye Sherlock". The final frame displayed a large "X".

Holmes reacted with a sigh and a nod of resigned deference. He wandered over to the mantelpiece, crouching down to place his hand on the photo frame's power supply. Pausing momentarily to register a thought, he stood up and returned to the centre of the room.

"Right," he said. "I need to get inside her."

"Well, I hope you have better luck than you did last night," I quipped.

Although a little disappointed in myself for the baseness of my witticism, I was imbibed by the sharpness of the retort. Holmes appeared unenamoured with both aspects and admonished me with one of the withered nasal exhalations I was now becoming familiar with.

Then, in a rather bizarre fashion, he started to ghost round the lower storey of the house. For the large majority of the time, his eyes were closed, his head circling in a clockwise loop. Occasionally his eyes would open and he would fix a vacant stare at a particular part of the room, before snapping his eyes closed again. Sometimes he would raise his left hand and massage his temple, other times he would stand perfectly still excepting the fingers of his right hand which he drummed in the air on the end of a semi-extended arm. Then, at regular intervals, he would wince, rapidly shake his head and spin on his heels to assume another direction.

Lestrade watched his every move, a look of perplexity paralysing his face. Periodically he would look to me for some sort of explanation, but I had none to offer.

Suddenly Holmes' peculiar staccato shimmy ended. His eyes lighting wide, he shouted, "Station. She's gone to the station. Twenty to twenty-five minutes ago. Inspector Lestrade, can I borrow your phone, please?"

Lestrade, still disabled by the confusion of what he had just witnessed, slowly lengthened his arm to pass his phone to Holmes, before moving to recoil it. As he had done to me the previous day, Holmes slipped the phone from his grasp before angling it such that the available light scanned across the screen. To Lestrade's obvious annoyance, Holmes typed in his access PIN, unlocking the phone at the first attempt.

He then spun round to take a picture of the digital frame, still mocking us from the mantelpiece. "Right, Inspector, can you send this picture to whoever's on duty back at the pigpen and get them to get down to the station to detain the lovely Irene here?"

"Which station?" grumbled Lestrade. "And how do you know she's using the train?"

"There are many reasons. The main one being that she only took one piece of luggage. Most other forms of transport you can take more, but on the train you have to hump it yourself, and the racks are always full, blah, blah, blah. Irene's not the type to travel light unless she has to."

"Which station?" growled Lestrade.

"Middlesbrough, of course," snapped Holmes, frustrated by Lestrade's absence of urgency.

10

We pulled into Middlesbrough Station to find Irene restrained by a couple of rather large policemen. Dressed in a patterned blue dress and denim jacket, she stood motionless with her shoulders slumped and her hands cuffed behind her back. Almost simultaneously, Agents Smith and Jones pulled up beside us.

Holmes addressed Irene with an air of disappointment. "What's this all about?"

Irene made no attempt to respond.

"You were never going to take on the feds and win, Irene. I fought the law, and the law gave my arse a right kicking. And that was just this bunch of head-the-balls," he said, his thumb gesturing towards Lestrade and a couple of uniformed officers milling nearby. "What were you trying to achieve?"

"Life is seldom about the destination, Sherlock," smiled Irene. "It's about the journey."

Holmes smiled, snorting an agreement. She leaned forward and placed a lingering kiss on his cheek."

"So where's the file?" asked Smith.

"In plain sight," replied Holmes. "You're looking straight at it."

"What d'you mean?" slurred Smith.

Holmes moved closer to Irene. He angled his neck one way and then the other, examining each side of her head. He then reached up and unclipped her right earring. Irene's earrings were cushion-shaped and quite large, perhaps a little shy of an inch square, sterling silver, set with a polished black stone.

"Whitby Jet," commented Holmes, as he examined the earring cradled in his hand. With the fingers of his other hand, he pinched the jewel causing the front of the earring to hinge upwards and reveal a small computer chip. "There you go," sighed Holmes. "Sorry, beautiful Irene, but these earrings are just not doing it for today's trendy indie look. They worked well last night when you were a vision in emerald, but I wasn't convinced with the vest stroke shorts combo you had on in the afternoon."

Holmes clipped the earring back together before handing it to Smith. "Stop the clock," he said, "the file you're after will be on that chip. If I'm not mistaken, that's the kind of chip you normally find in a memory stick." He then reached up and removed Irene's second earring. "You better take that too, she might have created a backup."

Smith nodded. "Thank you, Holmes, I think we have a few questions for Miss Alder now. Look me up if you're ever in the US and I'll buy you a Bud."

"Okay, Cagney, or is it Lacey?" he taunted. "I can never get that right."

Smith just shook his head. By now Holmes' mockery had worn tissue thin. Holmes then smiled at Jones who responded with a grunt of an acknowledgement.

"Fist bump," said Holmes, raising his knuckle in Jones' direction. Jones stood motionless doing nothing but hold the dead-eyed stare he was maintaining on Holmes.

"I'm stopping doing that," said Holmes. "I thought it would be good, but nobody seems to want to play."

As Jones loaded Irene into the back of the car, Holmes called across the car park. "Give my regards to the fellas back at Brokeback Mountain, won't ya?" his accent segueing into a faux southern American drawl.

As the car pulled away, Irene stared back at us doe-eyed through the rear window. Her look seemed to spark something in Holmes. A look of confusion snapped across his face. "Doc, what the fuck? What do they need her for? They've got the fucking file. Lestrade? Lestrade?" he exclaimed, shrugging his arms and rapidly shaking his face. His look of confusion was then replaced with a stricken look of deep panic. "Fuck," he exhaled, "fuck, Doc, they're not FBI. Rozzers don't wear two-thousand dollar shoes. Especially not for fucking work. Jesus, Doc, they're gonna kill her. We need a car, a fast one." He spun around surveying the street. "One of these will do." With that, he stuck his hand into his jacket pocket and after rummaging around in the rear of the coat's lining, he pulled out a smart phone. He then tapped furiously on the screen before giving it one final accentuated strike. With that, the lights of every car in the vicinity flashed as their central locking sprung open their doors. Lestrade spun around, unbelieving of what he'd just witnessed.

Holmes ran to one of the nearest cars, a Volkswagen Golf. I followed behind him, climbing into the passenger seat. He sat behind the wheel, again rapidly tapping the screen on his smartphone until the engine fired.

"Mirror, signal, fucking manoeuvre," he snarled before reversing the car out of the parking space at some speed. Coincidentally with the reversing manoeuvre coming to a halt, there was a thud. Lestrade, who had followed us across the car park, was sent sprawling. Taking little if any notice of the collision, Holmes then spun the wheels forward, screeching away from the station at breakneck speed. I looked over my shoulders to see Lestrade clambering back to his feet.

"He looks okay," I informed.

"Don't care," responded Holmes.

We accelerated down Zetland Road, braking at the last moment to negotiate the turn into Albert Road. Holmes kind of slid the car around the junction, recovering it just in time to make the opposite hand turn onto Wilson Street. At some speed, we slalomed around the traffic, narrowly missing both the oncoming vehicles and a youth in a grey hooded top.

The roundabout at the end of Wilson Street was hit with the car almost sideways. As the momentum of the vehicle subsided, Holmes slammed his foot down again taking the left turn at the next roundabout in a long screeching arc.

I tell you it was the strangest feeling. I was relieved that we'd negotiated the twists and turns of the side roads but there was no respite as we tore up the slip onto the A66. I was perfectly sure this wouldn't end well. I have never been so certain I was going to die.

I was suddenly struck by the recollection of Holmes' earlier failed attempt to drive the British Gas van.

"I thought you said you couldn't drive?" I shouted over the sound of the engine.

"Why did you think that?" he cried back as he weaved to make full use of the dual carriageway. "Apparently I'm quite good."

"Also where did that phone come from? You said you didn't have one."

"No, Doc, I said I wasn't allowed one. I never said I didn't have one. You weren't listening. Fuck, fuck, fuck, how did I miss that? Gee men can't afford shoes like that. They're fucking gangsters. You fucking twat, Sherlock."

As we passed the Zetland car park, Holmes noticed Lestrade and his men in pursuit.

"Oh shit," said Sherlock, "the Five O have got their lights on. That's not gonna help."

"Holmes," I shouted, "weren't you stone drunk not six hours ago?"

"Trust me, Doc," came the response, "that can only help. Don't you carry a hip flask? A single malt, sixteen-year-old Lagavulin?"

"Yes."

"You may wanna have a swig of that."

I reached for the hip flask concealed in my jacket pocket, but then thought better of it. To this day I'm not sure how he knew that.

As he zigzagged through the early morning traffic, Holmes glanced at me and growled. "Never tell me the odds."

"I didn't," I replied, somewhat confused.

"I know," he laughed. "I've just always wanted to say that. Actually I'm quite a fan of probability, and all that sacred geometry shit."

Fortunately, we caught up to the Americans and Irene before the intersection with the A19. If we hadn't, I'm sure not even Holmes would have been able to do much more than guess which route they had taken. By now they were also travelling at speed, presumably having recognised the blue lights of Lestrade's men as a pursuit. Holmes probably had the power available to catch them, however instead he slowed slightly, maintaining a constant distance behind them. Although our speed still rarely dipped below a hundred miles per hour, it felt somewhat safer than the madness that had proceeded. As in his earlier pursuance of Bradley, Holmes was happy to maintain a constant, determined velocity.

"When did you figure out the file was in the earring?" I asked.

"Last night," he said. "They were a candidate yesterday afternoon, but her watch and the MP3 player she had strapped to her arm seemed more likely. When she turned up last night still wearing them that nailed it. Sophisticated women like her tend to have more than one pair of earrings. The thing about the earrings not matching her outfit today was just bullshit. They looked fine to me."

"It impressed Lestrade," I pointed out.

"That's like impressing a hungry tramp with a sandwich."

"And Middlesbrough Station? How did you know that?"

"I didn't. It just seemed the most likely chance of us catching up with her."

"You guessed, you mean?"

Holmes was affronted. "No, I gambled. I never guess. It was only really gonna be Boro or Darlo. Not enough trains that go anywhere from anywhere else. If she'd gone to Darlo, we'd have never got anyone there in time anyway."

Holmes flashed a look of frustration at me. "This is gonna take forever," he complained. "He's not having to make any decisions. We need him to make decisions. If not, they'll end up in the fucking Lake District. The way their car was moving earlier it looks like he's got plenty of petrol. We're on half a tank. We'll run out long before them and I don't fancy Lestrade's chances of catching them. Not without harming Irene. Do you think I should try and ram him?"

"No, Sherlock, that would be a bad decision."

"I tell you what, Doc, give him a ring. Tell him if he doesn't stop, I'm gonna twat him."

I'm not sure how serious this suggestion was, but I looked at my phone anyway, to see there was no signal.

The necessity for Jones to make a decision came in the form of a rolling roadblock formed by two articulated lorries on the road ahead of us.

"Oh, here we go," said Holmes. "He's got about four choices here and he's never gonna pick the right one."

As Jones raced towards this obstruction, Holmes eased off slightly, the consequence being that Jones approached the artics, still travelling side by side, at a speed that reduced his choices. The option he took was to squeeze the car between the two lorries. With the space available to perform this manoeuvre limited, Jones clipped the rear bumper of one of the lorries, causing his car to veer sideways. The sideways traverse of the wheels made them gain purchase with the asphalt causing the car to flip and roll several times before coming to rest on its wheels, steam or perhaps smoke billowing from its bonnet.

Holmes slammed on the brakes, stopping someway short of the carnage. Ordering me to remain in the car, he jumped from his seat and ran towards the wreck. He pulled furiously at the rear door of the right-hand-side of the car before running round to try the other side. Fortunately he managed to get that side open. He reached in and pulled Irene from the car which, by now, was starting to release flames from several locations.

As he walked back in my direction, carrying Irene in his arms, the flaming wreckage exploded in a ball of fire. Holmes, who wasn't actually that far from the explosion, didn't flinch. I'll never forget that image of Holmes, with a comatosed Irene in his arms, silhouetted by a cinematic backdrop of fire and smoke. It was beautiful. Actually, that's not the right word given the scene extinguished the lives of two men. It was fantastic. Probably beyond any words I'm able to write.

As I sat frozen in the car, Holmes tapped on the window. It was as much as I could do to wind it down.

"Could I borrow some of that whisky, Doc?"

Without a word, I removed the flask from my pocket and handed it to him.

"Ta," he said, nodding.

With my heart still racing, I pulled myself from the car. It was all I could do to stagger to the rear of the vehicle where I found Holmes and Irene sat leaning against the boot. Holmes had his arm around Irene, who was wrapped in his jacket.

"Thank you, John," she said, handing me back my flask. She was bedraggled and covered in soot, but still looked incredibly beautiful.

"My pleasure," I responded, replacing the flask in my pocket and resuming my stagger.

As the adrenaline subsided, I was overcome with the enormity of what I had just been involved in. It must have been the shock kicking in. I stumbled to the side of the road and slumped on the verge. I watched as a less than angry wind gently buffeted the flames of the burning wreckage, distributing the smell of burning fuel and rubber to plant it resident in my nostrils.

I honestly don't know how long I sat there until my daze was broken by a shadow eclipsing the morning light. I looked up to see Holmes standing over me.

"On balance, I think that went quite well," he said, smiling and holding out his hand for me to shake.

"Let's not do it again, though," I sighed, grasping his hand from my seated position on the verge.

We shook hands and Holmes pulled me to my feet.

"Get yourself off that damp grass, Doc, you'll catch your death."

Given what we had just been through, I could do nothing but laugh with exasperation and slump forward, wrapping my arms around his shoulders.

"I think you need a swig of that whisky, my mate," he said, reverting me to the upright position.

I retrieved the flask, spun open the top and allowed the nectar to drain down my throat. Its warmth did do me some good.

At this point, we were joined by Lestrade.

"Oooh," said Holmes, "if it ain't the Sheriff of Nottingham."

"Where's Irene?" questioned Lestrade.

"I don't know," said Holmes. "I thought she was with you."

"Sherlock, she was stood right next to you."

"Oh right," protested Holmes, "now you're having a pop at my powers of observation. Okay, smartarse, take a look around you. See if you can notice something else that's missing."

Lestrade looked around confused.

"He'll get there in a minute," mocked Holmes. "I'll tell you what, Inspector, I'll give you a clue: it's big and metal and has the word 'police' written all over it."

"Oh shit," muttered Lestrade. "Hardwick," he shouted, "where's the M5?"

"The motorway, sir?"

"No, you idiot, the BMW."

"Dunno, sir," he replied. "I thought you had the keys."

A smirking Holmes then turned to me. Putting his arm around my shoulder, he smiled and said, "Come on, Doc, I think you need a beer. My round." He then looked to where the car we'd been using was parked. "Ah, I can't start the Golf. My phone was in my jacket pocket." The look on his face transformed into one of mock innocence. "Inspector Lestrade," he called, "any chance of a lift back into town?"

From that day to this, Holmes rarely referred to Irene Adler by name. On the odd occasion she trespassed into our conversations, she was only ever referenced in one of two ways. She was either the only person in the world with the power to destroy him or 'the woman'. To this day, I still don't know if Holmes could assimilate feelings of love, or for that matter, real friendship. His intense fanaticism for cold logic and reasoning seemed somewhat at odds with the softer passions. I will tell you this however, if, after this episode, if anyone was left standing at the station, it wasn't the beautiful Miss Irene Adler.

THE GOLDFISH BOWL

1

Although Holmes was endowed with some extraordinary talents for observation and reasoning, he was rarely disposed to demonstrating these skills. People perform in order to garner affection and attention. Holmes had no obvious desire to acquire either of these commodities. Of course, these skills were on display through the course of our various adventures, however, even then, he seemed intent on wrong-footing me by throwing in some doubt to cause me to question the legitimacy of what I otherwise regarded as unique genius.

An odd example of where he flexed his exceptional, if doubtable, skills for no practical purpose occurred one morning when we, as we did on occasion, were breakfasting in the Baker Street Kitchen. As sometimes happened, the conversation that morning had gone a little sporadic and then stale. As I sat sipping the remnants of my tea, Holmes sat with his back to me, staring out the window. You may think for your dining partner to not even show you the courtesy of facing you is a discourtesy, however I am quite sure this never crossed his mind. I was failing to hold his attention, so he simply found an alternative.

As we sat there, me with my nose marginally out of joint, he broke the silence by starting to call out professions. "Hairdresser, solicitor, offshore rig worker, off-duty policeman, instrument artificer, dole, shop fitter, dole, dole, dole."

"What are you doing?" I queried.

"Just observing and deducing," he replied. "There's bugger all else to do. Civil engineer, nurse, dole – no – unemployed accountant, dole."

When he got to proclaiming, "poet," I stepped in and called his hand. I wrapped on the window to beckon the man in. When I queried the gentleman on his profession, he did indeed profess to being a poet, before slinking off, somewhat confused at my questioning.

"How on Earth did you know that?" I questioned.

"Well, my mate," said Holmes, "from his grey, gaunt pallor he clearly isn't someone who is up and out for a six o'clock bus and all that bracing Teesside air. To me, he looks like someone who sleeps well into the morning and follows an unconventional working pattern that is less about regimented time periods and more about grafting when inspiration strikes. This is supported by his build and general physical condition which look to be the result of an irregular and unhealthy eating regime. The thought therefore being that he is involved in some sort of creative but perhaps solitary pursuit.

"Then we have his clothes. A shirt and tweed jacket coupled with those manky jeans tells me he's more art than science and what self-respecting musician would wear a tweed jacket? So we're left with some sort of artist or writer. The appalling colours he has dressed himself in scratch out any of the visual arts. Besides, painters and the like prefer to work outside where the light is better so he would have more colour in his boney little cheeks, therefore I'm left with the written word." Holmes rocked back in his chair. "He doesn't look like he has the energy to read a novel, never mind write one, therefore we have poet.

"This is backed up by the parcel he is carrying. He's carrying it in a manner that says it's clearly important to him. It certainly isn't a book of knitting patterns for his Aunty Eileen, and he's rushing to the post office so he obviously does not want its delivery delayed by him missing the next collection. Not that he knows when the collections are because he's just missed it by ten minutes and the next one isn't until three. Then there's the parcel itself. It's A4 size so clearly a manuscript of some sort, and yet not thick enough to be a novel. However improbable it may seem to find a jobbing poet in Middlesbrough, it's all there is left."

I was dumbfounded. The explanation portrayed such simple reasoning.

"Of course," continued Holmes, "the real clincher is that I've seen him before. He's called Karl and he runs the poetry recital evening in the Irish bar every second Thursday. What a bunch of tossers that lot are. There was a bloke there one night banging on about how it felt like being a conker. Knobhead."

"You fraud," I protested. "Why didn't you start with 'He's called Karl and runs the recital evening' instead of all that other gubbins?"

Holmes pursed his lips slightly, exposing the suggestion of a wind up. "Data is data, Doc. It doesn't matter how easy or hard it is to come by it. It's still data. Data is everywhere. Take this room. The two guys over near the specials board. The one with the beard is trying to sell the one without the hair his website optimisation services. The couple in the corner. They're in the process of reconciling. She's had an affair and he's blaming himself. He's telling her he will change. He won't. And she's telling him it won't happen again. It will. Oh, the couple of teenage girls drinking skinny lattes by the counter. They're discussing the potential sexual prowess of some two-bob scroat called Jason. Hang on, Jayson's spelt with a Y."

"How do you know all that?" I queried.

"Observation," he snorted frustratedly. "Data in."

"I never saw you observing. You've spent most of the time with your back to me staring out of the window."

"No," he said blankly, "the best way to observe is when nobody notices you are doing it. That way the data isn't corrupted. Those who are knowingly observed tend to perform. Those who are oblivious, well, don't."

At that, a group of teenagers entered the cafe. "What about them?" I asked.

"Mmm," sounded Holmes, "they've all got the same colour hair, but that's probably why you singled them out, and it's the red hair which is statistically interesting. They're clearly not members of the same family and so it looks like they've not come together, but rather been put together. They've also got money, new money. They're all wearing expensive clothes, new clothes. Nice shoes too."

With that, Holmes resumed his position staring out the window.

"Is that it?" I prompted.

"Yep," he replied, "that's all the data there is."

"So why have they been 'put together'?" I asked.

"I don't know," he replied, "but I suspect it has something to do with them getting all the dosh. I think we'll find out in a minute. They're trying to decide which one of them is going to come over and speak to us."

After a short while, a slight girl with long straight hair tentatively approached us, the remainder of the group following.

"Hello, are you Sherlock Holmes?" she asked.

"I am indeed, and who might you be?" replied Holmes.

"Jade Wilson."

"Now then Miss Wilson. Pleased to meet you. This is me mate, John Watson. What's got you all dressed up and no place to go?"

Holmes' persona seemed to change as if flicked by a switch. He was quite literally unrecognisable from the dour individual whose back I'd been surveying for the previous three-quarters of an hour. The ice cold veneer of previous disappeared to be replaced by a palpable warmth. This had the effect of putting the stammering teenager immediately at ease.

"Do you know a bloke called Bradley?" she asked.

"I do," replied Holmes. "Good lad, heart of gold."

Jade responded with a quizzical look, suggesting Holmes' testimony didn't ring quite true. "He reckons you're some sort of detective. So we were wondering if you could help us with something."

"Not really," smirked Holmes. "I just like to dabble a bit. Tell us what the matter is anyway."

Holmes gestured for Jade to take the remaining chair at our table whilst signalling to the others in the group to pull up chairs from the tables around us.

Jade explained that she and the others had been taking part in a reality show, something that was to be aired on Channel 4 called the Goldfish Bowl. The premise of the show was to take seven 'fiery redheads' and set them a series of week-long challenges. Sometimes the group worked as a team; sometimes they would be split, with them working against each other, three versus four. The challenges themselves covered a variety of endeavours from puzzle solving and model making, to the writing and acting out of short dramatic plays and the creation of original music. Each Monday at nine o'clock they would attend a room above some retail premises in town to find some written instructions pinned to the wall, along with a selection of paraphernalia associated with the task being set. At five o'clock, a buzzer would sound to indicate they should leave to return at nine the next day. When it got to Friday, they would demonstrate the results of their week-long labour and a large, gold, fish-shaped box slung to the ceiling in the middle of the room would rain cash, for them to distribute amongst themselves. The amount of money varied from six to seven hundred pounds to, on one occasion, three thousand pounds each.

I asked Jade how she had managed to come by such well-paid employment. That was the odd thing, she said, it was in response to an advert in the Evening Gazette. They had all emailed a photograph of themselves to the production company, and a few days later they received a response telling them where and when to turn up. There was no interview or screening process and at no point did they meet anybody from the production company.

Holmes stayed silent throughout, happy for me to drive the conversation whilst he oscillated between surveying the faces of the seven youths and staring thoughtfully into the middle distance.

"So what happened?" I asked.

"I'm not sure," said Jade. "We turned up this morning to find a big padlock on the door. No explanation. It just ended. We were halfway through a challenge to take turns pedalling the distance from Middlesbrough to London on an exercise bike. It's a total mystery."

"Nothing is total," said Holmes in a ponderous tone, "but this is a bit odd. I think we need to take a look at this 'Goldfish Bowl'. Come on, Doc, we've nowt better to do."

2

Jade and the others took us through the town and to the location of this room. Leading us through a door, unlocked to the street, and up a narrow stairway, we were confronted by a heavy door secured by a rather large toughened steel padlock.

Holmes took two thin, hook-ended pieces of metal from the pocket of his jeans and started working on the lock. Without a word except the occasional sigh and frustrated mutter, he worked away for nigh on twenty minutes.

Finally he jumped back, hands on head and stared angrily at the lock. He then started kicking manically at the lock and a good proportion of the surrounding doorframe.

"What's going on here, like?" came a voice from behind us. "If you don't mind, I would be grateful if you didn't kick the holy fuck out of me door."

We spun round to see an oldish, balding man, dressed in a style very similar to Holmes: jeans, training shoes, and the type of leather-yoked donkey jacket favoured by Holmes before Irene Adler had absconded with it.

At first Holmes' look was one of annoyance, apparently at the synchronicity of the man's attire to his, however this soon transitioned into composure. "And you might be?" said Holmes, his persona seeming to morph once more, him losing an element of his Teesside accent in the process.

"I might be David Arrowsmith. I might also be landlord of these premises. Why are you kicking shit out of my door?"

"Sorry about that," said Holmes, "I'm trying to assist these young people. I got a bit carried away with myself in my eagerness to help."

At that, I interrupted to relay a potted history of Jade's earlier story.

"Well I know nowt about that, like," said Arrowsmith, "but I don't mind you having a look at the room."

Arrowsmith pushed past us, unlocking the door with a quick turn of a key from a large bunch containing maybe thirty other keys.

"I loosened it," muttered Holmes as we followed him into the room.

Holmes' face was scraped with despair. The room was completely empty, with magnolia walls and a similar colour carpet. He stood motionless except for his eyes which darted around the void, sometimes taking his neck muscles with them. Given the sparseness of the scene, the only thing notable to myself was a smell of newness and fresh paint unbecoming of the rest of the aging building.

"The furniture's included if you're looking to rent," called Arrowsmith, his words echoing around the room. His facetiousness caused a break in Holmes' concentration, who flashed a look of frustration which he diverted into an unconvincing smile.

"I take it it didn't look like this at five o'clock last night?" said Holmes addressing the group, that were by now milling around the room in a collective state of bewilderment.

"No," replied three or four of them in unison.

"The paint is fresh and the carpet's just been re-laid. Is that something you've arranged Mister Arrowsmith?" asked Holmes.

"Nope," he responded curtly.

"Are you expecting the return of some sort of bond?"

"Nope," he said, "there didn't seem much point given the amount they were paying in rent. Three times the going rate and a month in advance."

"And how were you paid?"

"What the fuck has it got to do with you, like?" snapped Arrowsmith, growing tired of his interrogation.

"Please," Holmes encouraged, nodding towards the youths.

"The money was wired each month from a holding company."

Holmes switched his attention to the youths. "If you were making a television show, how was it being filmed?"

"There were these pods," answered one of the boys, "running around the top of the walls. I think there were cameras in them."

"Could you hear anything?" asked Holmes. "Electric motors whizzing as the cameras moved and refocused?"

"No," replied the boy.

"I could," said another of the males.

"And your name?"

"Vinnie," said the youth. "Vincent Spaulding."

Holmes showed his appreciation with a slow nod, before walking over to the side of the room and placing his face against the wall to allow his eye to track along it. Turning to address the rest of the group, he asked, "Did anyone else hear anything?"

His question was greeted with shakes of the head.

"Right," interrupted Arrowsmith, "I can't stand here all bloody day. Our lass will think I've got another woman on the go."

The prospect seemed unlikely.

"Can you lock up after yourselves? And try not to steal anything," he shouted, as he made his way down the stairs chuckling to himself.

Holmes turned to me. "Bit of a three-pint problem this, Doc."

"So what do you want to do?" I asked.

"Pub," was the response.

"It's only just gone eleven," I protested.

"Good," he said, "it's open. I won't have to pick the lock."

3

As we entered the Twisted Lip, Holmes gestured to the bar. "Get 'em in, Doc, you do the purchasing. I'll start the pondering."

I paid for the beers and joined Holmes who had cleared some chairs from around a table to leave just two facing each other. Sitting opposite him, I placed a pint of Engineer's Thumb in front of each of us.

"You see, Doc," he said, "problems like this are a bit like fixing a computer system. When you're debugging code, you can't possibly hope to understand what all the millions of lines of code do."

"Not even you?" I interrupted.

"Especially not me," he replied, unaffected by my goading, "I can't even remember when to take the bins out. No, you have to work at levels of abstraction. You have to break it down into components and then smaller components. If you find something that isn't quite right, you then dive down into the lower level logic. That's what we need to do here. Whereas programmers are looking for a bug, we're looking for a clue, probably a mistake of some sort. Some scab we can get our fingernails under and prise open.

"So what do we have? We have an empty room. The room, of course, has a location, which may be relevant. We have a bunch of red-headed kids, this TV show thing, and Mister David Arrowsmith, the landlord. You know, I think we can discount the television show. I don't think those kids were even being filmed."

"But Vinnie said he heard the cameras?" I queried.

"I'm not so sure. I think young Vincent was imagining it. His data is a bit of an outlier. Let's leave that for now. Obviously there's an element of intuition in this too."

"Guessing, you mean?" I responded, confused by his dismissal of what I considered to be valuable information.

"No," said Holmes, offended at the suggestion. "Intuition is as much based on data as anything. It's just that the data is processed by the subconscious rather than the conscious. Kind of background processing. I thought you would know all this with you being a head pickler. It's what lazy fat gets like Lestrade call a hunch."

Given that I wasn't sure if what he was talking about was a recognised aspect of psychology, I conceded, making a mental note to hit the books once I was back in the surgery.

"Okay," said Holmes, "let's start with the room. What do we know about the room?"

"Not much," I groaned.

"No," he agreed, sliding back on his chair and taking a large gulp of beer.

"Right," I said, "if the television show is not for real then maybe the room is being used for something else, outside the hours the kids were there. That's why the kids had to leave at dead on five every night. The kids are there from nine to five and for the rest of the time someone else moves in. If the television show is not for real, and just a cover story, then there would be no need to record it."

"Makes sense," said Holmes, rocking forward on his chair, "but what's this other thing someone else is using the room for?"

"Actually," I said, "the bank's not far from there. Maybe the TV show was a cover for some tunnelling."

"The thing is," laughed Holmes, "if you are gonna dig a tunnel, you probably wouldn't start from a room on the first floor."

I recoiled, my enthusiasm singed by the embarrassment of my oversight. "Look, Sherlock, if you're just gonna take the mickey, I'll go back to work."

"Don't worry, my mate," he reassured. "There are no wrong answers," he said, still laughing, "there are some bloody stupid ones."

My derision was broken by Martha who entered the pub carrying a large parcel wrapped in string and brown paper.

"Oy, rent boy," she said, addressing Holmes, "you're now three months behind. You need to liquidise some of those assets of yours. Mamma needs her honey."

Holmes flicked me a knowing nod, suggesting the 'honey' which Martha was referring to was not financial in nature.

"Oh, and this is for you," she said, handing him the package.

Holmes took the package, placing it immediately on an adjacent table, the humour of the previous discussion erased from his face.

"Aren't you going to open it?" queried Martha. "See what it is? It looks like it's from America."

"It's my jacket," said Holmes, clearly disturbed by something.

"How do you know that?" I asked.

"I've worn that jacket most days for the last four years. Spring, summer, winter, the other one. I know its size and weight," he replied vacantly, his mind seemingly elsewhere. "It's also been wrapped by a left-handed woman, 'the woman', and it feels like my phone's still in the pocket."

With that, Martha pulled out her phone and selected a number. After a few seconds, the sound of Prince singing, 'You sexy motherfucker,' rang out. Martha pursed her lips and rocked her head to one side feigning disgust. Holmes made no reaction, remaining silent and quite still.

After a few minutes, which had the feeling of longer, he took the package from the table and placed it on his knee before gently unknotting the string and taking care not to tear or introduce any further creases in the paper. He neatly folded the paper and balled up the string before unrolling the jacket. He stood up and put it on, before grinning a smile inconsistent with the dark remoteness portrayed by his eyes.

Whilst still standing, he reached inside the jacket pocket and took out the phone, placing it on the table face up before sitting back down.

"She's changed the PIN," he said vacantly. Given that he'd not attempted to access the phone, I queried how he knew.

"The screen's polished clean. She's removed any evidence of what has been keyed. No need to do that if…" Without finishing the sentence, he poked out a finger and tapped in some numbers.

The phone buzzed. 'Wrong passcode. Try again.'

"See, there you go."

A few seconds afterwards, the phone buzzed. It was a text message from Irene. 'You'll never find this.'

Holmes leaned over his still-locked phone to read the message before settling back into his chair without comment. He stared into some unseen middle distance motionless except for his eyes, which flicked around as if triggered by neurons sparking in his brain.

"You know why she did it, don't you?" he said, breaking a painful silence.

I just stared at him, struggling to frame a response.

"Why she wandered to her death so readily. Without resistance. It was her best chance. If Lestrade had carted her off, I would have happily let him. Instead she gambled her life on me, on us, pulling her back from the precipice. Out of the flames. It was the one scenario in which she escaped. And so she staked her life on it." He then smiled. "And she won her bet."

"Right," said Martha. "I've got to get back. Bradley's minding the shop and I'm not sure the little git can count change without some finding its way into his grubby pocket. Sherlock, rent," she said, as she rose from her chair.

"Do you not want to see her again?" I asked.

Holmes avoided my question asking a similar question of me. "Do you want to see your wife again?"

"How do you know I even have, had, a wife?" I asked. My breakup was not something I was comfortable talking about and I was sure I hadn't mentioned it to him.

"It was obvious," he said. "She left three or four weeks into our therapy sessions. You started to eat a little less, drink a bit more. Last night's booze is a familiar smell for a washed up drunk like me, and you must have lost six pounds in weight over the course of a couple of weeks."

Holmes' flow was interrupted by the barmaid, Mary, collecting our now empty glasses and offering replenishment.

"I was worried about you for a while," he continued, "but then you started to smarten yourself up a bit. Buy a couple of nice shirts and some half-decent shoes."

I haven't told you but my wife and I did split up quite recently, around the time that Holmes said. That he'd picked up on that during those therapy sessions, when it was I supposed to be analysing him, was quite amazing and not a little ironic.

4

I didn't see Holmes for a few days after the arrival of the package from Irene Adler, 'the woman'. The event in itself seemed quite trivial; however the effect it had on him was acute. I've never seen a person quite so withdrawn. A while later I reasoned that this out-of-body absenteeism he fell into was down to his planet-sized brain processing the new woman-related data. While it did so, the rest of him seemed to shut down.

Not that there seemed to be much information to process. It was after all apparently nothing more than the return of a couple of his personal possessions. What was he seeing that I wasn't? If a picture paints ten-thousand words, then that neatly wrapped package seemed to paint hundreds of thousands to Holmes.

My concerns on Holmes' state of mind were allayed when I left my surgery a few days later to find him leaned in a shop doorway across the street.

"Hi, Doc," he called. "I think we need to have another word with Dave Arrowsmith."

"Okay," I said. "How do we find him?"

"Well," said Holmes, "we could go and bray fuck out of that padlock, and hope he shuffles up again to see what all the noise is about, or we could just go around his house."

"How do you know where he lives?" I asked.

Holmes looked left and then right, as if to check he wouldn't be overheard, before whispering, "I looked him up in the phone book."

As we turned into Arrowsmith's street, I asked him what our approach would be.

"I think I'll use an approach favoured by Lestrade," he replied, "and ask some questions. The stupider the better."

Arrowsmith lived in a modest mid-terrace house nestled in an unremarkable street. He answered the door in a vest the grey side of white.

"Mister Arrowsmith," said Holmes reverting to the persona he adopted earlier, "I was wondering if we could ask you a few more questions?"

"Depends what they are, son," he replied.

"Can we come in?" asked Holmes.

"No," responded Arrowsmith, leaning arms crossed against the doorframe.

"Okay," continued Holmes, "you said the rent for the room was paid by a holding company. Can you remember the company name?"

"Saxe-Coburg or something," replied Arrowsmith. "Some place in the Cayman Islands? The wife calls it the James Coburn money. We're gonna use it for a holiday."

"Do you get a lot of people paying their rent from holding companies in the Cayman Islands?"

"Nah, first time ever. I didn't even know where it was until me mate Pat looked it up on the internet. Me and the wife are thinking about going there for a fortnight. We're trying to get a cheap flight there at the end of next week. Looks like a nice place."

"So how did they get in touch with you?" asked Holmes.

"Using some website, I think, Rentagaff dot com. It was all done via email. Magic stuff. I just emailed them the account details and the money started appearing in the account. Never met anyone in person, but someone was definitely around, pissing about with the room and that. I just kept out of the way. Three times the normal screw is all I needed to know. They could have torched the place for all I cared. Look, son, is this gonna take all night? The wife's got some corned beef panackelty in the oven."

"No," said Holmes, pensively. "Do you have the email address you used to contact them?"

Arrowsmith stuck his hand into a festering trouser pocket and pulled out a scrap of filthy looking paper. "Here it is," he said, "you might as well have it. I tried it this morning to see why they'd buggered off and it's stopped working."

"Cheers," said Holmes, "enjoy your dinner."

"Dinner, son," snapped a bemused Arrowsmith, "I had that four hours ago."

Holmes and I walked away baffled. If the creators of Goldfish Bowl weren't involved in some flagitious activity, and had nothing to hide, why go to so much trouble covering their tracks? As Holmes pointed out, it had the feeling of money laundering, but the money wasn't being laundered, it was apparently being given away.

"It would be easier to just burn the cash," said Holmes, "or stick it in the Bradford and Bingley and fuck off to sea in a canoe."

5

The next day, Holmes and I met in the Irish bar at an appointed hour to resume our three-pint problem solving. We entered to find Lestrade sitting at one of the tables devouring a massive pork parmesan. He was flanked by a uniformed policeman who remained standing and was clearly trying to distract himself from his superior's slaverous food consumption.

Without breaking chew, Lestrade gestured with his fork for us to join him.

"Are you eating again, Lestrade?" said Holmes as he sat. "You're like fucking Pacman."

"He's the same shape," muttered the uniform to Lestrade's visible annoyance.

"Listen, Holmes," he said, "this goldfish bowl thing you're dicking around with. Where you at with it? The super's interested in it. One of the lads involved, Vinny Spaulding, is his nephew or something."

"Nowhere," said Holmes. "It's all a bit weird. There's very little rhyme to it and even less reason. The best theory we have is something the Doc's come up with. A tunnel into the bank."

I glared at him, perceiving the groundwork for a comic slight on myself.

"A tunnel from a first floor room?" said Lestrade. "How the fuck does that work?"

"Not a physical tunnel," responded Holmes, "a virtual tunnel, through the communications network into their back office systems. You could do that from anywhere in the world, but if you're sat local, there are a lot less switches to go through. There's also the opportunity to combine an attack through the network with some social engineering of the locals. Employees and such like."

"So how do we check that out?" queried Lestrade, mid chew.

"I could take a look, a couple of hours on their systems should do it."

Lestrade laughed. "You?" he exclaimed. "I'd be surprised if they'd even let you open an account. You're a convicted bank robber, for fuck's sake."

Holmes pursed his lips in frustration.

"Okay," said Lestrade, "let me set up a meet. I don't think you'll be pushing any buttons but maybe you can give them some pointers on things to check for."

True to his word, Lestrade managed to set up a meeting with the bank the following morning. Both Lestrade and I dressed up in our most business-like attire for the occasion, whilst Holmes made no such concession remaining clad by his recently reacquired donkey jacket.

After a short wait in reception, we were led to a meeting room by an attractive young woman in glasses, dressed in a tight-fitting white blouse and navy blue skirt, slightly too short for business respectability.

"Shotgun," whispered Holmes on seeing her.

In the meeting room were two men: Bill Morris, who introduced himself as a senior manager, and Duncan Ross, who gave himself no title but informed us he worked in Information Security.

Morris initiated the conversation. "I'm afraid we have a problem here, gentlemen. We've run Mister Holmes and Doctor Watson through our vetting procedures and unfortunately Mister Holmes raised several red flags."

"Look," interrupted Lestrade, "this lad might be a bit of an arsehole at times but to give him his due he knows more about computers than Sir Clive Spectrum."

Morris' response was business-like. "A glowing testimonial, Inspector, but we simply can't expose details of our systems to a convicted criminal."

"Do you know what I did?" snapped Holmes. "I screwed over a payday lender that was charging an APR of two and a half thousand percent, and using a debt collecting agency that made Ronnie and Reggie look like Cannon and flaming Ball."

"Was that Wad Wappers?" interjected Ross.

Holmes nodded, clearly shepherding his frustration and annoyance.

"Some fine work," Ross continued. "I've seen it used as a case study on several courses. The way you reworked and pieced together some well-known techniques was close to genius."

"Close?" responded Holmes, still managing down his anger.

Ross turned to Morris. "Jim, Mister Holmes has quite some reputation in this field. If he can't find a vulnerability in our systems then there won't be many who can. It would be an excellent test, and a good opportunity for us to see how safe we really are. This gentleman created a whole new genre of computer hacking, organic attack."

After a short period of consideration, Morris conceded. "Okay, Duncan, but you can't expose any information which compromises our data security, and if this goes tits up, I won't be able to protect you, or either of us for that matter. We'll both be in for the high jump."

A conversation ensued that I couldn't begin to relay to you. Something about firewalls, ports and enumeration. There was also mention of "exploitation" and "penetration". Finding this a little kinky, and with the professional persona I was attempting to maintain dulled by boredom, I giggled, much to the derision of Holmes.

Ross seemed to spark off Holmes, feverously scribbling notes as they spoke. As I watched them work, I must admit to a feeling of paternal, that's-my-boy, pride for Holmes, who was clearly impressing both Ross, Morris and, perhaps to the greater extent, Lestrade.

The conversation concluded with an agreement that Ross and his colleagues would run certain tests. As we shook hands, it was obvious that Morris had thawed a little and was grateful for Holmes' assistance.

6

Later, in the evening, Holmes and I dined in the Irish bar. Having both borne earlier witness to Lestrade's ravenous consumption of a parmesan, we each elected to select alternative faire from the excellent menu.

Halfway through our meals, I took a call from Lestrade. Flicking my phone on to speakerphone mode, we listened as the inspector informed us that, "Those friendly bank manager types have done a full diagnostic of their systems and they're as safe as Fort Knox."

Holmes raised an eyebrow as if to deliver one of his contemptuous responses, but then thought better of it. "Another dead end then," he sighed.

"Seems so, lad," responded Lestrade. "Unless you've got any other ideas, it looks like we're running out of road on this one."

I closed down the call and we both sat in silence for a short while considering where we went next.

Holmes shrugged quizzically and resumed his dinner. "How do we move forward when we don't know which way we're facing?" he mumbled. "Mmm."

The silence continued whilst we completed the remainder of our meals and for a period afterwards.

"You know, there is something," exhaled Holmes, with the tone of someone whose memory had been jogged by a once dormant thought, "something I've been thinking about for a while. We could try reverse thinking."

"What's reverse thinking?" I queried.

"Well," said Holmes, "I got this from a book I borrowed off a lad years ago, a white one, with white writing on the front, still only read half of it. I should give him it back really. Anyway, reverse thinking is where you start at the end of a problem and work your way to the beginning. Edward de Bono!"

"Edward de Bono?"

"The guy who wrote the book. Think of it like this. You're at the base of a tree and you need to navigate up to a particular leaf. To get to that leaf, you need to make the right decision at every single branch. Kind of literally and figuratively. However," continued Holmes, his enthusiasm growing, "if you start at the leaf and work your way down there are no decisions to make. You hit all the logic in the other direction and, effectively, there isn't any. The route is easy to find. That's the route route, not the root, if you know what I mean. Am I explaining this well enough, Doc?"

Before I had a chance to respond, he was off again.

"It's like engineering where the best way to verify a calculation is not to go through the rigmarole of just doing it again. Then you just end up with two answers and either of them could be right. The best way is to start with the answer and find a way to check it. No, it's probably more like science where you dream up a hypothesis then try to go away and prove it. We need to start with a crime and then figure out how the hell a room full of kids getting paid wads of cash to do sod all helps in some way. We've pretty much ruled out bank robbery, so let's not waste any more time on that for the minute. What else is there?"

"What about the money?" I suggested. "Crime and money often sit hand in hand, and it was a little odd that the kids were getting paid in cash."

"Interesting," said Holmes. "I met Jade the other day to get hold of one of the notes they were paid with. Martha checked it with her special pen and it looked legit. I also got Miss Merryweather to run it past their guys and she confirmed it."

"Miss Merryweather?"

"Yeah, the bird we met at the bank. You remember. The one with the sawn-off skirt. I think we've ruled out money laundering earlier, as that normally doesn't involve giving money away. What, what, what?" growled Holmes.

"Giving money away is fairly unusual," I postulated. "Okay, this cash is kosher, but didn't the Germans have a plan during the war to flood the country with fake bank notes and destabilise the economy. The kids didn't need to be given money in the sort of amounts they were, and I'm sure Arrowsmith would have settled for a lot less."

"It's a plan, Doc. Make everyone in Boro rich so those wankers down south have no excuse to be so far up their own arses. If only, hey. Again, interesting. It gets me thinking about some sort of butterfly effect where the introduction of a lot of cash in a localised area causes magnified ramifications elsewhere. Actually, it would be a good way to get rid of those minimum wage, zero hour employer bastards. The thing is you would need to involve a lot more people than, what, eight, and probably need a hell of a lot more dosh. It's just too chaotic. You could never be sure you would achieve the desired effects. Besides, the butterfly effect is a load of bollocks. Anyway, how could a couple of little butterfly wings cause a hurricane, for fuck's sake?"

"Maybe it is all just purely altruistic," I sighed. "Some kind-hearted soul giving his fellow gingers a leg up?"

"Quite possibly," replied a resigned Holmes, "but Arrowsmith seems to have done the best out of anyone and he's not got red hair. He's hardly got any hair at all. And now we're back where we were before. Charitable souls don't expend that amount of effort covering their tracks. No matter how anonymous they want to be, people still really don't mind their good deeds leaking out. Besides, would someone like that have access to these types of skills? I checked out that email that Arrowsmith gave us and it's like it never existed. The URL has been wiped off the face of the internet. Amazing, really."

"What about the kids themselves? Could there be some seedy motive behind their involvement?" I asked.

"No," replied Holmes, "there's nothing to lead us there. I had a pretty long conversation with Jade and there was no suggestion of anything like that." He paused momentarily before adding, "Anything else? The room, the money, the kids, Arrowsmith, what crime have we not considered that would involve any of those?" He pursed his lips in frustration. "We need a domain of disclosure to whittle down. A list of crimes. It's a shame they don't do that scales of justice column in the Gazette any more. I miss that. That's the thing that first got me into crime."

"Investigating it or committing it?" I asked.

"A bit of both," came the response.

At that, Holmes stood up and went to the bar, returning shortly with a drink for each of us. "I think it's at this point you are supposed to say something that triggers a thought in me and solves the case. That happens every week on Jonathan Creek. Anything?" he asked.

"Nope," I responded.

"Bugger. I think I need to trade you in for a fit bird," smirked Holmes. "It works for Jonathan Creek."

"What Caroline Quentin?" I queried.

"Well, no, not so much her but Julia Sawalha and Sarah Alexander, whoa! Even Sheridan Smith is a do fer."

"A do fer?"

"Would do fer work."

7

I woke the next morning with a thought. Clearly my background processing had been working overtime. I threw on some clothes and ran most of the way to Baker Street. I banged on the door of Number Twenty-two which was opened by Holmes, already dressed for outdoors.

"Arrowsmith," we both chimed in unison.

"Give him a load of money, seduce him with thoughts of the Cayman Islands, and you have a ready-made mule," I blurted.

"Just what I was thinking, my mate," replied Holmes. "Give Lestrade a ring. The flight takes off in a few hours. Arrowsmith's probably already on his way to the airport."

We made our way to Albert Road where Lestrade picked us up in an unmarked police car. As we screamed up the A19, blue lights flashing, Lestrade called ahead to the Customs and Immigration people asking them to detain the Arrowsmiths. Not three-quarters into our journey, they called back to say they had searched the Arrowsmiths and found them clean.

We entered the airport's departure concourse to find an ensuing fracas involving Arrowsmith, his wife and several burly customs officials. Although hopelessly outnumbered, the Arrowsmiths seemed to be more than holding their own.

On noticing our entrance, Arrowsmith broke off from the melee and rushed towards us.

"You twat," he screamed as he drove both hands into Holmes' chest, knocking him off his feet.

"Sorry, mate," pleaded Holmes, from a seated position on the floor. "It was the only logical conclusion."

"Only logical fucking conclusion?" screamed Arrowsmith, by now restrained by Constable Hardwick. "She's had her fingers in our lass's bra and I can't tell you where that Geordie bastard's been sticking his finger."

"I was trying to protect you," said Holmes, climbing back to his feet.

"Protect me?" he yelled. "I'll protect you by sticking my finger up your arse, shall I?"

"Look, there was a danger that someone had tricked you into carrying something dodgy over to the Cayman Islands. Drugs, dirty money or even worse. If you'd have got over there, the coppers would have slung you straight in jail. No questions."

"Cayman Islands?" glared Arrowsmith. "We're going to fucking Tenerife. Pat said the food in the Cayman Islands would be all that posh shit so we knocked the idea on the head."

The ride back to Middlesbrough seemed inordinately long, with Holmes and I in the rear and Lestrade driven by Hardwick in the front. The only dialogue came from Lestrade. "I was starting to think you had something about you, lad, but it turns out you're a bit shit. All you've come up with is the square root of bugger all."

Holmes sat quietly and motionless except for the rocking of the car, his mind in another realm.

We were returned to our departure point on Albert Road, and following a suggestive glance from Holmes, we turned in the direction of the pub.

It was the lowest I've seen him without mention of Irene. I don't think he was particularly affected by Lestrade's smug barracking; it seemed more an internal turmoil seeded by his fallibility. His mood was a little too acute given the circumstances. After all, no one was hurt, well, excepting the obvious anatomical discomfort of the Arrowsmiths. Given Holmes' gloom was the result of a misadventure in which he stood no gain, I did feel a little sorry for the chap.

We slumped in silence in one of the booths of the Irish bar with our beers. Holmes broke the silence. "It's like it's the perfect crime, because there's no apparent motive and no fucking crime. It's like alcohol-free fucking lager. Completely fucking pointless. You see, Doc, when you have eliminated the impossible, whatever remains, however improbable, must be the truth."

"So we've eliminated the impossible?"

"Yup."

"And we've not missed anything?"

"Nope."

"So what's left?"

"Nothing. Absolutely bugger all."

Holmes stared into the vacant middle distance whilst picking at his outside incisor with his right thumbnail. He combed his fingers through his hair before rapidly rubbing his head and resting his hand on his brow, his forefinger and thumb spanning and pinching his temples.

"There is nothing left," he repeated. "It's like a purpose-built dead end. A puzzle with no solution. Oh beautiful…" He smiled, exhaling at the same time. "It's a goldfish bowl, and we're the fucking fish."

"Who? Why?" I queried.

"To test us, to confuse us, to frustrate us. To discredit us. One of those."

By now, he appeared to be slipping into some sort of perplexed daze, the soporific effect of the raw confusion excluding him from the moment.

"Which one? Can't you narrow the list, eliminate the improbable or whatever you just said?" I pressed, hoping to snap him out of his comatose state.

"No, Doc. No data."

"But who, Holmes? Why? Lestrade?"

"No, this is all far too sophisticated for that jumped up shit bag. He's more of a blunt instrument. Oh," he exhaled, his consciousness now returning, "someone to do with the late Smith and Jones, no longer of this parish, but still spread all over it. Their gaffer, maybe? We scuppered his plans to get hold of that file, kentucky-fried a couple of his best oppos, and generally made him look a bit of a twat. Oh, is he gonna be pissed off with us. Shit. We better start sleeping with the lights on."

Within a few weeks of Holmes and I accidentally teaming up to solve crime, we had our nemesis. Our arch enemy. Not that we knew who, or indeed, what he was. Was it even a he? It could have been a woman. Irene Adler, perhaps? Perhaps it wasn't even a single person. Perhaps it was an organisation like James Bond's Spectre or whoever the bad guys were in the Man from UNCLE. Okay, maybe my mind was running away with me, and the idea of an organised crime cartel operating across Teesside was perhaps a little too fantastic.

But still. Like two goldfish staring through the glass of the bowl, all we could see at best was a shadowy outline. In my mind's eye, I pictured him as Roger Delgado, the chap who played the Master in the early Doctor Whos. I'm not sure what image Holmes formed, or even if his mind was urged to reconcile the unknown like mine is.

As yet, this character didn't inhabit our known universe, but seemingly dropped things into it to manipulate and provoke us. I was sure his interest in us lay in Sherlock rather than me, however this did little to quell my concern. For perhaps the first time in my life, I was faced with a real fight or flight scenario.

You know me. Faced with the decision to fight or fly, I would normally take to the wing eleven times out of ten. But not this time. I was part of events. Circumstances had taken the choice away from me. Whatever lay ahead of us was for me to bear witness to, ha, and to chronicle in these accounts I send to you.

THE SECONDHAND BRIDE

1

"Do you remember something you loved? Not a person, an object. Something from your childhood. A toy, a piece of clothing maybe, that raggy old blanket. Something you loved above all else. Something you couldn't do without. Do you have it?

"Now do you remember the last time you used this thing? The last time you played with it, the last time you wore it? No? You loved it, above all other things and yet you left it stuffed or hidden or hanging somewhere and moved on. You never looked back; it never crossed your mind again. Your attention was on the next thing, the next object or perhaps person.

"People tell you they want to be loved. They don't. They're too self-absorbed to care what others are thinking or feeling. To be loved does nothing more than reinforce a person's idealised, self-sanitised image of themselves. You love your house, you love your car, you love your football team, you love sticky toffee pudding, shoes. None of those things love you.

"The truth of the matter is you want to love. You want to give yourself some point, some noble purpose. It doesn't. By its very nature, it's transient, fickle, sometimes even dangerous. And it's not preordained by some divine power, some cosmic chemistry. It's an illusion of the mind. A self-delusion of your own making. But if you're happy in that delusion then fine. Good. Very good. The trick is not to even think about it. To maintain the pretence. Then it is real. To you. And if it's real to you, that's all that matters.

"I've never loved, but from what I've seen, it looks interesting. A compelling addiction. It drives such bizarre actions and is responsible for such tragedy."

With that Holmes' head slumped forward, decapitated by a day's consumption of alcohol.

Too short a time later, the barmaid Mary approached with a pint glass filled with ice and water. With a resigned look that suggested this wasn't her first intervention of this type, she slowly tipped the contents of the glass over Holmes, who sprang back to consciousness, inhaling and pointing a finger at Mary as his head rose from its resting place on the table.

"Thank you, Mary," he gasped. "Same time tomorrow?"

Mary threw me a look of disdain, suggesting I was in some way culpable for a scenario that began long before I got there.

It's difficult for me to explain the relationships Holmes held with those few of us around him, without the risk of being unfairly harsh. I don't honestly know. Despite my training, I was never confident in my reading of him, so let me convey this as a hypothesis, a possible point of view.

Ostensibly, Holmes maintained practical relationships. Martha provided him with a place to stay and, if the inferences were to be believed, some other comforts. Mary imbibed him with the unoccasional beer. Even Lestrade had a role to play, albeit as a half-willing pantomime nemesis in a bidirectional predation.

As for myself, my primary usage seemed to be that of great man's assistant, general dogsbody and occasional liaison between himself and Lestrade, the given history decreeing that communication between the two was on the challenging side of strained. That said, as time moved on, I did feel I was growing into the role of collaborator. With each escapade, my contribution increased and I found myself closer to the centre of the intense discussions that invariably ensued whenever the investigations were afoot.

I forget the exact detail, but I remember once providing some additional insight on one occasion and this injection eliciting the response, "Doc, you shine like a star." I have to concede to that making me submit to some pride in myself. To this day, I look back on that comment as a milestone that confirmed my graduation to fully-fledged sidekick. I only wish I could remember and tell you what it was I said. I'm sure it was brilliant.

Please don't let me veil Holmes in too dark a light. He was incredibly loyal to those who surrounded him and would act to help without invitation. There was however little apparent in the way of sentiment. It was more akin to an instinct and I could never lay to rest the thought that each of us were eminently and instantly expendable. I fully expected to walk down Baker Street one day to find him disappeared.

Then there was Irene, 'the woman'. I'll stop short of calling her the love of his life, however she did seem to expose Holmes to something more than the purely practical, only to cauterise the wound she created in the same action with which she created it. Her brief sortie into his sphere left a lasting scar on an otherwise unscratchable alien. Call me an old romantic, but I like to think the reason for Irene's undoubtable impact on Holmes was that of a universal truth; love will out, and even the strange creature that was Holmes couldn't offer a defence.

Given the practical nature of Holmes' associations, it was surprising how he exhibited an extraordinary insight into the human condition. He had a remarkable understanding of the spectrum of human emotions, to the point where, given a person's mood and a particular scenario, he could extrapolate their actions with unnerving accuracy. I remember on one occasion he left me dumbfounded when he successfully predicted that a traffic warden would deliberately ignore an illegally parked car. This talent became particularly profitable, when it came to football matches, especially so in the event of a penalty shootout. The associated wagering he encouraged as we watched the odd match in O'Connell's invariably resulted in a spend-neutral night for the pair of us.

The only theory I can offer you for this extraordinary sagacity is that he had the luxury of a perspective not afforded to the rest of us. He somehow viewed human beings, us 'people', from the afar. He observed as if an alien interloper gathering data for transmission back to the mothership. To him, everything was of critical import, nothing was unworthy of note and nothing ever fused into an unfocused scrim.

2

I think it was a Wednesday. I was a little late in getting to my surgery and was hurrying along Albert Road when I saw the figure of Martha staggering in the opposite direction. Drenched in grief-stricken malaise, she scoured the faces of those who passed her.

As I approached her, I called her name. She looked back at me in a daze not seeming to recognise me. I grabbed her by the upper arms. "Martha, it's John, are you okay? Tell me what's the matter."

She just looked back at me blankly, handing me a letter she was carrying and mouthing the word, "Paul."

The letter was from the Ministry of Defence and concerned Lance Corporal Paul Hudson of Third Battalion The Rifles. After a lot of apologetic consolation, it explained that Lance Corporal Hudson was missing, presumed dead.

"He's not gone," whimpered Martha. "I can feel it. Sherlock, Sherlock will find him for me."

"Okay, Martha, we'll find him. Who is Paul?"

"My husband," she replied, confused at the question.

I escorted Martha back to the boutique where, in spite of her vapid protestations that she didn't take sugar, I made her a cup of sweet tea. Although reticent to leave her given her state, her desperately frail urging left me with no other course of action other than to try and locate Holmes.

A search of Holmes' usual mid-morning haunts proved fruitless. I stalked up and down the town seeing not a soul I recognised until I came across Bradley. I greeted him as if he were an old friend which affected him to recoil. The only other time we'd met was with me assisting Holmes in his apprehension following a misdemeanour of his in Martha's boutique, Hud Couture.

"Bradley, it's John Watson. I'm a friend of Sherlock Holmes," I reassured.

"Oh yeah, I remember you, like," he replied, his caution subsiding.

"I need to find Sherlock urgently. Have you seen him?"

"Na," he replied. Prompted by the desperation of my resulting sigh, he added, "Hang on, give us a minute."

Retrieving his mobile phone from the pocket of his hoodie, he tapped rapidly on the screen with his thumb before returning it to his pocket. We then stood in silence for a few uncomfortable minutes, the lack of union in our two lives apparent. Even our respective apparel was at odds. Bradley in his tee shirt, hoodie and low-slung jeans, me in my typical uniform of suit, boots and no tie. My mental search for a topic to break the silence was curtailed by a beeping from Bradley's pocket.

"He's in the museum, mate," he informed me. "MIMA, near the bottle."

I entered MIMA, the Middlesbrough Institute of Modern Art, to find Holmes sitting quite silent and still on a bench, surveying one of the paintings. As I took a seat next to him, he greeted me without a look to my direction. "Hello Doc, I'm thinking of taking up painting. How do you think you would get into something like that?"

"I'm not sure. Paint. Buy some paint, paintbrushes? Sherlock, Martha needs you. She's had a letter from the army saying her husband Paul is missing, presumed dead."

"Okay," he said pensively, "we better have a look then. Probably a bad idea anyway. There's better ways than that to waste your time."

We entered the boutique to find Matha rereading the letter and sobbing at its contents. Holmes took the letter from Martha and scanned its contents, his eyes flicking as he consumed the information.

"It's okay, Martha, 'presumed' just means they can't be arsed to look anymore. Let me and the Doc have a look into this." He moved over to her and wrapped his arms around her, smothering her as she buried her damp face into his chest.

On entering Flat 1B for the first time in a short while, it was noticeable that the random detritus that had once cluttered the mantelpiece had been cleared. In its place stood the electronic picture frame from Irene's place in Wynyard. The frame wasn't powered up, giving it the effect of a dark mirror.

Holmes removed a large hardback book from a pile of books on the windowsill. He opened it to reveal the pages hollowed out and a laptop computer hidden in the resulting void.

As the laptop fired up, I queried Holmes on the approach he was going to use. My excited assumption was he would use the nano thingies he'd used to such success when locating Irene Adler and the scandalous media file. My fervour was countered and duly doused by Holmes' phlegmatic response, "I was just going to google him."

Our more typical search of the internet revealed that Lance Corporal Paul Hudson, 3rd Battalion The Rifles, had gone missing some time ago. As had Martha's letter, the official statement cited by several sources reported Lance Corporal Hudson missing presumed dead. It was disgraceful really. The reports we were reading were three months old and yet the military had only just informed Martha, who, although estranged, was still legally his wife. Holmes didn't vocalise his views on this, however his annoyance was apparent from the clenching of his lips, exhalation through his nostrils and a dark, browed stare.

The information regarding Paul's disappearance, gleaned reading across several articles, was actually quite sparse. Paul was on his second tour of Afghanistan, stationed in Camp Bastion when he disappeared in the middle of the night. The military had conducted several searches over a period of weeks and turned up nothing. As Holmes had said earlier, they then seemed to just give up. The suggestion was that Paul had succumbed to some sort of camp fever, resulting in him walking out into the desert, where he probably encountered hostile forces.

Perhaps the most interesting aspect of our research was that Paul going missing wasn't an isolated incident. He was actually one of eight soldiers who had disappeared in mysterious circumstances in about as many weeks. Some of the more sensational news sources had even given the phenomenon a name. Quite crassly, the servicemen and women who had gone missing were referred to as "ghosts of the desert" or "sand spirits".

One name that came up repeatedly was that of Sergeant Isaac Wilson. Sergeant Wilson was commander of Paul's troop, and was often quoted in the articles relating to Paul's disappearance. Indeed, the theory that issues with Paul's mental state had caused him to leave the safety of the camp appeared to have originated from Wilson. Given the gushing testimonial he gave of his comrade, it also appeared that he and Paul had a relationship beyond that of colleagues. A quick trawl of the social networking sites confirmed that up until his disappearance, Isaac and Paul did socialise on regular occasions.

Holmes tapped his fingernails on the laptop screen. "That's where we need to start, Doc," he said. "Sergeant Isaac Wilson. Have you ever been to Sheffield?"

"Yes," I said. "I studied there."

"Cool."

"Why don't we just phone him?" I questioned.

"Because I'm not interested in what he has to say," he said. "It's the other stuff I need to see. The data we need needs a bit of bandwidth."

We ducked back into the boutique to find Martha still consumed by a soporific daze.

"We can't leave her like this," said Holmes, wrapping his arms around her again. "Let's shut the shop up, Marth, and get a cup of tea."

"I don't want any more bloody tea," she blubbed.

Holmes then shepherded her out of the door, leaving me wondering whether to go with or stay and mind the shop.

A few moments later, Holmes returned. "Okay, Doc," he said in an efficient tone, "I'll lock up here. Can you nip down the road and see if Mary is around and free to keep Martha company?"

"Me?" I queried. "She doesn't even know me? She won't come with me."

"She will," said Holmes, his face contorted with confusion. "She's well into you."

"Really?"

"Of course, you old hound, she's pegging for it. Well up for it."

"I've never noticed anything."

"Yeah," he sighed, "it's usually the one stood closest who can't see the full picture."

I went to collect Mary with a degree of trepidation. As I entered the Twisted Lip, she greeted me with a smile. It was probably the same smile I'd seen on numerous other occasions, however given the earlier revelations, it seemed to convey additional significance.

I explained the situation and she was more than happy to help. As we made our way back to Number Twenty-two, Mary linked her arm in mine.

4

Standing in Middlesbrough Station brought back memories of our previous visit, and the encounter with Irene Adler. "You know, Sherlock…"

"Yes," he interrupted, "last time we were here, the woman, blah, blah, yadda, yadda."

"I wasn't going to say that," I protested.

"Yes, you were," he retorted. "I could tell by the way you rolled your shoulders."

"So," I defended, "why shouldn't I mention her? You can't run away from a memory."

"Yes I can," he snapped.

"Why would you want to? She's clearly affected you. You should go and look for her. You need to find some closure."

"'Closure'," he winced. "Have you become American in the last ten fucking minutes, like?"

At that point, I conceded. There seemed little point in pursuing a discussion which was serving no purpose other than to antagonise him.

I took the opportunity of the ensuing silence to survey the stone architecture of the station building. I don't think I'd ever considered it before but it's a beautiful place, if perhaps typical of numerous other stations of that era. There must have been a fair bit of station building going on a hundred and fifty or so years previously. To the credit of the various engineers and craftsmen, they did an excellent job. As my old dad used to say, "Put your best into the job or nothing at all."

We boarded the train to take backward-facing seats at one of the tables. As usual, Holmes appropriated the seat closest to the window. His mood now mellowed, he sat with his face pressed against the glass. The effect of this was to cause the condensation to pool and drizzle down the window in isolated streaks.

Holmes assumed the mode he invariably took when confronted with a window-framed view, his eyes flicking to survey the vista. This time however, his vacant look suggested little was being registered.

Still looking out of the window, he addressed me in a distant, fragmented manner. "She's hewn into me, John, crashed into my soul, seared across my mind's eye. I've achieved peace. Some kind of peace. I just can't take any new information, no matter how speculative. Thinking of her blocks out thoughts of anything else. That's no good for me, mate."

"Maybe you should face your demons? Go and find her. I'm sure you'd soon track her down."

Holmes snorted, his blank expression transforming briefly into a smile. "I've considered it. I've run the scenarios. There is no sunny day. She's tied up in so many things. Things that will never unravel. She will never be mine. And I can't be around her if she's not. Even if she changed. But then she would cease to be her. There's just no way around this. Nothing to do, other than let her disappear. I've got to move out of her reach."

He was right. It all seemed so flawlessly hopeless. Such a crying shame given she appeared so singularly unique in his life.

"Well," I accorded, "I must admire your control. I don't think I could just walk away. I'd be off after her. Hang the consequences."

Again a smile made a fleeting visit to his face. "It's easy. As easy as not sticking your hand back into the flame."

The rest of that leg of the journey was pursued in a gloomy silence. Oddly it was Holmes, someone at home in the void, who disrupted the equilibrium with a frivolity. "You know what this is, Doc, don't you? It's our tricky third album."

On my querying of this, Holmes pointed out that this was the third of three 'adventures' we'd pursued together. I do however think the word misadventure would have provided a more accurate description. It was indeed true that this was our third outing in pursuit of mystery, however given the lack of tangible success delivered by our two previous forays, it was hard to see how this trip could be afforded the classification of 'tricky'.

To date, we had been involved in the retrieval of a media file of scandalous, albeit unrevealed content, only to see it blown to pieces along with our erstwhile clients, and we'd followed that up with a quite thorough investigation of a crime that was apparently never committed. In my view, in spite of some excellent work and some inspired reasoning, we were scoring somewhere in the region of nought for two.

"You know," said Holmes, "I'm not so sure about that Goldfish Bowl malarkey. I just can't get past the fact that we missed something. The problem is the more I think about it the more clouded it becomes. There is something, though. It's like an itch you can't scratch. One of the kids, or Arrowsmith, or whatever. There is definitely something. The one thing I am certain of is that it's the same gadgy behind all of it. Smith and Jones, the Goldfish Bowl. It's the same fella, and he's got himself down as a bit of a smart arse. I'll have the get, though. You can put your mortgage on it."

After switching trains at Darlington, we took seats in the quiet car. The consequence being that any further discussion of our mysterious nemesis, or for that matter Irene, was curtailed. As we sat silently opposite each other, Holmes slipped into quiet mode and resumed his stare from the window and the disinterested consumption of the northern countryside as it sped by.

When we got to York, a rather pompous, elderly, waxed jacket-wearing chap boarded the train, travelling with another gentleman of similar age. His first action was to set about evicting a young woman with a babe in arms from the seat he had booked. This in spite of the carriage being barely half full. I stood up to help her relocate the various baby-related accoutrements to a vacant berth. Holmes' only recognition of these events came via a derisive snort.

Then a youngish man, who had also joined at York, entered the carriage talking on his mobile phone. Clearly oblivious to this being a quiet car, he continued his conversation as he took his seat. I couldn't ascertain the full context of discussion however, from what I could tell, he appeared to be comforting whoever was on the other end of the line.

Waxed Jacket took umbrage at this. "Excuse me," he called, "this is the quiet car, you know!"

The man curtailed his conversation with a hurried reassurance to whomever he was calling and hung up. He then offered an apology to both Waxed Jacket and the other travellers sitting in his locale.

Given the value Waxed Jacket apparently placed in silence, and the strict preservation of rules, the hypocrisy he then proceeded to exhibit was galling. Having hushed the unobservant young man, who was clearly navigating some external distress, he then engaged in a conversation with his travelling partner at a volume that could only be increased through shouting. I say conversation, however it was a discussion in which only he appeared to be partaking. His companion's only response was to glance furtively around the carriage to gauge the opinion of the others on the train.

Holmes pulled his face back from the window before knocking his forehead back into it. He then rose from his seat, excused his passage past myself, and crossed the aisle to where Waxed Jacket was sitting. He leant over him to speak in a volume barely audible to me, just a few feet away, before offering a proposition. "The quiet car thing isn't just about mobile phones. It applies to gobshites too. This is gonna go one of two ways: you're gonna shut the fuck up or I'm going to kick fifty shades of shite out of you."

Waxed Jacket apologised profusely and the rest of the journey to Sheffield was enjoyed in a silence befitting a morgue on a bank holiday weekend. As we alighted the train in Sheffield, Holmes clicked a wink at the young woman and tickled her baby under the chin with the knuckle of his index finger.

"There you go, Sophia," he said to the baby, "you enjoy the rest of your ride on the chu chu train."

The baby, who was twisting a bit, instantly changed her mood and chuckled back at him.

The silence Holmes had established on the latter part of our journey had afforded me some time to reminisce. Having taken my medical degree in Sheffield, I was looking forward to it triggering some long dormant memories. Memories of life and love during my fleeting time there. Perversely, few of my memories were actually that fond, and many concerned revitalised recollections of the girl who cast me aside once my purpose had been served. The girl to whom I provided brief base human diversion, to contrast the more intellectual pursuit of bagging a medical degree, and the nights that ended in debauchery, tequila or sometimes both.

You might think me perverted but I often think the darker experiences in life give it a certain validation. What at the time may feel like a living hell, can somehow make life more tangible, less cinematic. Something to be experienced rather than observed.

Maybe this was what I got from Holmes: validation. In the short period of our acquaintance, I'd experienced a spectrum of negative emotions from, what do they call it, 'mild peril' to life-threatened terror, all interspersed with a gamut of intellectual stupefaction fostered of Holmes' oblique perspective. Nothing especially positive but all enlivening and life-affirming.

Actually, against a more recent canvas, the demons that had perhaps prevented me returning to this town seemed quite impudent.

5

As we left the station, Holmes sprang to life, his head darting around as he hoovered up each and every detail of the place. It was as if I could hear neurons sparking in his brain as he surveyed this, to him only, strange and fascinating place.

In just five minutes of us leaving the station, he was overcome with a look of exhaustion, the mental effort of his intake having taken its toll.

"I'm tired," he said. "I need a sit down. There," he pointed, "a pub. They usually have loads of seats."

We entered the Globe pub to find it empty, barring an elderly barman and a few stray students. This came as a relief to me as I feared if he were to click back into his observing mode, he would probably trip a fuse.

"You decide," he mumbled before slumping on a seat with his back to the window.

Working on the assumption that this decision concerned the choice of our libation, I ordered two pints of what I assumed was craft ale, Hobgoblin, I think. I joined Holmes by the window, placing his drink on a beer mat in front of him. He picked up the glass and consumed around a third of its volume in a couple of gulps.

"Thank you," he muttered, "I was running on vapour there."

I'm not sure whether he was addressing me or the beer.

Unusually for Holmes, he paid little attention to his surroundings. He sat with his head dipped, his eyes pointed at the brown patterned carpet. Young students, in groups of two to four filtered in and out of the bar, with Holmes affording no notice.

"So what was Martha's husband like?" I asked.

"What is he like?" corrected Holmes. "He's not dead. I think he's a complete doyle, but Martha's always been crazy about him. Ever since we were at school. They got married when we were about nineteen and pretty much straight after that, he cleared off and joined the army. The only proper job he ever had. It's a shame really because if he'd stuck around I reckon Martha would have come round to realising what a dick he is."

"You don't like him, then?" I asked.

"He's alright," said Holmes. "We used to knock around together at school. It's just Martha could do a lot better. And now she won't do anything because she expects him to rock back up one sunny day. To be honest, I always thought he would myself, if he was skint or in some sort of shit."

Holmes replaced his now empty glass a little too heavily on the beer mat.

"Would you like a refill, love?" called the barman.

"Yes, mate," Holmes replied, "but can we have a pint of the Brewdog this time, the one with the red label." Turning to me, he whispered, "It's okay, he's not a bandit. 'Love' is just what they call each other down here. I did some research into their language before we came." He shook his head. "It's well fucked up but there are some Boro words in there."

After the revitalising effect of a few more Brewdogs, we stumbled on up into the centre of town, Holmes' previous inclination to create a mental map of the whole city now subsided.

"Amazing place." he said. "Apparently there's a Greggs here that's open past chucking out time. It's like New York but with Greggs."

More by accident than design, we ended up at Leopold Square, a place of bars and restaurants that post-dated my student days in Sheffield. Agreeing that we had walked up enough hills, we decided that we'd complete the journey to Isaac Wilson's place by taxi. Fortunately, there were several stacked along Leopold Street.

As seemed to be a theme when we travelled, few words passed between us during that taxi ride. Instead, as was generally the case, Holmes sat transfixed to the window consuming the detail that sped by. Thankfully this hunger for information was lighter than it had been earlier in the day.

"I think I just saw Chrissie Waddle coming out of Pizza Hut," he muttered pensively as we drove along Ecclesall Road. "Actually, it might have been Carlton Palmer."

As we rounded Brocco Bank roundabout, Holmes called to the driver, "This'll do, mate."

The taxi drew to a halt and Holmes alighted, leaving me to provide payment.

As we both stood orientating ourselves to our location, Holmes spoke. "I thought it best if we walk the rest of the way. Get our heads squared off."

That was perhaps a mistake. From the roundabout, we walked up an incredibly steep road, before turning into a side street to be faced with an even steeper incline. Maybe three quarters of the way up Kilimanjaro Street, and much to my relief, Holmes stopped.

"That's it," he breathed, pointing to a house three or four doors up. He then took a few deep breaths before standing up and strolling the rest of the way.

Unable to mirror his recuperation, I staggered breathlessly after him.

Holmes brayed on the door and, after a short while, long enough for me to recover a reasonable amount of composure, a formidable-looking male arrived to open it.

"Isaac Wilson?" asked Holmes, before introducing himself and explaining he was a friend of Paul Hudson's.

Wilson's home was clearly that of a soldier. We were led into a reception room, adorned with various military paraphernalia in which every shelf and ledge was stacked with photographs of soldiers, some in regimental starch, some in less formal poses.

Holmes reconnoitred the room, displaying an observable appreciation. "That's Paul," he said, pointing to a photograph of Wilson with his arm wrapped around the shoulder of another soldier of similar build. As I went to remove the picture from its display position, Holmes give a short tug on the elbow of my shirt and a short surreptitious shake of the head to tell me I shouldn't be touching.

"Yep, that's him," said Wilson, returning to the room with two mugs of steaming tea. "Finest soldier in the British army, that lad."

"Aye," said Holmes, "a good lad."

"The best," responded Wilson.

"So what happened to him, Isaac?"

Wilson went on to regale a story that, although less sanitised, was much along the lines of what we'd discovered from various sources on the internet. Paul had gone stir crazy in camp and wandered out into the desert, apparently oblivious to the calls of the guards on duty that evening.

Pressed by Holmes for a more personal insight into the events leading up to Paul's disappearance, Wilson explained how Paul had been acting out of character. He described how Paul seemed agitated and distant and was often huddled away from others, whispering into his phone.

Perhaps the more bizarre aspect of Wilson's story were the accounts of a strange light emanating from the area of the desert where Paul had disappeared. Wilson explained how Hāfez, a local who worked as a liaison with the locals of the surrounding villages, had related this to an ancient legend of a mystical spirit known as the Hosmer Angel. Wilson recounted how local legend had it that those lost in the desert would be rescued by a benevolent angel and spirited away, never to be seen again.

I was expecting Holmes to respond to this fantastical element of the story, however his reaction throughout Wilson's tale was consistent. He listened intently, nodding appreciatively as Wilson relayed his story.

Oddly, the story of the Hosmer Angel seemed to stack up with some of the less other-worldly aspects of the story. Shortly after Paul had walked off, the camp colonel mustered a search party to go and look for him. They tracked his footprints across the sand until the point they disappeared. It was as if he had been whisked away. It had caused quite a stir on camp and, although much of the discussion had been trenched in humour, Wilson was convinced that a lot of people had been left believing in the legend of the Hosmer Angel.

At the conclusion of Wilson's story, Holmes rose to his feet, sighing pensively as he glanced at me to join him. He mooched around the room taking another look at the many photographs.

"It's odd how people dress up to kill each other," he mumbled before halting his traverse in front of the picture of Wilson and Paul. "Do you mind if we take a picture of this one?" he asked. "For Martha."

"Martha?" asked Wilson.

"His wife."

"Erm, no, of course," replied Wilson.

Holmes held out his hand indicating we would be using my phone. I handed it to him and he did his usual trick of allowing the light to scan across the screen before tapping in my PIN number. Given I had recently changed it, I was a little aggrieved at the ease of his access.

6

"What did you think of all that?" I asked Holmes as we made our way down the bank towards Ecclesall Road.

"I think that everything he told us was true. He just stopped short of telling the last couple of chapters. It's a good way of doing it. Easier than making something up and remembering it. I think he's been schooled by someone. Someone who knows what they're doing."

"So what did he neglect to tell us?" I asked.

"That Paul is alive and well and has been in that house in the last day or so."

"How on earth did you draw that conclusion?"

"Paul's fingerprint was on that picture."

"You could tell Paul's fingerprint just by looking at it?"

"Yes."

"Really?"

"No."

Holmes explained how whoever had picked up that photograph had done so because they felt some connection to it. It wasn't

Wilson. He religiously dusted and polished his various artefacts and was therefore unlikely to dab his own fingerprints on the glass of the pictures he polished. The pity, reflected Holmes, was that both Wilson and Paul were right handed. The print Holmes spotted was on the right hand side of the frame. Had Wilson been left handed that would have clinched it. Don't ask me how he drew the conclusion that Wilson was right handed.

As Wilson had told his tale, another potential scenario formed in my mind.

"There's another possibility," I said, trying to apply what Holmes had taught me during the preceding weeks. "That light on the horizon Wilson spoke about. The accounts of it may well be apocryphal, but I think if we understand what that is, the rest will fall into place."

"Okay," said Holmes, clearly humouring me.

"So," I continued, unperturbed by his doubt, "let's rule out the impossible and see what remains. As that will be, erm, what remains is, erm, the remainder. So what's impossible?" I continued, not quite having remembered the adage he'd regaled to me on numerous other occasions. "Well, it wasn't anyone on our side. Everyone in the camp was accounted for, there were no patrols out, and the nearest other friendlies were hundreds of miles away. It also couldn't have been Afghans, they would have left tracks. So whatever made the light created no impression in the sand. Therefore whatever took Paul, came from the sky. There was no sound, so it couldn't have been an aircraft, and whatever it was didn't land or it would have left tracks. Alien abduction! It's the only possible answer."

"Bloody hell," laughed Holmes, shaking his head in disbelief.

For a brief moment, I thought his doubt was sparked by a disbelief in the accuracy of my reasoning, however it soon became apparent that this was not the case.

"Couple of things: the light on the horizon could be anything, we can't rule anything out, or in, apart from aliens, because there are no such fucking thing. Well not from another planet anyway. Pretty much everyone in Hartlepool's an alien, but that's never been useful."

"You don't believe in extraterrestrials?"

"Do I buggery. I'm more likely to believe in angels than ET. You've just got to look at how people go on to see the chance of anyone travelling between planets, or indeed out of Hartlepool, are the square root of bugger all.

"If the people on other planets are anything like the ones on this one, and there is no reason to believe they aren't, alien races will never meet. At this very moment we may well be alone in the universe, however its sheer size means that somewhere out there life will or will have existed. The balance of probability tells you that. Whether a civilisation could become advanced enough to travel the stars before it extinguishes itself? Definitely not.

"The force that pulls us, that drives us to advance, is what will ultimately destroy us. We edge forward, and with each step, we move closer to disaster. Our lust for life will be the death of us. I'm certain of that, you see it everyday, in the newspapers, in the street, and there's no reason to deduce it would be very much different anywhere else. It's the only logical conclusion. It's as if whatever it was that convinced us to pull ourselves from the primordial mud, that very thing that created life, is the bringer of death. It's a perfect and quite beautiful paradox. If creation is the design of some divine being then he's an ironic sod."

As we entered the Nursery Tavern, Holmes looked over his shoulder at me. "Aliens? I think you'd better stay on soft drinks."

"Is there anything you don't have a theory on?" I asked as we took our seats in the corner of the bar.

"Yes, headphones, tangled headphones. No matter how carefully you ball up the wire, it always comes out of your pocket all tangled up. They only need to be in there for a few seconds and they're in about ten knots. How the hell does that happen?"

"Okay," I said, trying to return the discussion to the matter in hand, "we need to reduce the improbable."

"Reduce? We eliminate the impossible!" Holmes scolded. "We're undertaking an investigation not boiling down a stew. Do you know when you ruled out Paul being whisked off by an aircraft?"

"Yep," I replied, singed by my admonishment.

"You shouldn't have done."

"Why?"

"Because it was a helicopter. The gust of the rotor blades combined with the wind that night were what smoothed out the sand. There was no sound because the prevailing wind was strong enough to carry it out into the desert."

"But you're guessing, you don't know what direction the wind was blowing that night."

"I'm making an assumption. I never guess."

"So how did you come up with that?" I asked.

"Reverse thinking. Begin at the end. I started with smooth sand, light and no sound and worked backwards. Besides, what happened to Paul's footprints from his big old size twelve army boots? It's not that the tracks disappeared, it's that they were blown away."

7

Holmes stood up, before draining the remainder of his drink. "Right," he said, "you need to buy a laptop."

"I need to buy a laptop?"

"Yep, we need to check out that fingerprint you've got on your phone and have a root around for Paul."

"But I don't need a laptop," I protested.

"Show me your fingertips."

I held out my hands.

"See. Shiny. Those fingers have been tapping on a well used keyboard until the early hours of the morning. Actually, the quite late early hours by the looks of it. How long have you had your laptop?"

"I'm not sure. Five maybe six years."

"There you go. Time for an upgrade."

We flagged a cab and made our way back into town. On the way

Holmes suggested that I should pay for the laptop with cash in order that we didn't leave a trail. When I pointed out that I didn't have that much cash and so would need to visit a cash point, he told me that wouldn't be an issue as he could fix that. On that, I felt it prudent not to take the discussion any further.

Not long after, we were sitting in Leopold Square outside Popolo's with six hundred and fifty pounds worth of shiny new laptop computer paid for in crisp cashpoint cash. There had been several cheaper options, however Holmes had convinced me not to buy cheap and end up buying twice.

As we sucked down a couple of ice cold Peronis, Holmes tapped ferverously on the keyboard whilst emitting sounds ranging from puzzled interest to mild annoyance.

"That's a bit odd," he said before rocking back into his seat.

"Have you found something?" I asked.

"Yeah, but it's a bit Safestyle Windows."

"Sorry?"

"Ya buy one, ya get one free. That fingerprint belongs to two profiles. Both of them with the sort of encryption levels normally reserved for nuclear secrets and the prime minister's cross-dressing preferences. This is well suss," he said, interrupting himself. "The encryption doth protect too much."

"Can't you crack it?"

"Na. It would take months. Mmmm," sighed Holmes, "we need another way of looking at this. Let's assume he's somewhere in Sheffield and cut down the search space."

"But he could be anywhere," I queried. "He may have just been passing through. If indeed that fingerprint even belongs to him."

"You're not wrong, Doc, but we need to start somewhere. You can't pick yourself up by your boot laces. That fingerprint was left in the last day or so, so there's a good chance the owner of it is local. We can kettle the fish later. Right, we need to profile it."

"How does that work?" I asked.

"Everyone follows patterns," he explained, "we just need to profile Paul and see who in Sheffield acts in a similar manner."

"I don't follow any patterns. I'm an individual, I have my own free will."

"How often do you get your hair cut?" retorted Holmes.

"Whenever it needs cutting."

"You get it cut every three weeks on a Wednesday afternoon."

"Yeah, but that's just because it's convenient."

"And that's exactly my point," said Holmes. "It's convenient. It stops you having to decide. It strips away the mundane and leaves your thoughts for more interesting things. Einstein was the same. He had a wardrobe full of the same suits, shirts, ties, and shoes, so that he didn't need to waste his thoughts on figuring out what to wear each morning."

"Actually that's not true."

"Isn't it?"

"No. Actually he spent most of his time mooching around Princeton in a big old sweatshirt and a pair of flip flops."

"Flip flops?" protested Holmes. "I hate flip flops. Especially on men. In fact, I hate all shoes that are named after the sound they make. Except loafers. You'll be telling me he never slept with Marilyn Monroe next."

"Nope, they never even met."

"Right," said Holmes, dismayed by the inaccuracy of his knowledge, "but the point is you are all individuals, but you shouldn't confuse that by thinking you have free will. You're eighty-five, ninety percent instinct. You're like flowers that follow the sun, or moss skulking in the shade. People are unique, but their habits are not a kick in the arse off being fingerprints. They might only buy tuna when packs of four are on offer, skip going to the gym after a bank holiday, buy far more bottles of extra-hot chilli sauce than they could possibly use by the sell-by date, draw cash out of the cash point in two or three set amounts…"

"Okay," I conceded, "how long will this take?"

"Enough time for you to get another couple of beers in," grinned Holmes.

I returned to the table to find Holmes sitting back in his seat with the laptop pushed to one side. Although the text was scrolling down the screen at a speed that made it unreadable, Holmes would still glance at it occasionally.

"How come you know so much about Einstein?" asked Holmes.

"I didn't think I did," I replied. "I think it's more to do with you getting all your facts from dodgy films and conversations with pub drunks."

Holmes narrowed his eyes and responded with a look of confused suspicion before directing his attention to the illegible output of the laptop.

After a short period of silence, Holmes leant forward and prodded a few of the laptop keys. "There we go," he said, "one thousand four hundred and seventy three matches."

"In the country?" I asked.

"No, just Sheffield."

"Okay then, you take the top half, I'll have the rest and I'll meet you back here in, say what? An hour and a half?"

Holmes, unimpressed by my facetiousness, shook me his withered, I'm not finished yet look. I suspect he was also still smarting from the Einstein clarification.

"Ya see, Doc, that's the thing with big data."

"What's that?"

"It's fucking massive. It's also not easy when the only thing you have to go on is he wears size twelve shoes and drinks rosé wine."

"Rosé?"

"Yeah, he gets away with it though because he's a bit of a hard bastard. Anyway," continued Holmes, "among these teeming fish we have dodgy big old trout swimming widths. Namely, Isaac Wilson. If we can find some instances where he bumps heads with some of these other little fishies, the deep blue sea becomes as shallow as the grief he pretended to show earlier. So if you just give me a few more seconds, pearl one, loop one and there we have it, a Mister James Whinney-Banks."

"James Whinney-Banks, who's he?"

"Put it this way, Doc, Paul Hudson might have got into that helicopter in the Afghan desert but it was James Whinney-Banks who climbed out of it."

Holmes drummed his fingers on the table either side of where the laptop was sitting.

"Penrhyn Road, just a couple of streets away from Wilson," he said. "Interesting."

"How?"

"It was only purchased in the last three months and it has no mortgage on it."

Holmes furrowed his brow and sucked air through his teeth before rattling a few more of the laptop keys. "The payment for the house was transferred from the account of some obscure government department. What's all that about then?"

"What shall we do?" I asked. "Go round there?"

"No, Doc," said Holmes pensively. "I think it's some sort of safe house. I don't think we'd get anywhere near him. We need to catch up with him when he's out and about."

"How do we do that?"

"Pub quiz," said Holmes. "Hud loved a pub quiz. Especially if it had a music round. I'm not really sure why, he was absolutely crap at them."

Holmes resumed his rattling of the laptop keys. "James Whinney-Banks' bank account seems to get some regular hammer on a Wednesday at a place called the Psalter Tavern," he said. "And guess what. Wednesday is quiz night. Last week, the big gay used his card to buy a couple of bottles of a cheeky little rosé. Clearly he's still comfortable with his sexuality. What day is it today?"

"Tuesday."

"Okay, it looks like we're staying over," he said as he flipped the lid shut on the laptop.

We made the short trip across the square to the Leopold, an attractive four star boutique hotel built from the yellowy brown stone they used to quarry locally. As we stood in line, behind a married couple from Birmingham, it became apparent that we would struggle to get a room. The World snooker championships were being held in Sheffield at the time and the pretty receptionist was explaining how the hotel was fully booked and, given the influx of people for the snooker, it would be difficult to find a room elsewhere in the city.

As the couple struggled away with their luggage, I expected us to follow likewise. Oddly, Holmes approached the desk to have, what I imagined, would be the same conversation. This was one of those many occasions that I felt it better to observe Holmes rather than intervene.

"I have a room booked in the name of Lestrade," said Holmes.

As the receptionist attempted to locate the booking, Holmes appended, "Detective Inspector Lestrade. The room's pre-paid."

"I'm sorry, sir," responded the receptionist, "we don't seem to have a booking in that name."

"The booking will be there. Look again. You will find it," asserted Holmes.

"No, I'm sorry, sir. We have nothing under that name."

"You must have, it was booked by one of the girls back at the station. My colleague and I are here on some important police business. We really don't have time for this. Please find us a room, any one will do."

Again, the receptionist was very apologetic and relayed the story she had told the previous people.

Holmes tightened his lips and gave the poor girl a long serious stare before turning on his heels. As he left the building, with myself in tow, he muttered to me over his shoulder, "I learnt that trick from old Ben Kenobi. He does it better than me."

Holmes strode back across Leopold Square to take a seat on the wall that surrounds the water feature.

"Laptop," he commanded, holding out his hand, before softening his order with a grin. After just a few minutes, he slammed the lid shut, saying, "Booked," and handed me back my laptop.

On our return to the hotel reception desk, Holmes greeted the receptionist with an embarrassed grimace.

"Bit of a cock up back at the ranch," he said. "Can you please check booking reference nine, three, seven, six, seven, six?"

"Certainly, sir," said the receptionist, her patience clearly tightening. "Ah yes, sir, we do have a booking for that reference for a Mister Lizard."

"That girl," replied Holmes. "I'll put her over my knee when we get back."

The receptionist glanced a look that indicated that she was unsure if his threat of corporal punishment in the workplace was a serious one.

As we entered what I was relieved to find was a twin room, Holmes ducked into the bathroom.

"What the fuck's wrong with this water?" he shouted.

"It's fine. It's just different," I called back. "They extract it from the hills here, whereas back home we get ours from Kielder."

"Well they need to un-extract it because it tastes like piss."

"Sherlock, have you never been out of Teesside before?"

"Yeah, of course. I went to Blackpool once but we drank dandelion and burdock. It was ten bob a can, which was expensive back then. I've also been to Whitby, Lilt, and Beamish on a school trip. Lilt again."

Holmes re-entered the room with a look of disgust strewn across his face.

"Why don't you just grab something from the minibar?" I suggested.

"There's a bar?" whooped Holmes as I glanced over to where I thought it may be. "Oh, Doc, you gave it away," he said, as he crouched down and opened the fridge. "Hello ladies. Don't mind if I do," he continued in an accent that was more Southern States than South Bank.

"You do realise that stuff's quite expensive."

"Don't worry about that, Doc, Mister Lizard is picking up the tab tonight. Anyway, it can't be any more expensive than flaming Blackpool."

"So that's as far as you've been? Blackpool, Whitby and Beamish?"

"Pretty much. I never needed to go anywhere else. Besides, look what happened to Captain Cook. He went legging it off around the world and ended up getting his head cut off. Apparently some of the locals got a bit shirty when he wouldn't share his parmo with 'em. That wouldn't have happened if he'd stayed in Guisborough. Well, unless it was a Friday night and the woolybacks were on the rampage."

We left the hotel late the next morning, me with my new laptop tucked under my arm.

"You probably want to get shot of that," said Holmes.

"Get shot of what?" I asked.

"The laptop. Its MAC address will have been logged on more sensitive government websites than, well, I don't know what. You log on with that at home and you'll have more spooks round than an episode of Rentaghost. You probably want to ditch your phone too."

"You're kidding."

"Yeah, but ditching the laptop doesn't seem so bad now, does it?"

"It actually feels no different."

"Okay," said Holmes, "bit ungrateful. Look, Doc, it will hurt me more than it hurts you. In our short time together, me and this little baby have seen some sights, I tell you. Oh, before you do there's one more thing I need to do."

"What's that?" I asked.

"Corrupt all the CCTV footage of us bouncing around this place."

As we made our way up West Street to grab some lunch,

Holmes took the laptop from me and approached a police constable pounding the beat in the direction opposite to ours. In an unconvincing Irish accent, he explained how we'd found the laptop in a pub and would be grateful if it could be put in lost property until the rightful owner showed up to collect it. We would take it ourselves, he said, but we need to get to the station to catch a train back to the Emerald Isle. That we were heading away from the station was lost on that particular boy in blue.

"I can't believe you've given such an incriminating piece of evidence to a policeman," I whispered as we walked away.

"I just thought it would be funny," said Holmes.

"Funny?"

"Yeah, well, if he's honest and hands it in, he'll be fine. If he wraps it up for Christmas then, well, that's his lookout."

You may recall a story in the news of a policeman being arrested in Sheffield for hacking into the systems of several banks and numerous sensitive government departments. The officer in question pleaded his innocence and that he'd been given the computer used by a couple of Welshman, unfortunately however, there was no CCTV footage available that day to corroborate his claim.

9

We got to the Psalter Tavern quite early to take a table in a secluded area out of general view. Holmes craned his neck to view each of the Wednesday night quiz crowd as they filtered in.

After an hour or so, Wilson and Paul arrived, accompanied by two rather handy looking heavies, to take a table just out of our view. Their two escorts positioned themselves behind a couple of half lagers at the bar. At that, Holmes sat back in his seat, holding his hand out flat to signal we should stay seated.

After twenty to twenty-five minutes and the first round or two of the quiz, Holmes looked at me before flicking his gaze down at our near empty glasses and raising his eyebrows. His instruction for me to replenish the drinks had now progressed to a non-vocalised arrangement.

I turned around from the bar with some fresh drinks to see Holmes approach Paul's table. Uncertain what to do, I leant back against the bar and observed the unfolding events. Paul was quite literally gobsmacked, his jaw dropping as he recognised Holmes.

Holmes flashed a knowing grin. "Hello, my mate."

At that, one of the half glass heavies from the other end of the bar moved to join them. Taking that as my cue, I crossed the floor to position myself behind Holmes' shoulder. The menace I was adding seeming rather disproportionate.

Holmes stared back at the heavy with a look of wide-eyed surprise. He then dipped his eyebrows to add some threat. "Who are you, like, his designated twat?"

At that, the heavy squared off to Holmes, his stature expanding in the process. He rocked his head to one side fixing a confident dead-eyed stare on the nonplussed Holmes. Assuming a fracas was to ensue, I maintained my position at Holmes shoulder, shuffling involuntarily from one foot to another.

"It's okay," said Paul, "he's an old friend. Leave it with me." At that, Paul rose from his seat and gestured for us to follow him.

Paul led us outside to a table at the far end of the external seating area.

"What the fuck are you doing here, Sherlock?"

"Martha sent me. For some reason, she wanted to check if you were still alive."

"How did you find me?"

"Ah, that was the easy bit. I just typed 'wanker' into Google. You came up first."

"Look, Sherlock," said Paul, directing the discussion in a more productive direction, "this is serious stuff. I'm supposed to be off the map, man. I'm under a witness protection programme, for fuck's sake."

"I've already figured that out," said Holmes. "What I can't

understand is why anyone gives a shit about a two-bob twat like you."

Paul responded with a look of resignation. He then stuttered to consider how much of his story to reveal.

"I was recruited," he sighed. "Two Americans from one of the regiments we shared camp with. They pitched it as some sort of security gig. It was my way out of the army and the money was fantastic."

"A quick fix with some easy money. That doesn't sound like you, Paul."

Paul paused to glare back at Holmes in frustration.

"So what happened?" prompted Holmes. "Not enough days off?"

"Don't be such a twat, Holmes," responded Paul. "This is serious shit, man. I could be taken out at any minute. Look," he continued, "this gig wasn't looking after some sheik's Rogger Royce. It turned out to be some serious crime shit. Assassinations and all fucking sorts."

"So you bottled it?"

"No," Paul sighed, "it just got a little too warm and a little too close to home."

"Close to home?"

"They were recruiting me to get to you. That was my first job. To get you onside."

"Me?"

"Yep, the Americans wanted me to get you to do some computer shit. Something about a file they needed."

Holmes rustled around in the inside pocket of his jacket and pulled out a scrap of paper. He unfolded it in front of Paul to reveal a sketch of Agents Smith and Jones.

"This them? The Americans?"

"Yeah, where did you get that?"

"Mary drew it. They spent a short time drinking in the Lip. You won't be getting any bother from them anymore."

"I know," said Paul. "I heard they ran into some trouble. It's not them I'm worried about. It's their boss."

"Their boss?"

"They only ever referred to him as the Professor. I never met or even spoke to him. But he's some serious shit. The army, Two Two, the secret services, the whole fucking lot of them are looking for him. I'm pretty sure they're only keeping me here until they need some bait."

"So why didn't you just come and get me?"

"Because as soon as you'd have finished the job, they would have capped you."

"What, and you're arsed about that?"

"No, but if you're hovis, who's gonna look out for Martha."

Holmes laughed. "You're worried about Martha yet you're shacked up with some other bird."

"Other bird?"

"Yeah, this Mary Sutherland. Did she come with the house?"

"No, she's my wife."

"Your wife? You're still married to Marth?"

"That was another life. That person's dead. There's paperwork to prove it."

"For fuck's sake, Paul, or whatever your fucking name is, this isn't about sodding paperwork. It's about Martha. We've known her since we were kids."

At that, the antagonism that had been ebbing and flowing between them evaporated. Paul looked Holmes in the eye as if to plead for some sort of exoneration.

Holmes broke the stare and swivelled his head to look out into the road, his head nodding gently to himself. He then stood up, shoved the crumpled sketch back in his pocket and buttoned up his jacket.

Returning his view to Paul, he scratched the middle of his brow before drawing some audible breath in and out of his nostrils.

"Are you gonna tell her I'm alive?" asked an uncertain Paul.

"No," replied Holmes. "I'm gonna tell her you're dead." He took a few steps down the street before turning back. "Oh, by the way, the answer to question seven is the Comsat Angels, you stupid twat."

10

That was that. Holmes and I were to keep Paul's secret until we were lying in our graves. As you might imagine, I was never comfortable with this arrangement. My view was that it wasn't within the gift of Holmes to cosset Martha in this way. The only mitigation was that Martha not knowing provided extra protection to Paul. I didn't see how he deserved it. However, if his cover was broken and the result was fatal, we would have circled around to a similar situation. A paradox if ever there was one.

I attempted to discuss it with Holmes several times, but he refused to engage. He did however pass one comment that seemed to make sense of it all, "It's not the despair that gets you, it's the hope." I'm not sure where he plucked that quote from. Probably a song lyric somewhere. But we extinguished Martha's hope and that somehow made things better. Perverse, really.

It was Holmes that broke the silence as we traipsed along Baker Street. "This is fucking brilliant, isn't it? We've finally cracked a case and we can't tell any bugger about it. Fucking bollocks."

We turned into Hud Couture to find Martha once again straightening the shelves. Holmes didn't speak. He just pursed his lips and shook his head, his eyes misting over.

"What's happening with you?" laughed Martha, her eyes shot with tears. She moved to embrace him, before stepping back, her hands clasped on his upper arms. "Sherl, I lost him when he stepped on the plane all those years ago. I watched him, laughing with his mates, all togged up in his army gear with his kitbag and everything. He never even looked up to wave back at me. I knew he would never come back. I thought he'd be killed on the way over there or as soon as he jumped off the plane. He wasn't, but he was lost to me. I knew he was. I knew it. I just didn't know how it was supposed to happen. Thanks, Sherl. I know you did your best."

As the pair resumed their embrace, I quietly exited the shop. To this day, I'm torn. Is a lie justified by the illusion it creates? You tell me. I really don't know.

THE VALLEY DRIVE MYSTERY

1

There are certain events in your life you remember for its remaining duration. Fixed points in time. My first proper date with Mary was one of these. We'd had the occasional drink together, and it wasn't uncommon for us to share a bottle of wine after she had locked up the Twisted Lip of a night, however this was the first time we dressed up and went to a formal event as an official couple.

She looked absolutely gorgeous in a black figure-hugging party dress that fused sophistication with a subtle sensuality. Adorning her look with little makeup and a few pieces of small understated silver jewellery, she was the kind of sight that made eyes sore. I couldn't take my eyes off her. She was so beautiful, I didn't want to blink. On first sight of her, I parked my worry that the party might end up being a damp squib. I wanted to get there and show her off, even if it was to a bunch of strangers.

The guests at the party were a mixture of flash new money types and those with more legitimate and explainable professions. I saw myself firmly in the latter of those two groups, however with the recent distractions provided by a certain Sherlock Holmes, my patient list of late had been dwindling to the point where the link to my chosen career was growing more and more tenuous. If it were not for Doctor Anstruther, the chap I shared rooms with, being so happy to cover for me on occasion, I think I may have been forced to leave the medical profession altogether.

I hadn't seen Charlie McCarthy since our days at university. Time had not been kind to him. At university, he sported long flowing hair which he tied into a ponytail. Now the only hair he sported, on his head at least, was his eyebrows. He also had the sort of face that had been leathered by the exposure to excessive sun and cigarette smoke. He was perhaps five or six years younger than me but looked at least fifteen years older.

Although we lived in roughly the same area, our circles had not overlapped in the nineteen or so years since we graduated. Indeed, had I not signed up to various social media websites after I had split up from my wife, I expect that period would have extended significantly, if not indefinitely.

Given Charlie's time-ravaged appearance, it was a slight surprise when he introduced as guest of honour, his rather stunning wife Lana. That said, looking at his house, he clearly had money. The strange thing was, she didn't appear to be the type to be swayed by wealth. They really were an odd pairing. As he always had done, Charlie controlled the conversation, his favourite subject being himself. It was however the occasional interjects from Lana that carried the most interest. There also appeared little in the way of affection flowing between them in either direction.

Halfway through a dull story concerning the creation of the next arm of his business empire, Charlie shouted, "Mister Spaulding," and left us to talk to another guest. His wife, who was really nice, apologised for his ignorance, shook our hands and dutifully followed.

Although the party was to celebrate Lana's birthday, she was far from the centre of attention. As McCarthy milled around the large reception room, steamrollering through other people's conversations, Lana was never far from his side. She was the type of person you were instantly drawn to. Both vivacious and intellectual, she lit up the room like a Hollywood star from the fifties. It was such a shame how McCarthy had her caged.

Actually I need to check myself there. It's starting to sound like

Lana threw a shadow over my Mary. She didn't. To my eyes, and I think to many of the other men and women in the room, Mary was the true beauty.

As I stood enjoying both Mary's exquisite company and a reasonable Prosecco, we were approached by a young couple who introduced themselves as Jordan and George. Jordan, the male, explained how he was a journalist from the Evening Gazette.

"We dress up in disguise and come to dos like this to spy on the well-heeled of Teesside," interjected George. "Our friends all think we're crazy, but he gets paid for the evening and I get all this free booze." She raised her glass with a, "Cheers," whilst double-crossing her eyes.

"Yeah," remarked Jordan, "a hack like me couldn't afford clobber like this. The paper pays for this get up."

"I can't wait to get out of these things and get my Docs on," added George.

They were a nice couple who tended to speak as a partnership in alternating sentences. I felt more an affinity with them than any other of the partygoers, and Mary seemed to enjoy their company too.

"You're a friend of Sherlock Holmes, aren't you?" asked Jordan. "I sometimes see you with him in the Lip."

"That's us," I replied. "Mary runs the Twisted Lip."

"Of course," said George, "I knew I knew you from somewhere."

"Mates rates from now on," added Jordan, smiling.

Mary smiled back, but made no concession.

"Yeah, I saw him again inside the cafe at the end of Baker Street this morning. What's it called?"

"Baker Street Kitchen," informed George.

"He's quite a character," continued Jordan, "we're often hearing about his antics at the paper. I'd love to run a series of articles on him. You don't fancy getting involved with something like that, do you, Doctor? You could write a column."

"Please, call me John," I insisted. "It would certainly be an interesting read, however I'm no author."

"That's no problem; I could get one of the lads to edit it for you."

"I can see it now," said Mary, "The Adventures of Sherlock Holmes."

"And the Intrepid Doctor John Watson,"' I appended.

"Yeah, whatever," replied Mary.

2

The conversation between myself, Jordan, George and the wonderful Mary was interrupted by the sound of a woman screaming and her manic pounding on the outside of the room's French windows.

A young man, who I later found out to be Charlie's son, James, rattled the door in his urgency before managing to open it.

"Lana's floating in the pool," screamed the woman.

James pushed past her and into the garden. The terror in her scream urged me and three or four of the other party guests to follow. We reached the pool to find James in the water pulling a lifeless body to the side.

Myself and another guest pulled her out and laid her by the side of the pool. As I moved to administer CPR, my shoulder was pulled back by James.

"Let me," he said. "I'm a nurse." He took his jacket from where he'd dropped it and placed it across Lana's body. He then started to pump air into Lana's lungs, breaking off periodically to massage her heart.

Grabbing his mobile phone from the pocket of his jacket, he handed it to me and told me to ring an ambulance.

"It's okay," I said, "I can use mine."

"No, you won't get a signal," he said as he continued to work on Lana. "Mine's linked to the landline."

I fumbled with his unfamiliar handset until James grabbed it back off me and hit a few keys before handing it back. The display read 'Emergency'.

The ambulance arrived in a matter of minutes. One of the

paramedics relieved James of his CPR activities and used a hand-operated respirator to continue the support of her breathing. The two medics then lifted her onto a stretcher and, with James now operating the respirator, made their way back towards the driveway where the ambulance was parked.

As the ambulance fired up its blues and departed, I looked to the chap who had helped me pull Lana out of the pool and shook my head. "She's gone," I said mournfully.

He nodded in agreement. "Superintendent Malcolm Spaulding, Cleveland Police. We need to lock this place down. I'm not seeing this as an accident. We can't let anybody leave. I'm gonna go back and join the others. See what I can pick up. Can you ring the station and ask for Detective Inspector Lestrade?"

"I know the inspector," I responded.

Spaulding and I re-entered the reception room to find Mary comforting the girl who had discovered Lana in the pool.

"Hello everyone," I said, addressing the room. "My name is Doctor John Watson. As you will appreciate, tonight's incident is a serious one. I therefore need to ask you all to stay here until the police arrive. I'm sure they won't take any longer than they need to, and I really would value your cooperation."

The crowd in the room displayed mixed responses. Some agreement, some frustration and some stony, stunned stillness.

Gesturing to one of the female guests to take over comforting duties, I moved Mary from earshot. "Can you ring the Lip and see if Holmes is there?" I asked. "I think we need him here. I'll ring the police and get Lestrade."

Coincidentally both Holmes and Lestrade reached the scene around the same time, their arrival being heralded by the ensuing bickering between them. As they made their way towards us, I caught the culmination of their discussion.

"That's all I'm saying," said Holmes. "If we turn up together, people are going to think we're shagging. A five minute delay, that's all it needed."

In response, Lestrade returned a dismissive shudder of the head.

"Bloody hell, Mary, you've scrubbed up well," said Holmes, licking his index finger and running it across his eyebrow. "I think it's time for you to leave this chump and get yourself a real man."

Holmes broke off his lamentable seduction to stare at the spot where Lana had once lain.

"Here, was it?" he asked, crouching down to his haunches before we had chance to respond. He tilted his head from side to side, picking his incisor with his thumbnail.

He then stood. Shepherding myself and Mary to a more private area of the veranda, he whispered, "Somebody's watching me. Can you two keep your eyes open? Observe everything, forget nothing."

Mary and I looked at each other, both perturbed by his instruction.

"Right then," he said, addressing Lestrade, "we need to move all these people to a neutral area. Stop 'em walking all over the evidence. Round the front on the drive, maybe. Can you get a couple of your lads to watch 'em, in case they nick off over the wall?"

Lestrade moved to address the assembled partygoers, some of whom were watching from a distance and others who had remained in the house to comfort those upset by the dreadful event of the night.

"Hello everyone," he called. "My name is Detective Inspector Lestrade of Cleveland Police. I would be grateful if you could please move to the front of the house. We'll try to make this as quick as possible, however you must understand there has been a serious incident here this evening, and we would therefore appreciate your cooperation."

Holmes nodded his approval, however his endorsement was tainted with a tinge of instinctive mockery.

As the party guests started to form into groups and gravitate as directed, one of the female guests asked if it was okay for her to get her coat from the house.

"Of course," responded Holmes, "but make sure it's your own. I know what you posh bastards are like."

The woman recoiled at the unfairness of his accusation.

Charlie McCarthy did not follow the crowd but instead

broke from the group and joined us, introducing himself as the homeowner.

"I'm Sherlock Holmes," came the response, "and I own fuck all. Why don't you shit shoe shuffle round there with rest of 'em? The adults are talking."

"Excuse me," replied McCarthy, "my wife just been found floating in the swimming pool."

"Look," said Holmes, "it's your party and you can cry if you want to, but right now I need you over there with the rest of the Teesside glitterati."

McCarthy looked to Lestrade, who returned an embarrassed nod. He then turned to join his migrating guests, however his progress was interrupted by a growl from Holmes. "Lestrade, take his shoes and bag 'em."

"You think they could be evidence?" asked Lestrade.

"No, they're shit."

Holmes' antagonistic manner then flicked like a switch. "Excuse me," he said politely to one of the scene of crime officers who were now scavenging around the garden, "can myself and the Doctor here each get a pair of those latex gloves that you use?"

Without speaking, another chap pulled a couple of pairs from what looked like a tissue box, handing us each a pair. Holmes pulled his pair on with an exaggerated mime before turning to address Lestrade. "Right, Inspector, touch yer toes, it's payback time."

He then adopted a serious demeanour. Standing with his feet together and his hands in his jacket pockets, his eyes darted from side to side. Every couple of minutes he adjusted his feet to re-orientate before resuming his survey. All the while, his eye movements were accompanied by neck twitches occurring at a less regular cadence.

I suppose the odd thing with his technique, which by now I'd seen on a number of occasions, was its irregularity. He never scanned the panorama in a methodical sweep but seemed to harvest random segments which he then pieced together in his mind. To me, this exposed the risk of something being missed, however in all the time I spent with Holmes I don't recall a single example of this ever being the case.

After a time period of perhaps ten minutes, Holmes walked over to a small shrub growing in the edging between the lawn and the paving that surrounded the pool. Pulling back the leaves, he exposed what looked to be a small bottle of tablets.

"SOCO," called Holmes, "can you bag this, mate? Careful though, there's a decent thumb print on it."

The scene of crime officer obliged, carefully placing the item in what looked to me like a freezer bag.

Holmes then made his way across to the outer edge of the lawn, which was bordered by some medium-sized trees. He skated around the boundary, pausing in several locations to stare at the ground before dipping through the trees and out of sight. Mary, Lestrade, myself and a couple of Lestrade's men stood rooted for what must have been ten minutes, awaiting his re-emergence.

"Someone's been over there in the last few hours," he said, appearing unobserved from behind our shoulders. "He's left his footprints by that tree." He then handed Mary a beaten up daffodil, before gesturing to one of the SOCOs and miming the action of a photograph being taken, whilst mimicking the sound of a camera shutter. "Mate," he nodded, pointing in the direction of the tree.

"Anything else?" sighed Lestrade, apparently unconvinced by Holmes' investigative technique. This in spite of Holmes uncovering the seemingly crucial piece of evidence that was the tablet bottle.

"Yes," said Holmes, "the bedroom. And don't get any ideas, Ricky Martin."

"What are you talking about?" scowled Lestrade.

"You being gay."

"I'm not gay. I'm a happily married man. I've got three kids."

Holmes responded by pointing a knowing glance.

As we made our way through the capacious house, with Lestrade ahead of us and out of earshot, I queried Holmes' earlier assertion.

"Do you think Lestrade is gay?"

"Nah," he smirked, "but he's not so sure himself now. I'm enjoying this."

"What? Goading Lestrade?"

"Nah, I'm getting bored with taking the piss out of him. I mean all this. We're real detectives. It's like being on the telly."

The surreality of the situation hadn't escaped me.

As we entered the bedroom, Holmes glanced around briefly before taking a seat in an ornate chair positioned by the window. Looking rather disinterested, he sat with his head resting on his knuckle. Much of the time he spent staring at the bed, his inaction only interrupted to acknowledge a SOCO who photographed a dressing table before removing a half-filled wine glass that was resting upon it.

Holmes then moved to examine one of the bedside tables. Kneeling down, he cocked his head and closed one eye to look along the surface of the table top. He then licked the little finger of his latex-gloved left hand before dabbing the surface of the table. Licking the same finger again, he displayed a thoughtful grimace.

Returning to his feet, he moved around the bed to make a similar low-level observation of the other bedside table, before swivelling and entering the en suite bathroom, located on the other side of a walk-in wardrobe, dressing room affair. As I watched him through the corridor, he stood staring at the sink before again using his little finger to sample something on the rim. He then glanced sharply around the bathroom before re-joining us in the bedroom.

"The girl who discovered the body, what was she? The maid, or housekeeper or something?"

"Maybe," I responded, "she was dishing out drinks and canapés at the party. She may have been hired for the night, but I did notice a certain level of familiarity between her and both Charlie and Lana."

"Can we get her up here?" he asked Lestrade.

Lestrade nodded a confirmation to a uniformed officer by the door, who then left to retrieve her.

"Doc," asked Holmes, "did you notice Lana leave the party?"

"No, but I did overhear her saying she felt a little tired and was considering a lie down."

"Did she look tired?"

"Not that I recall, but we were all starting to feel a little worse for wear by that time. Odd that I feel relatively sober now."

"She didn't look too bad to me," added Mary.

"That's the thing with canapés," said Holmes. "They don't soak up the booze. You'd have been better off with a parmo in a bun each."

"Delightful," remarked Mary.

Our discussion was interrupted by the officer returning with Patience Moran, the girl who had discovered Lana. She was indeed the live-in housekeeper.

"Hello," said Holmes. "It's nothing to worry about. I just wanted to ask you a few questions about Missus McCarthy. Is that okay?"

Patience nodded.

"Do you know which side of the bed Missus McCarthy slept on?"

"Yeah, that side," she said, pointing to the left of the bed as we looked at it from its foot.

"How do you know that?"

"She sometimes asked me to wake her. She was a very deep sleeper and would sleep through an alarm. If she ever had an appointment, I used to come up and shake her."

Holmes paused. "Did she take a drink to bed?"

"Yes, every night."

"Not water?"

"No, usually some orange."

"Juice or cordial?"

"Cordial normally. Mister McCarthy always drank all the fresh stuff."

"Thank you," said Holmes, before gesturing to the officer to escort her back.

After they had left, he continued. "If Lana was in the habit of taking a drink to bed with her, why didn't she grab something from the party. I never saw any cordial down there but there was plenty of other stuff. She could have made do."

"Maybe she intended to return to the party," I postulated.

"Yeah, cos that always happens, doesn't it? Get pissed, take a quick ten minute nap, and party on. And how did she get from here to the pool?"

"She might not have come up here."

"What and that wine glass made it up here on its own, did it? Maybe she sleep walks," muttered Holmes with no real conviction. "Kitchen," he continued. "If you want to find out what goes on in the bedroom, 'ave a look in the kitchen."

On entering the kitchen, with Mary, myself and our assembled police entourage in tow, Holmes made his way straight to the dishwasher. He pulled open the door with a single index finger and stood staring into it, his eyes darting around the numerous items of glassware, crockery and cutlery.

"More forks than knives," he muttered.

"What does that mean?" asked Mary.

"She's had a man in. Or maybe Alanis Morissette."

"Can you bag all those glasses? The ones that size," he said, pointing to a short, thick-based tumbler.

He then squatted to his haunches to pull out the bottom drawer of the dishwasher. "These too," he said, picking out a terracotta mortar and pestle.

Once Holmes had completed his investigation of the house, we exited by the front doors to where the party guests were amassed. Holmes milled among them, looking them up and down. In response, most people just stared back bemused, barring the odd individual who shook their head in extended frustration.

All during this little pantomime, we stood a short distance away, Lestrade with a look of perplexity set into his face.

"Someone's got their eye on me," said Holmes as he returned to us. "Is there anyone there you recognise, Lestrade?"

Lestrade scanned the group. "Shit, Superintendent Spaulding," he said before stabbing a look of anger in the direction of the two uniformed policemen on station.

At that, Spaulding broke from the group and joined us, his cover blown.

"I'm sorry, sir," said an overly-apologetic Lestrade. "I never noticed you there."

"That's quite alright, Lestrade," he said. "I thought it best if I remained incognito. To see what I could uncover. I'm not convinced this was an accident. Missus McCarthy disappeared off to her bedroom and twenty minutes later she turns up floating in the pool. There's something not quite right here."

"There are a few other things not quite right here," said Holmes. "What's a police superintendent doing at a gig like this, and how come nobody here knows you're Five O?"

"Pertinent points," smiled Spaulding. "I'm here in my capacity as school governor and I rarely broadcast my day job. It leads to a lot of unnatural behaviour. If anyone asks, I tell them I'm a civil servant, which of course I am."

"Did you uncover anything?" asked Holmes.

"No, nothing of any worth," he replied, "however from what I've seen of your methods, I'm reasonably impressed. Did you uncover anything of interest inside the house?"

"A few things. A bottle of pills we found by the pool seems key, however we'll know more when your lads perform some tests on some of the other stuff."

"Thank you, Mister Holmes. Lestrade, you can fill me in when we're back at the station tomorrow morning. Can we now allow these people to go home? They're starting to grumble and I don't think we'll get any more out of them tonight. At the moment, I'm afraid there's no tangible evidence to suggest this is anything more than a terrible accident."

Lestrade broke off to take a call. "That was the station. The woman taken in to James Cook tonight was dead on arrival."

Mary yelped at the news. Even though I was sure she wouldn't make it, my insides hollowed.

The three of us, Holmes, Mary and myself walked through the garden gate into the pending darkness to be confronted with the issue of how we were to get home. Holmes walked over to a black cab parked about thirty yards up the street before beckoning us to follow him.

"Come on," he called.

Somewhat confused, we followed him as he jumped in the driver's seat. Not wanting to get in a vehicle, which I presumed stolen, I followed him around to the driver's side.

"Where did you get this?" I asked.

"I borrowed it," he replied.

"From whom?"

"From Martha," he responded, slowly and deliberately.

"From Martha?"

"Yeah, well, it's Paul's but he won't be needing it anymore."

I wandered back around to the kerb where Mary was now standing and helped her into the back of the cab, feeling a little ashamed at my wayward assumption.

"This should be an interesting one, Doc," called Holmes through the sliding window in the partition between the driver and the passengers.

"It could have just been an accident, Sherlock," I responded.

"It could," he said, "but it's still an interesting little mystery."

"A difficult one to crack?"

"No, not really. As long as we try to avoid focusing on what happened and concentrate on why it happened, the root cause and/or causes, it should all become clear. I'll tell you one thing, though. By this time tomorrow, Lestrade will have put two and two together, got out his little Casio calculator watch, and arrested Charlie McCarthy for the murder of his wife."

"Murder?" exclaimed Mary.

"Yep, Lestrade won't wait around for lab results. It's not his style. He likes to get people locked up ASAP. Lana was drugged and thrown in the pool. That's how he'll see it. We could end up working for McCarthy if we're not careful."

"I somehow don't think he's gonna pay you, Sherlock."

"No, probably not."

3

The next morning I strolled up Baker Street to find Holmes having a tea with Martha in her boutique. My mood was a strange one. It was exciting to be involved in a case like this, but it was all a little too real. It did after all involve the murder of someone. Someone I'd had a brief chat with around an hour before her death. There was however nothing for me to do but follow the path we'd already begun, and hope for a successful outcome. What success looked like, I knew not.

"Marth, can I borrow Hansom again?" asked Holmes as I entered the shop.

"Hansom?" I puzzled.

"That's what she calls her cab," he responded.

"No, bugger off," interrupted Martha. "You brought her back empty last night."

"You only went to Marton in it?" I queried.

"Yeah, after I dropped you off I picked up a few fares. Better than that though, I also picked up a bit of information about your mate, Charlie McCarthy."

"From whom?" I asked.

"Some of the people I gave lifts home to. Anyway, McCarthy was a director of a company called Boscombe Metals along with another gadgie called John Turner. The company was funded with all sorts of government grants, but between the both of them, they ran it into the ground. There's a lot of bad feeling about it. Basically they pissed millions of pounds of public money down the drain. There must also be a fair bit of bad blood between them. Lana was Turner's wife before she knobbed off and left him for McCarthy."

"Lana Turner?" quipped Martha.

"Yeah, suppose it must 'ave been," replied Holmes, "but don't cry yourself blind, darling. Turner looks to be doing alright. He lives in a big place called Hatherley Farm up near Thorpe Thewles."

"Really?" said Martha. "Perhaps I should invite him over?"

"Martha, he's about a hundred. Are you into mantiques, like? Actually, I can see you and him on a Saga holiday. Do you want me to put a word in for yer?"

Martha's response was all visual and quite frightening.

Holmes, immune to her venom, grinned back. "God bless the

millionaire that shares your wedding day. Howay, Marth, chuck us your keys. I'll put some petrol in it."

"It's not an it, she's a her, and if you put petrol in her, I'll break your legs. She takes diesel."

We trundled up the farm track to Hatherley Farm to find Turner fixing a tractor by the side of the farmhouse.

"I haven't ordered a taxi," he said, confused, as he approached us, wiping the oil off his hands and lower arms with a rag.

"Good," responded Holmes, unseating himself from the driving position, "I'm not licensed to carry passengers."

Turner's uncertainty elevated yet further as I alighted the passenger compartment to join Holmes.

"John Turner?" asked Holmes.

"Yeah," nodded Turner hesitantly.

"My name is Sherlock Holmes. My colleague here, Doctor John Watson, is an associate of your ex-business partner Charlie McCarthy. We would like to ask you some questions."

"Surely you're not the police?"

"No, we're kind of freelance."

"So I don't have to answer your questions then."

"No. If you'd prefer, we could get a few dozen plod round here to ask some questions for us. And maybe have a look around."

"Is this about Lana?" asked Turner. "I got a call last night when I got home."

"Yeah, there's a possibility she may have been murdered, and if so, we're gonna find her killer. Either way we're gonna get to the bottom of this. Is there any reason you wouldn't want to help us with that?"

Turner paused to consider. "None that I can think of. But what would I know? Lana left a year and a half, two years ago."

"So how did you feel when your business partner started screwing your wife?"

As you might imagine, Turner railed at the coarseness of Holmes' question. "How do you think I fucking felt? I was devastated."

"Were you still working with McCarthy at that time?"

"No, the company had been wound up by then."

"Are you sure?"

"Quite sure. I lost my wife and my business. I remember that quite well."

"Boscombe Metals. That wasn't great, was it? How much of the taxpayers' money did you piss down the drain? Ten, fifteen million?"

"That money wasn't pissed down the drain, it was siphoned away."

"Where? Into this place?"

"No. I saw none of it. I inherited this farm from my late father. While he was dying, and my mind was elsewhere, Charlie McCarthy bought crap, paid for consultancy services and all sorts of other shit we didn't need. All of it from companies he owned or at least had a stake in. When I got my head together, there was nothing left. Nothing to do but lay the lads off and call in the receivers."

"Isn't that embezzlement or fraud or something?" queried Holmes.

"Probably misappropriation of public funds, but if there's one thing Charlie McCarthy knows how to do, it's cover his tracks. Besides, what could I do? I countersigned most of those deals. I just didn't know what I was signing. My head was all over the place, so I trusted him."

Turner turned to walk away before reverting back to face us. "Look, believe what you want," he sighed, "but it's not me you should be talking to. It's Charlie McCarthy."

"No need," replied Holmes. "By now, he should be banged up and fielding some tricky questions from me Five O mates down the station."

Turner responded with a knowing nod, suggesting he felt justice was being done.

"What's up with your leg?" asked Holmes, his tone segueing into something less accusatory.

"Ah, it's nothing," replied Turner. "Just an old diving accident. A manta ray decided to give me a bit of a tickle."

"Do you still go diving?"

"No, that was Lana's thing. I only went to make sure she was safe. The thing is she was ten times better at it than I was. It ended up being her looking after me."

"Did you not think about marrying again?"

"No," he smiled. "I'm done with that sort of thing."

"Thank you, Mister Turner," said Holmes. "I'm very sorry for your loss."

Turner nodded his appreciation.

As we jumped back in the cab, I took Holmes to task. "You were a bit harsh on him there, weren't you? I know he was divorced, but someone he was close to has just died, for god's sake."

Holmes was unapologetic. "Yeah and it wasn't until I eased off that he told us the useful stuff."

"What useful stuff?"

"That he's still in love with his ex-missus and they liked to go diving together. In water."

"How's that useful?"

"Well it's useful if you noticed the two brand new diving masks."

"Diving masks? Where were they?"

"Hung up in the garage."

"I never saw them."

"Yes you did, you just didn't observe."

"Right, I presume you're thinking what I'm thinking. That John and Lana were in the process of reconciling and McCarthy killed her?"

"Nope," said Holmes wistfully, "we've nowhere near enough data to start forming conclusions. You don't put the batter in the oven until the fat's hot."

4

As we sat in the Twisted Lip, I couldn't see past the conclusion that Charlie had murdered his wife. From what I'd seen, there wasn't an awful lot of love flowing between them, and there was clearly more to John Turner's story than he'd chosen to divulge.

"A three-pint problem, Sherlock?"

"Mmm, maybe. Too early to tell."

"I mean, would you like another beer?"

"Oh, yes please, my mind is racing. I could do with putting the brakes on."

I returned to the table just as Lestrade entered the pub. He was clearly riled about something.

"Ah, Inspector Lard," said Holmes, "no need for me to get up."

"Sherlock, what the fuck are you doing questioning potential murder suspects?"

"Is there such a thing?"

"What?" snapped a confused Lestrade.

"Well you're either suspected or you're not. You can't be potentially suspected. That's a tautology or something. You're really not very good at this, are you, fat boy? In't that right, Doc?"

I wasn't sure whether that was actually an example of a tautology but I thought not.

"Look, it doesn't fucking matter," snarled Lestrade. "What matters is you not interfering in my investigation."

Lestrade stomped away from the table, before turning around and pacing back.

"What did Turner tell you?"

"Haven't you spoken to him?" puzzled Holmes.

"I have, but I want to know what he told you."

"Well, he blames McCarthy for their company going tits up. Reckons McCarthy squirrelled all the money away."

"Yeah, I got that," replied Lestrade, his mood quelling.

"Things with Lana weren't completely dead in the water either."

Lestrade reeled with a look of synthetic indignation.

"Sorry," continued Holmes, "I mean a reconciliation was in motion. In fact, they may have already been back together. I also got the feeling he was about to bugger off somewhere. He was fixing some crappy old tractor. It seemed like he was killing time."

"Maybe he was trying to take his mind off the death of his ex-wife?"

"No, it was more than that. The way he was working was too methodical to be just about distraction. It was a labour of love that he'd come back to. That tractor hadn't been touched in years. It's like he's all of a sudden found some peace of mind."

"Maybe that's down to McCarthy's pending imprisonment," I interjected.

"Nah," replied Holmes, puckering his lips as if to shepherd a thought, "he started work on the tractor before Lana died."

"Okay," said Lestrade, "I need you to come to the station, Sherlock."

"Fuck off. Unless you're gonna arrest me for something. And what are the charges? Having a better grasp of grammar than the local constabulary?"

Lestrade's response was somewhere between apathy and frustration. "Look," he sighed, "we arrested Charlie McCarthy earlier and are going to carry out a formal interview. Spaulding wants you to be involved."

"Me?"

"Yeah, you. Someone's convinced him you have some observational superpowers or something, so he wants you to sit in. But remember, you're only there to observe. I ask the questions, and if you fuck this for me, I'll string you from Newport Bridge."

"Alright," chirped Holmes, "I've never been on that side of the table."

Being in the interview suite at Middlesbrough Police Station was quite bizarre. It was exactly as I'd seen on various television programmes. A bare room with a simple table and chairs was partitioned by a one-way mirror. The sound from the interview area was piped through to the observer's side of the glass, allowing us to see and hear everything. Our vantage point was elevated yet further by several monitors relaying video from cameras trained on the interview table.

A uniformed officer I didn't recognise led McCarthy in,

accompanied by his solicitor. Taking their seats at the table, the solicitor dipped his head towards McCarthy, appearing to issue instructional reminders.

A good while later, Lestrade and Holmes trooped in. Before taking his seat, Holmes winked at me through the glass. Given the observational area was quite spacious, and I could have been stood in any position along the glass wall, I can only wonder how he knew where I was stood.

"What's he doing here?" exclaimed McCarthy.

"Mister Holmes is here purely in an observational capacity," responded Lestrade.

"Well, I don't want him here. Get him out."

"Who we include in these interviews is entirely up to us."

McCarthy's solicitor nodded a confirmation.

"Okay, let's get straight to the point here," said Lestrade. "You drugged your wife and threw her in the pool."

"I'm sorry," responded McCarthy's solicitor, "this is all supposition. What evidence, if any, do you have to support this accusation?"

Lestrade maintained his focus on McCarthy. "We have the bottle of pills, found at the scene, with your thumbprint on them and we have witness statements that you weren't in the room at the time Lana's body was discovered. The autopsy takes place on Monday and I'm sure that traces of the pills found in that bottle will also be found in Lana's stomach. Are you going to wait for that or are you going to save us all some time and confess?"

"Why would I want to kill my wife?"

"Because she was fed up with your philandering and in the process of leaving you to go back to her ex-husband. Because she knew all about the Boscombe Metals fiasco and had enough information to bury you. That's just for starters."

McCarthy responded with a look of confused disbelief.

"Where were you at the time Lana's body was discovered?"

"I was in the garden on the other side of the house, getting some air."

"Alone?"

"Yes, alone."

"It's not looking good for you, Charlie. You're the only one there that night who doesn't have any alibi, your fingerprints are all over what looks likely to be the murder weapon, and no one else but you seems to have a motive, but you have at least two, maybe more." Lestrade stood up to leave. "If I were your barrister, I would be looking at a plea bargain." He flashed a look at the solicitor before scraping his chair back under the table.

Holmes remained seated. "Have you been away somewhere?" he asked, calmer than the prevailing mood.

"Yeah," replied McCarthy, "a business trip."

"You have business in Burma?"

"I was sourcing some suppliers. I've been there a few times. They're not the easiest people to do business with."

Holmes nodded indifferently.

"Any more questions?" asked Lestrade, shaking his head in exaggerated disappointment.

"Nope," said Holmes, "I've got all I need."

"So what did you observe then, boy wonder?" asked Lestrade as he and Holmes joined us in Lestrade's office.

"Not much," replied Holmes. "You did all the talking."

"Yeah, I like to unsettle them first. Sometimes that's enough to get them to confess."

"There was one thing, though. That pill bottle came from Burma. It would be too much of a coincidence if it wasn't McCarthy who brought them over here. Have you searched the house to see if there are any more?"

"Yes," responded one of the assembled uniforms, "there were a couple more bottles like it in McCarthy's office."

"Did you check the bins too? For empties?" asked Holmes.

"No," he responded with an embarrassed shuffle.

Lestrade nodded to confirm that that should be his next task. "He's banged to rights," he said as he rose from his chair.

"Let's not go at this like a shagging dog," said Holmes. "You've already waltzed past one key piece of information."

"What's that?"

"There was another person missing from that room at the time the body was discovered."

"Who?"

"The person who discovered it, Patience Moran."

Lestrade's expression indicated he thought that an irrelevance. His struggle to articulate a response was interrupted by the entrance of PC Hardwick.

"Boss, the tests on the bottle of tablets found at McCarthy's place were inconclusive."

"What does that mean?" jibed Holmes. "You couldn't get the top off?"

Hardwick, incognisant to Holmes' mockery, placed a file on Lestrade's desk.

"Let's have a look," said Holmes, grabbing it ahead of Lestrade's grasp.

"It's the same substance that we found in the wine glass, the glasses from the dishwasher, and the mortar and pestle. We just don't know what it is."

"Right," said Holmes, "it's organic, a type of moss, I'd say. Hamiltoneius Ricardendumi, I reckon."

"Really?" I asked. "You can tell what type just from looking at that graph?"

"Can I bollocks. I just made that up."

"Okay," interrupted Lestrade. "What now, Bill Oddie?"

"We need to get some of those pills to a lab. A proper lab. There's a good one in Billingham, erm Belasis Park, Belasis Pharmaceuticals. Inspector, summon my driver. Oh, you're already here," said Holmes, his finger raised in Hardwick's direction.

5

Belasis Pharmaceuticals was an impressive place, perhaps incongruous to its Billingham location. We wandered through the pristine reception area to be greeted by an eminently efficient and seriously attractive young receptionist.

Lestrade announced himself as a detective inspector and requested an audience with whoever was in charge.

A short time after, we were joined by a tall well-presented gentleman who introduced himself as John Openshaw and the CEO of Belasis Pharmaceuticals.

"Hello, Mister Openshaw," said Holmes, shaking his hand. "My name is Sherlock Holmes. I'm working with Detective Inspector Lestrade here, and my associate Doctor John Watson, on the investigation of a serious crime. We have some pills that we need analysing. Are you able to help us with that?"

"Of course," said Openshaw, "let me take you through to the lab."

Openshaw led us through a series of immaculately white corridors before turning through some large double doors and into an expansive laboratory. One person, whose appearance lacked harmony with his surroundings, tinkered at the far end of the room.

"Alastair," called Openshaw, "can I introduce you to these gentlemen?"

Openshaw introduced us all and explained the nature of our visit. The lab technician, dressed in cargo pants, trainers and a dull white lab coat, offered no response, except to nod and hold out his hand to receive the bagged pills we had brought for analysis.

"Alastair Bruce," exclaimed Holmes. "Professor Alastair Bruce. I read about you in the Gazette when you came over from Yale. Quite a story."

"Just Alastair will do," responded Bruce. "The professor thing just makes me feel old and is something best left in academia."

"Alastair here is a local lad, his parents still live up the road in Norton."

"Yes, it was quite a coup prising Alastair from Yale," added Openshaw. "I still can't figure out why he came here," he smiled.

Bruce raised his eyebrows and nodded. "Shall we have a look at what you've got there?" he said, curtailing some uncharacteristic small talk from Holmes.

He wandered back down the lab with us in tow. A hawk-eyed Holmes watched his every move as he ground up the pill before dividing up the resulting powder and distributing it across various apparatus.

Sat atop a tall, wheeled stool, he skated between the apparatus, studying dials and making various adjustments, the electronic whir of his equipment obscured intermittently by the sound of the stool wheels rolling across the hard tiled floor.

"How long will this take?" asked Lestrade.

"Not long," responded Bruce in a near whisper, his expeditious activity uninterrupted by the intrusion, "this equipment is state of the art. I designed it."

After no longer than fifteen minutes, Bruce propelled himself to the end of the bench and started tapping furiously on the keys of an expensive-looking laptop, in a manner not too dissimilar to that I had observed of Holmes.

"Right," he said, "the main component is organic, bryophyta. It's a rare one though. Not something we have on our database. Let me see what Yale have to say about it."

Bruce resumed his cacophonous percussion of the laptop keys. It wasn't long before he skidded back on his chair. "There you go. 'Neckera Rangiferina, Dead Man's Moss'. Very rare but found across a few countries... Myanmar, Thailand, Vietnam."

"Why would you find it in a medicine?" I asked.

"It's a sedative. A strong one. Over do it and it can induce a death-like state. Really overdo it and it's fatal. It's not what you'd call a mainstream pharmaceutical, but apparently it's still known to be prescribed by some of the more, erm, traditional, backstreet apothecaries."

"Well, there you have it, Lestrade," said Holmes. "Herbal tranquilisers that could knock out Nellie the Elephant."

"Thank you," said Lestrade, shaking the hands of both Openshaw and Bruce. "Please draw up an invoice for your work and forward it to myself at Middlesbrough Police Station."

Lestrade handed Openshaw his business card, which Openshaw afforded some time to study. "That's okay, Detective Inspector, the first job is gratis. We're just glad to be of help."

As we headed back down the A19 to Middlesbrough, it was apparent that Lestrade's mind was set. Confirmation that the pills were tranquilisers, originating from the same region of the world from which McCarthy had just returned, served as the clincher.

In all honesty, I wasn't that far behind him. McCarthy grinds up a few of these pills and slips the powder into Lana's wine. She feels a bit groggy and retires to her room to sleep off what she thinks is the effects of the alcohol. McCarthy sneaks out of the party to find her comatose on her bed, throws her over his shoulder, she can't have been more than eight stone, and deposits her in the pool. It all seemed to slip so seamlessly into place.

"Is this what they call an open and shut case?" I asked after Lestrade delivered us to our now traditional dropping off point on Albert Road.

"No," came the reply, "we don't have nearly enough data to start talking luggage."

"But it all fits into place?"

"It fits into a place," said Holmes, "but it may not be the right one. Think of it like this: if carbon is arranged in one way, you get graphite. Arrange it in another way and you get diamond. You probably couldn't get two more different things but they are built from the same basic elements. This is the same. It's elementary, Doc. We have some of the elements and we sew them together in a particular way, but we're more likely to find the correct way if we uncover more data, some more of the elements or even the bonds that bind them."

"So what about Alastair Bruce, Professor Alastair Bruce? Should we be worried about him?

Holmes laughed. "You think that fella is the criminal mastermind that has been stalking us."

"Smith and Jones did refer to their boss as 'the Professor'."

"Somehow I don't think it's gonna be that easy, Doc, besides I don't think criminal overlords wear Adidas Gazelle. He's more into Jamiroquai than organised crime."

"Look, Sherlock," I protested, "he is a clever guy, he's a professor and he's local."

"He is a smart kiddie, but in a particular niche. There is nothing about him to suggest he could groom international assassins and bring down governments. It would be a good way to track this fella down though. Just draw up a list of all the professors in the country and work our way through them. I can't imagine there's that many. Obviously we cross off all those who just call themselves professor like Professor Green and that Brian Cox gadgie."

"Brian Cox is really a professor."

"Is he?"

"Yeah, he's a professor of astrology or physics or something at Manchester University."

"Really? Well, bugger me. With that hair? Who knew?"

Holmes and I returned to the McCarthy place to find any evidence of a police investigation gone. My assumption was that Lestrade, happy with the conclusion he had drawn, had spooled up his crime scene tape and withdrawn his men.

Holmes knocked on one of the large front doors which was answered by Patience Moran.

"Do you mind if we come in and ask you a few questions?" he asked.

"No," said Patience, beckoning us in and leading us to a spacious, well-appointed sitting room.

"Are you here alone now?" asked Holmes as he sat on one of the plush settees.

"Yes," replied Patience. "The police were here until around dinner time, but then they just upped and left. At least when they were there, I could busy myself making tea but now...? I've been staring at the walls all afternoon wondering what I should do with myself. I don't even know if I should still be here."

"Have you worked for the McCarthys for long?"

"Coming up to a year in November."

"And Mister McCarthy, did you get on well with him?"

"Yes," she replied, tears welling in her eyes.

"It's okay," said Holmes, moving to sit beside her. "You've done nothing wrong," he reassured, his arm wrapped around her shoulder. "Doc, can you make Patience a cup of tea?"

When I returned to the room, Holmes had resumed his seating position opposite Patience. "Go on, get that down yer. It will do you the world of good."

As Patience drank, Holmes rose from his seat and milled around the room. When Patience was about halfway down her cup, he turned to address her. "Why were you out in the garden? When you found Lana?"

"I was just putting some rubbish in the bins."

"But the bins are round the other side of the house. There's no need to walk past the swimming pool."

"I know, I was just wanting some air. It was getting a bit stuffy inside."

Holmes shook his head. "Sorry darling. You weren't in that garden to take the rubbish out. I checked the bins on the night and there was nothing from the party in them. They hadn't been touched in days. You were out there with someone. The reason you walked past the pool is because you both didn't want to be caught coming back in through the same door together. Do you want to tell us who you were with?"

Patience's only response was to stare back at us blankly.

"Do you want me to tell you who you were with?" said Holmes, retaking his seat opposite her.

Again, no response was forthcoming.

"Charlie McCarthy."

Patience's face was immobilised with fear.

"That scent you're wearing now. Charlie McCarthy was covered with it on the night of the party."

"It's a common perfume," responded Patience.

"It's all too common, sweetheart. None of the well-heeled nobs at that shindig would have been dousing themselves in something you can pick up for about a tenner a bottle. They spend more than that on their wash wiper fluid. Why are you protecting him?"

Again, Patience made no attempt at a response.

"Reasonably-priced perfume wasn't the only thing you were both wearing that night. Both of you had mud on your shoes from the garden. I checked everyone else, and you were the only two who had done a bit of off-roading. He's going down for murder. Do you want to go with him as an accessory?"

"Okay, he was with me. He never murdered anyone."

"And it wasn't the first time, was it? You two have been messing around for a while, haven't you?"

"Yes," said Patience, tears draining down her face.

"So how did you work that with Lana in the house?"

"Lana was a deep sleeper. Charlie used to come to me in the night after she'd dozed off."

"The orange juice she kept by her bed. Did you bring that up?"

"No, Charlie did that."

"Did he often fuss around her?"

"No, not really."

Holmes paused. His thumb and forefinger scraping the stubble on his chin. He then rose from his seat to leave.

"Am I in trouble?" asked Patience.

"Not with us. We're not the police and they seem hell-bent on putting Charlie away. What you do from here is up to you."

"So does that give McCarthy an alibi?" I asked as we made our way back down the driveway.

"Not really. He could easily have dumped Lana in the pool before he hooked up with Patience."

As we rounded the tall wrought iron gates, Holmes stopped to lean with his back against the stone wall that surrounded the house. "If McCarthy knew Lana was floating in the pool, does it make sense for him to send Patience off in that direction to find her, and given she might present some sort of alibi, why has he not offered it? It's a queer one this, Doc. It's like his whole existence is a lie. He even lies about the truth. I've never seen anything quite like him."

7

Given the franticity of our day, we adjourned to the Twisted Lip to recharge.

"You see, Doc," said Holmes, "the trick is to see more than what you want or are expecting to see. Lestrade only sees the obvious. He's walked straight past the glasses in the dishwasher that also contained traces of the sedative. It's the little things that often tell you the most. Not that those are little things. They could be massive. There are so many things that he isn't noticing, and seeing things isn't enough, they need to be observed. How many times have you been up to my flat?"

"I don't know," I said, feeling this was somehow a number Holmes was expecting me to have to hand. "Twenty, maybe thirty times."

"Yes," he said, "something like that. So if you've climbed them stairs dozens of times, how many are there?"

"I'm without a clue," I sighed.

"See," said Holmes, "you've been up and down those stairs loads of times and you don't have a clue how many there are. Do you see? It's the things we see the most that we take least notice of."

"How many are there?" I asked.

"I don't fucking know," he replied. "Why would I need to know that? I'm not a flaming carpet fitter. It's not even my carpet. It's bloody horrible."

My tutorial in observational technique was curtailed by the entrance of Lestrade. "There's been a development," he said. "Lana's body has gone missing from the mortuary."

"You're fucking kidding," said Holmes.

"I wish I was," said Lestrade. "A massive part of the case against McCarthy has gone with it. The pathologist has been off sick so there's been a bit of a backlog."

"And the autopsy wasn't done?" appended Holmes.

"Nope," replied Lestrade sheepishly.

"Contents of the stomach?"

"No, nothing."

"Brilliant."

Lestrade joined us, taking one of the vacant seats at our table, and we all sat there subsumed by a deflated silence.

"Mary," called Holmes, "a beer for the inspector, please. And a couple more for me and Lover Boy."

"I'm on duty," said Lestrade.

"Not for much longer, I reckon," sighed Holmes, "given the cow's arse you're making of this."

Holmes was oblivious to Mary as she arrived with our tray of drinks. As she unloaded three pints of Engineer's Thumb, he sat with his head back, his eyes scanning the ceiling. So as not to interrupt him, I placed the payment for the drinks on the tray. Mary smiled and gave me a knowing shake of her head.

Holmes inhaled and exhaled through his nostrils audibly. "What would someone do with a body? Specifically, someone connected to McCarthy. Let's go with the obvious. The really bleeding obvious."

As we approached the now derelict site of Boscombe Metals, it was clear it had been abandoned some time ago.

Lestrade swung the car into the debris-strewn car park and we jumped out to make our way towards a collection of three buildings.

"This one," said Holmes, directing us towards the least interesting of the three, a shabby-looking outhouse. "Shall I pick the lock?"

"You pick locks?" replied Lestrade suspiciously.

"Of course," responded Holmes. With that, he stepped back and drove the heel of his boot into an area just below the door handle. The door swung open in a single blow. "There you go," he said. "You never saw that, right."

We crept our way into the dust and gloom of the factory space.

"Doc, phone," requested Holmes.

I handed it to him for him to switch on the camera light and hand it straight back. Lestrade, who was trailing behind us, sighed and turned on his police-issue torch, creating a luminance that rendered my light source irrelevant. In response, Holmes flicked on a light switch to light up the whole area.

"Over here," he said, leading us to a large rectangular metal tank covered in sizeable wooden boards. He shuffled back the timber to reveal the tank full to almost the top with a water-like liquid.

I reached my hand forward to sample the liquid, but was prevented by Holmes who threw his arm across my chest.

"Whoa there, Doc," he said, "you don't look with your hands." He targeted me a look of puzzled concern before turning to Lestrade. "Have you got any food on yer?"

Lestrade dug into his pocket and pulled out a semi-consumed bag of pork scratchings.

"Perfect," laughed Holmes, "you never stop eating, you. You're like fucking rust."

Taking the bag from Lestrade, he tipped the contents into the bath and we all watched as they fizzed and bubbled before disintegrating into nothing.

"Right," said Holmes, "get your SOCO boys down here and I'll bet you a penny to a pound they find more than enough evidence to suggest Lana's body was here."

He pointed to a reddish brown stain on the metal of the bath, which to my eye looked like dried blood.

"Check that out for a start," he said.

Back at Albert Road, I expected us to head down Baker Street to partake in a few more pints. Instead Holmes had "one more visit" for us to make. The visit being to the Nunthorpe apartment of James McCarthy, Charlie's son from an encounter previous to Lana.

As we approached the communal front door, Holmes turned to me. "Let's have a bet," he said. "I bet you a pound, no, a pint. I bet you a pint of Peroni he's up there with a girl."

"Yeah, a good-looking lad like him having a girlfriend. That would be quite a prediction."

"No, the bet is that she's Lana and John Turner's daughter."

"Given I pretty much pay for every round anyway, does it really matter?"

"Yeah," protested Holmes, "this means you get one back."

I sighed and Holmes pointed to the doorbell of Apartment Six. The legend next to it read, 'James McCarthy / Alice Turner'.

"I'm not paying," I protested, "you got that off the internet somewhere."

Holmes looked back at me disappointed.

The contrast between James and his father was immense. Whereas Charlie was vulgar and brash, James was reserved and well-mannered. As soon as I was afforded a look at Alice, it was clear that she was her mother's daughter. Also well-spoken, she shared many of her mother's features. Her eyes, the shape of her nose, her chin, even the colour of her hair.

Holmes aimed the first questions at her. "Why were you not at your mother's party?"

"I was ill with stomach cramps. I made James go without me."

"Did you get on with your mother?"

"Very much so. I loved her. We were like sisters."

"What about your stepfather? Charlie?"

"I can't stand him, he's a creep."

"Is that why you didn't go to the party?"

"No, I told you I had stomach cramps. I don't like being around him, but as long as I'm with James, I'm fine."

James, who was sitting in close proximity to Alice with his arm around her shoulder, pulled her closer into him.

"So what's your relationship with your father like, James?"

"Not good. We're what you might call estranged."

"But he pays for this flat?"

"Yes."

"And you went to the party?"

"Yes, I went for Lana's sake."

"You pulled her out of the pool, didn't you? Was there any sign of life?"

"Not really. Perhaps a faint pulse."

By this point, the tears were tipping over the wells in Alice's eyes.

"James, did anyone try to revive her?"

"Yes, I did. It was too late, she was gone."

Holmes stood up, prompting me to do likewise. "I'm sorry. From what the Doctor here tells me, she was a wonderful woman."

"Thank you," said James, leaning his head to one side to rest it on the top of Alice's, who was by now in some state.

"They were a nice couple," said Holmes as we made our way back to the bus stop. "Which is good, as it means they're not used to, and absolutely useless at, lying."

"They were lying? Those tears looked pretty real to me."

"The tears were real, but the story was bollocks. He wouldn't have left her to go to a party when she was ill. Can you imagine that? 'Oh where's my daughter tonight, James?' 'Oh she's back at the flat writhing around in agony, but insisted I come and show my face.' No chance. She didn't look very ill to me, and the flat smelled of last night's prawn chow mein. There's some bad medicine going on there. Badder than Doctor Brown's, especially between Alice and Charlie. It wouldn't surprise me if he's had a pop. Tried to get a mother-daughter combo going on."

I admonished myself for not making similar observations, however I was distracted from my self-administered castigation by the memory of Holmes' earlier comments: "Seeing things isn't enough, they need to be observed." Clenching my teeth with annoyance, I almost broke a molar.

9

Holmes was very silent that next morning. This was not uncommon. When there was little in this world to occupy his mind, he would drift off into some alternative realm. That morning however, it was different. If at all possible, it was a different kind of silence. One with less malaise about it.

Even his selection of breakfast was different. Gone were the soft-boiled eggs and soldiers to be substituted by poached eggs, fried chorizo and bacon, sans brown sauce, chorizo sausage being perhaps the most exotic fare I'd ever seen him consume, and brown sauce being the obligatory accompaniment to anything that had spent time in a frying pan. Unfortunately for Holmes, his feast of atypicality was interrupted by the arrival of Lestrade.

"Time to wrap this up," he announced.

"Go on then," said Holmes as he studiously examined the chorizo pronged to the end of his fork.

"No, not here. Back at the McCarthy house."

"Ah, yes," said Holmes, "the criminal always returns to the scene of the crime."

"That's unlikely," responded Lestrade. "Charlie McCarthy is locked up in one of my cells."

"I meant you."

"I'm the investigating officer."

"We've only got your word for that."

"Look just get in the car, will yer."

We pulled up outside the McCarthy place to find Superintendent Spaulding waiting for us in his altogether more impressive chauffeur-driven police car.

Lestrade unlocked the front doors of the house and led us to the large reception room where the party had taken place.

"Okay," he said. "Barring the odd couple of minutes to turn her bike round, Lana stuck to McCarthy like wallpaper paste. Witnesses at the party, including the superintendent here, reckon she rarely got more than five feet away from him all night. McCarthy also made a point of topping up her glass. He was the only one with any real opportunity to pop her one of the sleeping beauties he brought back from Burma. It was these drugs, a few more full bottles of which we found hidden in his study, that made her feel tired and decide to nip upstairs for a lie down."

Without an accompanying direction, Lestrade then strode out of the room to lead us up to the bedroom. Holmes, the superintendent and myself all glanced at each other, confused, before realising the idea was for us to follow.

"The bedroom," announced Lestrade.

Holmes looked around and nodded in agreement that we were indeed in the bedroom.

"Lana staggers up here, with the drugs McCarthy has spiked her with beginning to take effect. She's just about compos mentis enough to place her wine glass on the dresser before collapsing on the bed. Meanwhile downstairs, McCarthy slips away from the party and makes his way up here to find Lana, as he expects, knocking out some serious uppercase zeds. He picks her up and makes his way down to the pool."

Lestrade held out his arms to mimic the carrying of Lana and stomped out of the bedroom and back down the stairs. As we hit the bottom of the stairs and passed along the hallway adjacent to the reception room where the party had taken place, Spaulding called a pause to proceedings. "Inspector, isn't this a tad on the risky side? He's carrying his unconscious wife past a room containing forty or fifty guests. It's all a bit brazen."

"McCarthy doesn't worry about risk. He takes chances. Besides, what's spoiling? If someone sees him, he just says he's taking her outside for air or something."

Spaulding, although not looking particularly convinced, didn't present a counter argument.

"Right," said Lestrade, "he gets to the pool. If you stand here at this end, you can't be seen from the windows of the room where the party was. He lowers her into the water, face down, and floats her out into the middle. In the process, he drops the bottle of pills which rolls under that small shrub. Hearing them drop, he looks around, but doesn't have time to look for long. He knows if he's caught here with Lana floating in the pool, he's buggered. He heads back into the house through the kitchen, where he bumps into Patience. Figuring she gives him a convenient alibi, he drags her off into the garden for a fumble. After a quick tickle, he directs Patience back into the house past the pool, under the premise that they are not seen together and, well, you know the rest."

"Motive," said Holmes in a monosyllabic tone that suggested he was either bored or under-impressed.

"She was going to go back to Turner. They were going to team back up and destroy him. Between them, they will have had enough information on Boscombe Metals to bury him."

Holmes expression relayed an element of concession to Lestrade's reasoning.

"Very good," said the superintendent. "It seems plausible. However, a lot, if not all of what you have here, is conjecture. You have a fingerprint on the pill bottle and that's about it. Do you have anything of use from Turner?"

"No, sir, he's unwilling to make a formal statement. He doesn't want to risk implicating himself in the Boscombe Metals fraud."

Spaulding sighed. "It's going to be hard to get this one to stick, Barry."

"Barry!" laughed Holmes. "Oh, that's crap. But it does confirm you're not gay. There's no such thing as a gay Barry. Welcome back to the world of totty, my mate. Jeffrey, Calvin, I even met a gay Dave once. Never a Barry."

Spaulding was unimpressed by Holmes' jibing. "Mister Holmes," he said, "I think we need to thank you. Your contribution to this case has been instrumental. If it were not for you, we may never have appreciated the role of John Turner in all this. It's just a shame he's refusing to be of more help."

"That's Charlie all over," replied Holmes. "He only exposes a soft side to those who he thinks can do nothing with it."

"Perhaps Turner could be summoned to give evidence," interrupted Lestrade.

"It wouldn't help," replied Spaulding, "he would just clam up. The last thing he wants to do is have a defence barrister question him about his role in the Boscombe Metals debacle. Mister Holmes, we need to recompense yourself and Doctor Watson for your assistance in this case. We do have a budget for consultancy, expert witnesses and the like."

"It's okay," replied Holmes. "I don't need the money."

I was surprised at his response given he had no obvious source of income.

"No, it's right that we pay you. You bring something new to the investigation."

"Okay, five hundred quid a day plus expenses."

"Four-fifty a day and no expenses. I'm not paying your bar bill. Lestrade, when you get back to the office, can you put the necessary processes in place?"

"Excuse me, sir, but I don't think we need any hired help."

"I think we do, Detective. We're all too bound by our training, procedure and process. An outsider like Sherlock here can bring a different perspective on some of the things we have to deal with. Lord knows we need it at times. It's a fact. Other people can see some things better than you or I."

"Stevie Wonder, for example," added Holmes.

"Mister Holmes, if we are to work together then it needs to be a two-way street. That means no taking the mickey."

Holmes nodded slowly.

"Are you happy for us to call on you should we need your assistance in future?"

"Depends what it is. We are selective. How you going to get in touch with us? Should we have some sort of bat signal?"

"No, I think we'll just stick our head around the door of the Twisted Lip. That should be sufficient."

Holmes grimaced in mock offence.

Back at Baker Street, the Twisted Lip had exactly the amount of people I had come to expect of a Tuesday lunchtime. Holmes, Mary and myself.

"Do you think Lestrade has got this right?" I asked. "There seems to be so much he has just ignored."

Holmes pretended to consider a while. "Probably not."

"So you don't think McCarthy did it?"

Holmes responded with a shrug of his shoulders. It wasn't until a long time afterwards that I understood that gesticulation. Think of me what you may. You won't have thoughts I've not laboured over myself.

Events were taking their course. I had doubts as to McCarthy's guilt and Holmes was keeping his own counsel. He didn't subscribe to Lestrade's interpretation of the events leading up to Lana's death, but wouldn't provide a view either way on McCarthy's exact role in her demise. I had severe doubts and was concerned injustice was to be left undone.

Holmes wasn't a campaigner. He wasn't about to set off on a crusade to ensure the true story of the evening was exposed. In the end, Lestrade's version of events became the de facto interpretation and I was swept along with the burgeoning consensus.

It might have been the truth. It was after all difficult to measure Holmes. Was his reticence to engage just him being his sometimes enigmatic self, or had Lestrade just beat him to the punch? There was the possibility that while he filtered through the minutiae, Lestrade had allowed what was actually a relatively simple story fall into place before us.

"You can't just let things fall into place, you have to put them there." Holmes said that on many an occasion.

The evidence they found at Boscombe Metals was actually a lot less conclusive than Holmes had expected. The blood they found was tested against the DNA of Lana's daughter and found to be a good match, however given she was drowned, not stabbed or shot, where did it come from? There's nothing more haunting than a fact that has nowhere to sit.

The unexplained blood was one of the many oddities that Lestrade was happy to skate past. It served his purpose to do so.

As I was later to learn, it is a capital mistake to ignore a fact. If the facts don't align with the story you are telling, it's all too easy to bend and twist them to fit.

Holmes' method was to arrange the facts, all the facts, into as many valid scenarios as he could build. He would then use the balance of probability to determine where to look next. As he dug, some of the stories would be invalidated and discarded. Information that others would dismiss as irrelevant, because it didn't support their case, was often the most useful to Holmes. It was this that allowed him to pare down the possibilities to leave but one. The truth. That was the process he referred to as 'deduction', or at least my best understanding of it.

The following evening we found ourselves back in the observation area adjacent to Middlesbrough Police Station's Interview Suite Two. Holmes was excused interview duties, his place next to Lestrade being filled by a slightly-built female detective I had not yet come across.

"It's not about what a jury thinks," sneered Lestrade. "Before we get to that point, there's a decision for you to make. Do you want to confess and get eight years with good behaviour, or plead your innocence and go down for a twenty? Twenty years is a lot of bum sex in the showers. Have you not seen Sherlock Holmes in action? The super's got him on the fucking payroll. He'll have him digging up evidence on every trick you've ever played. You couldn't be more fucked."

McCarthy looked to his solicitor who offered little in the way of support.

"I never killed her," he pleaded. "She said she was tired and disappeared off upstairs. That was the last time I saw her. Look, between then and when her body was found, I was with Patience. We were having an affair. Yeah, I did use those drugs to knock Lana out, but only so I could hook up with Patience. I didn't use them on the night she died."

"Your fingerprint was on the bottle found near the pool."

"I don't know how that got there."

"Come on, McCarthy. Who else would want her dead?"

"I don't know. I can't imagine."

"What happened to her body? Who did that bit of dirty work for you?"

"I don't know what happened. I had nothing to do with it."

"You don't know much, do you?" Lestrade stood up abruptly. "Confess," he snarled. "Do us all a favour. Including yourself. Interview terminated twenty twenty-four."

"Well done," said an aghast Holmes as Lestrade joined us in the observation area. "I don't know about McCarthy, but I'm ready to fess up. You seem pretty certain he's your man."

"I've never been more certain. I'll have his confession within the hour."

Lestrade was indeed right. A short time after, Charlie McCarthy signed a written confession admitting to the murder of his wife. His confession expunged any lingering doubts I had, but did nothing to remove the dark, hollow feeling I felt from having someone I knew reasonably well convicted of a crime such as murder.

10

Months later, after McCarthy's trial, I rounded the entrance of the Twisted Lip to find Holmes sitting with the early edition of the Evening Gazette laid across the table. Two pints of Engineer's Thumb weighed it down against the draft of the door.

"Pull up a beer," he said as I entered. "That one's yours. This is brilliant."

He was reading my article about the Lana McCarthy murder.

"Do you think it's alright?" I asked.

"Yeah," he replied. "I've read it three times. Where did you get all those big words from? I keep needing to get Mary to translate. By the way, she's not happy. She thinks your story makes her bum look big."

Holmes was genuinely laughing out loud. In all the time I knew him, he might have done that three perhaps four times.

"It's not a story, Sherlock, it's a serious news article about a horrendous murder. A crime leading to a twenty year life sentence, ten before he'll be assessed for release under license."

"Aw, right," he responded, relinquishing his joviality. "Do you still think he did it?"

"Of course he did it."

"Yeah, he did, yeah right, yeah nailed on," he said, flicking the paper over to read the back page. "I see the Boro threw it away last night. Ah, an injury time goal. Bloody typical."

"Sherlock," I pressed, "you don't think McCarthy did it, do you?"

After a long pause, he scrunched up his face and looked up at me. "No, not really. Well, not at all. He never killed her. She's not even dead. That's why there was no body."

"Not dead?" I interrupted. "I saw her lifeless body with my own eyes."

"No, you didn't. It might have looked lifeless."

"What?" I snapped. "Her body was taken from the mortuary and disposed of in that acid bath at Boscombe Metals. Probably by someone on McCarthy's under-the-counter payroll. It was McCarthy's unwillingness to give his accomplice up that led to such a long sentence. That was the conclusion we came to months ago!"

"It was never mine. That was Lestrade's theory. I just let him roll with it. Her body wasn't taken. The drugs wore off and she got off the bench and walked out. Into the arms of her adoring ex-hubby."

"Turner?"

"Well yeah, she's only got one," he said with confusion.

"I don't understand. What? Why?"

"To get some of the money back, I suppose. Look Doc, Lestrade did alright but he put two key pieces of data together in the wrong order. He thought she was drugged and thrown in the pool. Actually she wasn't drugged until she was pulled out of the pool."

"By who?"

"James McCarthy. One fork, no knife. Who else could have turned up for some scran everyday without Charlie suspecting they were knocking off his beautiful wife? Those who can't be trusted, tend not to trust any other bugger. But he'll have thought she was safe with his son. Ironic really, given he'd tried it on with Alice. That was the spark that got them both plotting. That's what got them both wanting to ruin him. For Lana that was always the case. Why else would she marry that cock?

"Remember there were more knives than forks in the dishwasher? Charlie had himself down as something special. Wannabe middle class that invites school governors to his shindigs. He's a knife and fork man. James on the other hand. Not so bothered. He's happy with where he comes from. One-forkers tend to be the working class or upper class. The unpretentious or the not really that arsed.

"The clever bit is they used the drugs Charlie was using to knock Lana out while he was having it away with Patience. Genius. Cut down by his own axe.

"So Lana, who's actually a free diver, and pretty good at holding her breath, sneaks past the party people and lowers herself into the pool. The hope is, one of the party guests will notice her floating there. Failing that, James will raise the alarm. In the end, the job ends up falling to poor Patience, fresh from a session with Charlie in the garden. The rest is easy. On cue James dashes out, pulls her from the pool and slips her a carefully measured dose of Charlie's super strength rhynohypnol. Just the right amount to induce a death-like state. Viola, everyone in the party thinks she's kippered. Including you. Oh yeah, James gets you to phone the ambulance. Except you don't. He has a different number programmed into his phone. Did you notice the ambulance man had a limp?"

"Actually he might of had, yeah."

"Same height and build as Turner?"

"Possibly."

"Did you notice he had mud on his boots?"

"No."

"Shame. Always look at the shoes. They can tell you so much. That footprint I found by the tree in the garden. It was made by someone who dragged their feet. Someone with a limp like Turner. I reckon he watched events unfold from by that tree, waited for you to make the call, hopped back over the wall and into the ambulance he will have, up till this point, had stashed in one of the barns at his farm. He had to keep a watching brief in case things didn't go to plan. He didn't want Lana to drown. He'd only just got her back.

"There were about four sets of tyre tracks on that track leading up to Hatherley Farm. One looked like an ambulance, Turner's Audi, the postman maybe and some that I'd bet you money came from a hearse. Once Turner had whisked Lana away in his ambulance, he transferred her to the hearse and took her straight to the morgue. I went to the hospital. She was never there. Given James works at the hospital he could have easily gotten hold of a death certificate and anyone could have rang the police to tell them Lana was DOA. They gambled on everyone being too busy to check with the hospital.

"The only thing then to do was create an explanation for where the body went. Where better than the acid bath at Boscombe Metals? But who, other than Charlie McCarthy, had a key for those outbuildings? John Turner. Shame they smeared the bath with Lana's blood. Some hair would have been more convincing. And probably less painful and prone to infection. Ah, one more thing. The wine glass in the bedroom. Lana will have plopped the pills in there herself, before realising you generally don't get drugged by a glass that stays full. That's why she chucked half down the bathroom sink. There were splashes of wine around the rim."

"Sherlock, a man is in prison for a murder he didn't commit."

"We never put him there."

"But we could probably get him out."

"Why would we want to do that? It might matter if he was innocent. But he's not. He's a thieving little scroat who deserves to be banged up. Besides, if we tell anybody now, your Evening Gazette gig will be right up the swanny, and we'll be down four-fifty a day less expenses. Four-fifty a day, Doc, you can't fall off. Plus we'd look a right pair of tits."

I was deadened by his explanation and the resulting revelation. It was as much as I could do to raise the glass to my lips. Holmes on the other hand just resumed his review of the Evening Gazette's sport pages.

"How did you see all that and I saw none of it?" I asked, wrecked by my ignorance.

"You saw all of it. Well, nearly all. Maybe you don't lie awake at night like I do?" he said, glancing a knowing nod in Mary's direction. "Doc, your only competition is yourself. Just don't let him beat you."

He then quelled my consternation with a kind of paternal smile. Before raising his glass, draining the remaining contents, and asking me if I would like another.

"No, I don't think I do."

"Come on," he said, "sup up and we'll go and see them. They should be living it up in Panama by now, with a canoe full of her life insurance money. But the insurance company hasn't paid out yet. Don't ask me how I know that. Long story. Well, actually a short story but it's probably better you don't know. Chances are they're hiding out at the farm, away from any prying eyes until the man from the Pru shuffles up with a cheque. We can't use Mary's cab. I forgot it took diesel and put petrol in it. Got any cash? We'll have to get a minicab."

The minicab dropped us off on the road and we made our way up the farm track on foot.

As we approached the farmhouse, Turner appeared. "Here's Mister Benn," muttered Holmes.

"Sorry, I'm just off out," said Turner.

"Going anywhere nice?" asked Holmes.

"No, just off to get some shopping. I've got nothing in for dinner."

"Where you gonna put it? Your boot's full. Those aren't clothes for shopping. They're comfortable clothes for travelling in. How's Lana?"

"What the fuck's up with you? She's dead."

"No, she isn't. Has the insurance money come through yet? The cheque went out yesterday. Can we go inside?"

We wandered into the kitchen behind a very nervous-looking Turner.

"If Lana's dead, is it you who's taken to wearing her shade of lipstick?" asked Holmes, fishing a wine glass from the kitchen sink. "What's this then? Some sort of tribute?"

Turner provided no response except to stare back at us. His only animation came from the flicking of his eyes from below a brow furrowed with concern.

"I tell you what, mate, let me tell you what really happened. See when McCarthy ruined you, the lovely Lana felt a bit guilty. You were in no state to keep an eye on McCarthy and she blamed herself. Whatever it took, she was gonna put things right. To do that she needed to get close to him. That was easy. McCarthy will have tried it on with her loads of times. All she had to do was stop saying no.

"Of course you knew nothing about this. At some point, she was gonna have to let that scumbag jump her, and there was no way you were going to allow that to happen. It was the ultimate sacrifice, but she was willing to make it. She could have ruined it between you and her permanently, but had to take that gamble. Don't worry though; the ink on the marriage certificate would have been still wet when she had him on bread and water. He soon turned to Patience to fill that need.

"Then things just fell into place. Fate has a habit of providing opportunities. Charlie has a pop at Alice and that gets his son James on the team. Over a number of cosy lunches, they cook up their plan. Frame Charlie for murder and get him sent away for a very long stretch. Over time, Charlie will have no choice but to transition his business interests over to James and you get the proceeds of a life insurance policy you'd probably forgotten about.

"Clearly this wasn't ideal from your perspective. You ended up hating Lana for what she'd done to you. But hate is a powerful anaesthetic. She knew that and was willing to sacrifice her marriage to put things right. She couldn't bear to see you ruined. Not by McCarthy. And then at the end, she brings you in. Her and James had a good plan but it was too big for just two people. It was a gamble but there was no one else. Alice couldn't help, she doesn't have the temperament. It's a narrow line between love and hate, and from what I've seen people can move in either direction, although it is harder to escape hate."

He paused to allow a response. With nothing forthcoming, we stood in silence, Holmes with his gaze fixed on Turner. The long silence was broken by the sound of the internal door opening to reveal a very alive-looking Lana. You don't get any closer to seeing a ghost than that. The last time I saw her she was laid lifeless on the ground.

"Hello," said Holmes. "It's nice to finally meet you."

"So what happens now?" asked Turner.

"Nothing," replied Holmes. "We're not the police. You carry on with whatever you were planning to do next. Panama, is it?"

"South Africa."

"South Africa," chimed Holmes. He nodded, signalling to me that it was time for us to leave. We ambled back down the farm track in silence. Me with my mind replaying the story I'd had reworked before me, Holmes with his mind on wherever he goes when the silence falls.

FIFTY ORANGE PILLS

1

There was nothing much happening that afternoon. It was a not atypical Teesside Wednesday with the wind propelling a drizzling rain to exaggerate its effect. Sherlock Holmes, ensconced in his mute mode, was providing little in the way of distraction. The conversation passing between us would have been naught had it not been for the obligatory pleasantries on my arrival. We hadn't arranged to meet, I'd just noticed him sitting in the window as I wandered past the Twisted Lip and decided to stick my head around the door. It was soon apparent that a signalled acknowledgement, and the continuation of my journey into town for the haircut I was requiring, might have resulted in a more conducive use of my time.

It was a familiar scenario. Holmes sat staring out of the window, motionless except for his eyes which flicked as people traversed to and fro across his view plane. He didn't even break off to take a sip from the beer I'd bought him. How I wished Mary was working that afternoon, however she had left town to visit her sister. She'd actually asked me to join her, however due to an unhealthy backlog of patients, I was unable to progress to our relationship milestone of meeting the family.

The monotony was broken by the entrance of a tall well-presented gentleman whom I vaguely recognised. He took off his raincoat and shook it out with a billow before approaching us.

"Sherlock Holmes, isn't it?" he asked, holding out his hand. "My name is John Openshaw. We met a few months ago. I am the CEO of Belasis Pharmaceuticals. We had a break in last night and some of our experimental drugs were stolen. I'd like you to help us recover them."

Holmes maintained his stare a while, causing Openshaw to shuffle on his feet, before responding. "We charge four-fifty a day, expenses included."

Openshaw smiled slightly, before pursing his lips and giving a barely noticeable shake of the head. "That's fine," he replied after a short pause.

"Each," added Holmes, before reanimating and spinning around from the window to rise from his chair and shake Openshaw's hand. "Sherlock Holmes at your service," he said, gesturing that Openshaw should sit and join us. "Doc, could you please get our client a drink?"

Openshaw explained that his organisation had been developing a drug to aid in the treatment of mental illness. These drugs could be used to manipulate the way the brain worked. By combining certain enzymes in different ratios, they had found a way to force the brain to undertake an activity in a different part of the mind to that which would normally be used. In experiments, they had blinded rats by destroying their occipital cortex, before restoring their sight by shifting the visual processing to a different area of the brain.

The problem they had was keeping the rats alive. In all cases, the rats had died within days of the drugs being administered. Consequently they were so far behind schedule that they were on the verge of abandoning the programme. Then, two or three weeks previously, they'd had a breakthrough and identified a compound that they thought could be used as a regulating agent. The work since had concentrated on the use of this agent. Unfortunately, thus far, the rats were still not surviving, but were now experiencing what Openshaw described as a "slow descent into madness."

The medical applications should they be successful, said

Openshaw, were endless. The drugs could be used to treat anything from brain injuries to autism and bipolar disorders.

"So who would want to steal some half baked drugs?" asked Holmes.

"We don't know," replied Openshaw, "that's why I want to bring you chaps in. Our first thought was industrial espionage, but given the stage of development we're at, it's difficult to see what use they would be. They'd have been better off stealing the computers."

"How many pills have gone missing?"

"We think fifty."

"Fifty," mulled Holmes. "So if you were selling them for a tenner, fifteen quid a pop, it doesn't even add up to a grand. None of the local dealers would get excited about that. Never mind go to the trouble of a break in."

Openshaw led us along the bricked terrace of Baker Street to his chauffeur-driven Maybach.

"Shotgun," called Holmes before climbing in the passenger seat beside the driver. I must admit I was glad for him to do so, the luxury in the rear seats being somewhat of a phenomena.

"So there's a few bob in the drugs business then?" asked Holmes.

"It is quite profitable, yes," responded Openshaw.

"Quite profitable," chimed Holmes, examining the interior of the car. "I bet you kill a few rats to get one of these bad boys."

When we got to Billingham, Openshaw led us through the sterile white corridors I remembered from our previous visit. We turned into the laboratory to find it in a state of disarray. Several lab stools were turned on their sides and some of the equipment lay broken on the hard tiled floor.

"I told Alastair to leave it like this until you chaps had had a look."

"Alastair?" I asked.

"Alastair Bruce," reminded Openshaw, "our resident scientist. I think you met him on your previous visit."

Holmes stood in the middle of the room, feet together and hands in his pockets. His eyes darted from side to side, occasionally accompanied by jerks of his neck. It was the routine I'd seen before, including the periods where he crunched his eyes shut.

"What is he doing?" asked Openshaw.

I signalled for him to be quiet, however I'm actually uncertain if noise served as a distraction to Holmes. In all honesty, I just wanted to position myself as integral to the investigation, in order to be sure that Openshaw thought I had a role in the team, and I was therefore deserving of my four-hundred and fifty pounds per day fee.

On completion of his staccato scan, Holmes stepped over to the window. "The glass is on the inside," he said.

"What does that mean?"

"It means it's where it should be." He then shifted his gaze to look through the broken windowpane. "You can see where the burglar walked across the grass. One person, male, five foot ten, eleven and a half stone. Someone who's recently returned from some time living abroad. Cigar smoker and, if I'm not mistaken, a lover of pickled gherkins."

"You can tell all that from some flattened grass?" remarked Openshaw.

"Can I bollocks. But I can see they came straight to this window. I'd have tried a few before breaking one. There might have been one left open. Were the pills not locked away at night?"

"Usually but Alastair was working late last night and a batch was left out."

"What about the alarm? Did that trigger?"

"No, we, erm, let the maintenance contract lapse. Alastair was going to have a go at fixing it, but he's been too wrapped up in his work and hasn't gotten round to it."

"You fellas are not exactly covering yourselves in glory, are you?"

Holmes looked to Openshaw to gauge his response. To my assessment, this conveyed little in the way of information.

"Right," he said, "I've seen enough. Can I speak to Alastair?"

"No problem, I think he's decamped to the canteen," replied Openshaw, unperturbed by Holmes' analysis.

"One thing though, you need to get the Five O involved. They need to be aware of this."

"I was hoping we could keep this amongst ourselves," replied Openshaw.

"There's nothing I would like more, but if those drugs get out on the street then it's bye-bye Maybach and hello shitting into a bucket in a tiny little cell."

"Point taken. I'll ring that Lestrade chappie. I have his card in my office."

As with the rest of the building, the canteen was an impressive affair. Rows and rows of pristine white tables and break out areas of fine Italian leather settees surrounding marble-topped coffee tables. I was however struck with the thought that it was a little large given that, from what I'd seen, the number of staff at Belasis Pharmaceuticals numbered no more than three or four.

Bruce sat in the corner, as far away from the door as you could get.

"Mister Holmes," he said, rising to his feet to shake Holmes' hand before turning to me. Apparently Bruce had developed personality and manners since our last meeting.

"John Watson," I reminded, as I offered my hand.

"Mister Watson," nodded Bruce.

"Doctor Watson," corrected Holmes. "These drugs, what would happen if a person was to take one?"

"I don't know. We've only ever used them on rats."

"Can you extrapolate?"

"Not with any certainty. They change the way the brain operates. The problem we've seen is the brain apparently tries to correct itself. It's this process that we think dements the rats."

"This regulating agent isn't working, then."

"It's making things better, we're not quite there yet."

"How long will it take?"

"I don't know. The rats are so limiting. We need to use the monkeys."

"Yeah," said Holmes. "Micky Dolenz hasn't done anything in years."

"Alastair," interrupted Openshaw, "you know the policy of this organisation. We do not use primates until we're confident that there will be no ill effects."

Bruce didn't respond.

"Can I get some of these pills?" asked Holmes.

"What for?" replied Bruce.

"I need to know what I'm looking for," snarled Holmes coldly.

Bruce looked to Openshaw who provided a confirmatory nod.

"So," said Holmes, "if someone was to pop one of these pills, is there any way to reverse the effects? Some sort of antidote?"

"We have been developing one but when we tested it on the rats, they all died."

"That's quite an antidote." Holmes stared back in silent disappointment. "You should always have a back button."

2

Openshaw led us back to the main entrance where he stopped to shake our hands.

"We'll let you know as soon as we have something," said Holmes.

"Thank you," replied Openshaw. "I am worried about them falling into the wrong hands. Please let my driver know where you need to go, she'll take you wherever you want."

"Nice one," said Holmes. "Ibiza it is, then."

As we both climbed into the rear of the Maybach, Holmes leaned forward. "The Diogenes Club, please," he said.

"You're not serious about Ibiza, are you?" I laughed.

"No, it's in Stockton," he replied, before calling to the driver, "Brunswick Street, Stockton."

The Diogenes Club was the type of club I used to enjoy during my younger days. One of those places with a low ceiling into which you descend down carpeted stairs. It reminded me a lot of the Beluga Club I used to frequent during my student days in Sheffield.

It being early evening, the place was not yet open to the public. We stepped into the spacious main room to find a handful of people busying themselves in preparation for the night ahead.

Holmes stepped across the dance floor, stuttering to hold up his arms in front of him and perform a strange shuffle, I assumed to be some sort of dance move, before approaching a chap who looked to be making repairs to the DJ equipment.

"What you doing here?" sighed the man.

"Cheers, Kidda, I've missed you too," replied Holmes.

"You only come over here when you want something."

"It'd be a bloody quick visit if I popped over when I had nothing to see you about."

The man then looked in my direction to prompt an introduction.

"Doc, this is Mycro, my brother. Mycro, this is my mate, Doctor John Watson."

"A mate? That must put you up to what? One?" Mycro offered me his hand. "Mycroft Holmes. It's good to meet you, man. Any friend of Sherlock's is a rare sight."

"We need some help on a case we're looking at," said Holmes.

"A case?" smirked Mycroft in recoil.

"Yeah, someone turned over a lab in Billingham last night and nicked a load of drugs. Me and the good doctor here are trying to get them back."

"What, and you're getting paid for this?"

"Yeah, four-fifty a day."

"Bloody hell! Four-fifty?"

"I want to check out the local dealers. See if some scroat's been trying to palm them off for a quick quid. Who are the top boys at the minute? Where's the best place to start?"

"Sherl, I run the cleanest club in Teesside. How would I know?"

"Come on, Kidda, the reason you manage to keep it so clean is you have a bead on these lowlifes. That's how come Zammo over there is happy to do a shift glass collecting. I'm kind of out of touch, since, you know, well…"

"Yeah, I know alright. I'd try Colin."

"What Colin the Barbarian? That doyle's still in business?"

"Yeah," sighed Mycroft, "he seems to go from strength to strength."

"Does he still drink in the Chump?"

"I don't know anywhere else that serves Iron Brew on draft."

Colin the Barbarian was a distance from aligning with my preconception of what a drug dealer should look like. This was largely due to an absolute absence of menace. If I were to categorise him, I would have placed him in the dinner-money-getting-stolen type, rather than someone who peddled death via his abhorrent profession.

His appearance, perhaps, was the essence of his business model. Who would suspect that a studious-looking nerd with thick-rimmed glasses and a haircut the square side of conservative would be the area's most successful apothecary of illegal substances.

"Hello Col," said Holmes gleefully as we entered the Camel's Hump. "You haven't changed much. You hardly look a day older. How old are you now, about twelve?"

"What do you want? A score?" muttered Colin.

"No, just a few words."

"Okay, how about 'fuck off before I hurt you'."

"Oh, Colin," sighed Holmes, before grabbing him by his jacket with one hand and slapping him about the face and head with the other. There was no real force in the blows, the intention being more to humiliate.

On the cessation of the sham violence, Holmes threw him back into his chair and dug into his jacket pocket to retrieve a bag of the orange pills which he placed on the table in front of Colin.

"Seen these before?" asked Holmes.

"No," replied Colin, without even looking down at the bag.

"Col," sighed Holmes, "I'm getting the feeling you're not wanting to collaborate with me on this."

"No, Sherley, I want you to fuck off."

Holmes grabbed him by the neck. "See these?" he growled, holding one of the pills in front of Colin's face with his thumb and forefinger. "These little fuckers can kill people. Do you want me to demonstrate on you?"

"Get off me, you twat."

Holmes forced his thumb into Colin's mouth and then covered his mouth with his palm. Colin struggled, his cries muffled by Holmes' hand. Holmes then grabbed Colin's drink and poured it into his mouth, the majority of it spilling over Colin and drenching his jacket, tee shirt and jeans.

"What the fuck," grimaced Colin, as Holmes relinquished his grip. "What the fuck was that?"

Holmes took the bench opposite him. "Do you know what those drugs do?" he said in a cold deliberate tone.

Colin stared back with a look of confused terror.

"They alter the way the brain works. The bit that makes your knees tremble when you're surfing those tacky little websites will have just swapped jobs with the bit that tells you you need a crap. The next time you see a pair of tits, you'll probably shit yourself. Don't worry though, given how old you look that's not gonna happen unless someone tries to feed you. Oh yeah, by the way, all the rats they were tested on went bonkers and died within three days."

"Okay," cried Colin. "What the fuck do you want me to do?"

"If you see any of these pills out on the street, you come and find me. Within minutes."

"What good's that? I'm fucking dying."

"No, Col, look in the bag. There's still three pills in there. You need to pay more attention. I was only practising. You know, in case you decided to be unhelpful. You just had one of these," he said, shaking a box of orange Tic Tacs.

He threw the box at Colin. "Here you go, you can have the rest. Your breath stinks."

3

The news I feared came a week or so later. Ralphie King, a twenty-seven year old bank clerk, was on her way home following a Wednesday night out with colleagues, when she drove her car into a tree. She died on impact.

To most, this looked like any other tragic traffic accident, however Holmes seized on the incident straight away. Witness reports of the incident, occurring on Norton High Street, said that Ralphie was driving erratically and at some speed at the time she crashed.

Holmes asked me to call Lestrade to clear a visit, and we made our way to the mortuary where poor Ralphie was now lain.

As we entered the morgue, we were greeted by an attractive middle-aged woman who introduced herself as Doctor Shreya Pondicherry, Forensic Pathologist. Directing us to the slab where the body lay, she explained how the cause of death was severe head trauma and Ralphie's injuries were typical of a road accident of the type she had been involved in.

Holmes showed little interest in Doctor Pondicherry's assessment but instead queried the contents of Ralphie's stomach.

"We've sent the stomach contents off for analysis and should have the results within seven or eight days."

"That's too long," responded Holmes. "Someone else will be dead by then. Murder's a compelling thing, Doctor. Once a man like this has killed, he kind of gets a thirst for it. He'll soon be ready to kill again."

"Murder? All I've seen suggests this was an accident."

"And what you haven't seen suggests something else. Twenty-seven year old bank clerks don't joyride home along Norton High Street. Something made her crash, and there's a reasonable chance it was one of the little orange pills Doctor Watson and myself are trying to track down."

"Orange pills? I heard something about them in the canteen."

"Do you have a spare sample of the stomach contents?" interrupted Holmes.

As we made our way out of the building, Holmes turned to me. "Do you have a car? We need to get over to Belasis and I can't be arsed to keep trollying round in police cars. People are starting to talk."

"No, sorry," I replied. "I just have a bicycle."

"Aw great. Can you give me a croggy over to Billingham?"

We made our way back over to Belasis Pharmaceuticals in a mini cab. I phoned John Openshaw en route so that he was expecting us. We entered the laboratory to see some of the equipment which had been broken during the break in stacked neatly against one of the walls.

We were only a few strides in when Alastair Bruce broke off from what he was doing and bounded over to greet us. "I believe you have a sample for me to test, gentlemen."

"We do," responded Holmes. "We need you to see if it contains any of those little orange pills you were so careless with."

"That should be straight-forward," said Bruce, before moving over to one of the many lab benches. He decanted some of the sample into a small test tube which he then placed into a centrifuge. We all stood, watching the machine whizz round in the performance of its task.

The centrifuge whirred to a halt and Bruce transferred the test tube to another less familiar piece of equipment. He then flicked on a monitor and rattled the keys of an adjacent keyboard.

"It's a good job this kit never got smashed up in the robbery," said Holmes.

"It is indeed," muttered Alastair, without diverting his focus from his work. "There you go," he sighed, "this sample contains three hundred and thirty-four milligrams of neurokineodroxaline. The active ingredient of our 'little orange pills'."

We all stood in silence, Bruce alternating his look between us as if trying to gauge our reaction. Holmes nodded slowly before thanking Bruce and smiling with all the passion of an emoticon.

We made our way back to Middlesbrough in the Maybach. Holmes lay back in his seat, staring at the roof of the car.

"What on earth has anybody got against a bank clerk? A bank executive, yeah. One of them bastards should be shot daily. But not her, she's never done anyone any harm. We need to go and see that Miss Merryweather. She works at the same bank, doesn't she?"

"Yeah but did they even know each other?"

"I don't care. Have you seen how nice her arse is? You'd better ask the questions, I need to concentrate on observing."

We got to the bank and asked for Miss Merryweather, who showed up promptly and led us to a meeting room a short distance from reception.

Holmes sat back in his chair and looked at me to prompt me to start my questioning.

"Did you know Ralphie King, Miss Merryweather?"

"Yes. We went out quite often with work. Once a month usually. I can't believe what happened."

"Were you out with her last night?"

"I was. Ralphie drank water all night. She said she had an early start in the morning."

"Who else was out?"

"Just some of the girls. The same crowd we always go out with."

"Did you attract any male attention?"

"Of course, we always do."

An until then motionless Holmes moved in his chair.

"Did any of those men seem strange in any way?"

"Yeah, they all did. Have you not been in the Highland Laddie?"

"No."

"You should both come. I think you'd like it."

"Did you stay in the Highland Laddie all night?"

"No, we moved on to Canteen and Cocktails for some tapas."

"Same question. Was there anyone in there that seemed strange?"

"Same answer. No more than any other night."

"Did anyone pay particular attention to Ralphie?"

"Yeah, a couple of lads, but she was a pretty girl."

"Did you notice anything unusual?"

"Nothing. It was a normal night out. We can't believe what happened. When she left us, she was fine. She was the nicest person you could ever meet. Half the girls haven't come in today, they're so distraught."

"Sorry," interrupted Holmes, "who exactly didn't turn up today? We need a list of names and addresses urgently."

Miss Merryweather left the room, returning minutes later. I was ringing Lestrade as she returned. She handed Holmes a piece of A4 paper, which he passed on to me. I explained the situation to Lestrade and read out the list to him. When I finished, Holmes stood and shook Miss Merryweather's hand.

"Thank you, I'll be in touch," he said.

As we made our way back to Baker Street, I questioned Holmes. "I'll be in touch?"

"Will you?"

"You said, 'I'll be in touch'. What about me?"

"Well, if you wanna be a raspberry, you come too. I just thought you were cramping my style a bit with your clever questions."

"I think you mean a gooseberry."

"What?"

"It's a gooseberry, not a raspberry."

"Ah, tamado tomato."

The next day the news of Ralphie's death was all over the front pages of the local papers. The Northern Echo led with 'Girl Dies in Drug-related Accident' whereas the early edition of the Evening Gazette had the slightly more sensational 'Killer Drugs on Teesside Streets'.

Lestrade had actually published a press release, warning of the theft of the drugs and how dangerous they were, a few days earlier. It wasn't until Ralphie's death that their mention moved from a small column on page six or seven to the front page headlines.

"Does it take a death to get people interested in something these days?" I snapped, as I read the early edition front page.

"Yes," replied Holmes, matter-of-factly. "Of course it does."

My disdain was interrupted by the entrance into the Twisted

Lip of Lestrade. "We've rounded up all those girls. The hospital's checked them out and they all seem fine."

"I'm sorry," said an exasperated Holmes. "I was worried that…"

"It's okay, son," interrupted Lestrade. "Better to be safe."

"I backed myself to clear this up before we got to this point," continued a despondent Holmes.

"Do you have any ideas?" I asked.

"Not really. We need to suspect everyone and no one."

"No one? What does that mean?"

"I don't know," he sighed. "I just thought it sounded clever."

Shortly after Lestrade had left to return to the incident room at Middlesbrough Police Station, we were visited by Colin the Barbarian. His avoidance of Lestrade seemed more than coincidental.

Without invite he joined us, sitting in the chair Lestrade had previously vacated. "I've asked around my main competitors and nobody's seen your orange pills. I've also put out a warning. If anyone's offered them, they'll come straight to me. And I'll come straight to you. Then we can go find the bastard and break his fingers."

Holmes looked back at Colin with a look of puzzlement.

"You're keen, like," he said.

"Killing customers is bad for any business. Even mine."

"Was Ralphie King good for business?" I asked.

"A bank clerk? They don't have the cash for gear. Them poor fuckers make their own sandwiches."

Colin was clearly someone who knew his target demographic.

"Bad for business," sneered Holmes. "I think it might be time for you to make a career change. I'm in the mood to fuck someone up today and there aren't any reasons why it shouldn't be someone in your line of work."

I think Colin had expected more of a plaudit for his work.

"I also had a word with Kitkat to see if he knew anyone who'd be up for a job like the one on the lab. He said it was a non-runner. The security was too good and there's nowt really worth nicking apart from a few laptops."

"Kitkat?" I asked.

"He's a local thief," responded Holmes. "There's not that much that little fucker won't nick."

"Why do they call him Kitkat?"

"He's only got four fingers. Well, three and a thumb. Some weird birth defect."

Holmes fixed a silent thought-filled gaze on Colin, who took this as his cue to leave.

"I think Col's right," said Holmes on Colin's exit. "The local sole-traders aren't involved in this."

"So why did you threaten to kill him?"

"Because he's still a twat."

Holmes dipped his head down, contorting his face as he squeezed his forehead with his thumb and forefinger, before looking back up at me. "John, I need more time than we're gonna get."

4

Stanley Rayburn was a minor local celebrity. News of her death came a day or so later. Neighbours had called the police when they'd heard the screams coming from inside her house. They broke down the door to find her floating naked in the bath.

We entered the mortuary to find Doctor Pondicherry in conversation with Detective Inspector Lestrade. She took us over to the slab where Stanley was laid and pulled back the cover to reveal the serene face of the beautiful young actress. She didn't look like she'd been through any trauma. She was a little pale but other than that you could have mistaken her for being asleep.

"I recognise her," sighed Holmes pensively. "She was in Downton Abbey. I think she lives down at Ingleby Cardboard with all the Thornaby wannabes."

"You watch Downton Abbey?"

"No."

"The Doctor here tells me that she jumped in an ice cold bath and froze to death," said Lestrade.

"Really?" responded Holmes.

"Yes," said Pondicherry, "my initial analysis indicates she died of hypothermia. Her condition is very similar to that of those who have died after falling through the surface of a frozen lake. I'll know more when we get the lab results back."

"Did you send over a sample of her stomach contents?"

"Of course. That's standard procedure."

"Can you also send over a sample to Belasis Pharmaceuticals?"

"There's really no need. The lab we use is really very good."

"But stifled with bureaucracy and really quite slow. Belasis have a whizz kid, with a brain the size of a planet, who can tell us what's in there within a matter of minutes, using state-of-the-art equipment that he designed and built himself."

We travelled to Rayburn's house in our familiar transit of Lestrade's police car. As we entered, Holmes switched into his step through mode. From the front door, he moved down the hallway. Sometimes with his eyes open, mostly with them closed. Essentially he followed the path of Stanley's clothing that was strewn about the house. Occasionally he would stop, extend his arm and drum the fingers of his right hand in the air. For Lestrade, who'd seen Holmes do this before, this was routine, Doctor Pondicherry however was fascinated.

To me, the scenario seemed obvious. Rayburn had entered the house in some deranged state and stripped off her clothing as she'd moved through it.

We entered the kitchen to find the fridge door open and some of its contents scattered on the floor in front of it. We then followed the remainder of her garments up the stairs and into the bathroom, where the bath was still filled with water. Holmes stood staring into the still pool.

"She just wanted to cool down," he muttered through a tone of disappointment.

As we travelled back up the A19 in the back of an unmarked police car, Lestrade took a call regarding a report of another suspicious death. Gia Davies, a dental nurse from Acklam, had burned to death in her first floor apartment. The duration of Lestrade's call took us past the Acklam turn off so we turned round at Middlesbrough and headed straight to the scene.

The Chief Fire Officer briefed us on arrival. Davies had apparently broken up her furniture, doused it in some sort of accelerant and lit a fire that the officer estimated would have killed her in a matter of minutes. From the position of her charred remains, it appeared she was sat cross-legged in front of the furnace when she expired.

"Shall we take a look?" I asked.

"Bugger that," responded Holmes. "I think I've seen all I need to see from here."

Lestrade and Pondicherry headed into the building, leaving myself and Holmes outside.

"This is starting to depress me," said Holmes. "He's leaving no time for the thoughts to ferment."

"You think the killer's male?"

"I don't even know that," replied Holmes. "A poisoner. It could well be a woman. But why? And who would be able to get close enough to all three to pop them a pill? They're also so spread out. I can't imagine they copped it in the same place and there doesn't appear to be anything connecting them. Internet dating, maybe? I'll have a scoot round cyberspace when we get back."

Holmes wandered over to where a group of onlookers had congregated, gesturing for me to follow.

"Did any of you know Gia?" he asked.

"Yes, I did," said one of the men.

"Was she in a relationship?"

"Yes, her boyfriend works away. Offshore, I think. He went back last week."

"What does she get up to while he's away?"

"Not much. She keeps, sorry, kept herself to herself, really. I think she spent most nights skyping him. He's going to be devastated. It was her birthday a few weeks ago. We all went to the Dosa House in town. She even drove us there. I can't believe she's gone. She was only twenty-seven."

"Thank you," said Holmes with a consoling nod.

We moved back to where the car was parked, for Holmes to sit on the bonnet. "That's at least something in common," he said. "They were all twenty-seven, and, of course, female."

"Rayburn was only twenty-three," I pointed out.

"Was she bollocks. Actresses always take three or four years off."

"Do you think we have some sort of weird serial killer bumping off twenty-seven year olds?"

Holmes' non-committal expression suggested it was a possibility.

"But why go to the trouble of stealing experimental drugs?"

"I haven't a clue, Doc. Not one."

"To trash the reputation of Belasis Pharmaceuticals, maybe?"

"Maybe," sighed Holmes. "I'm not sure about the twenty-seven thing, though. Maybe twenty-seven is just an unlucky number."

"You believe in luck?"

"No, but I'm wary of it."

Lestrade was visibly shaken when he returned. "It's quite a scene in there," he said.

"I can imagine," I replied.

"We need to keep this one out of the papers," said Holmes. "We can't let them connect this to the pills. Just tell them it was a house fire. Have you mentioned the pills to the Trumpton?"

"The fire brigade?" responded Lestrade. "No."

"Okay, let's leave it like that. It gives us an edge. And at the minute, we don't have much else."

Our aimless postulations continued into the evening and to our usual perches at the Twisted Lip. As we sat behind a couple of pints of Engineer's Thumb, Holmes examined one of the orange pills between his thumb and forefinger.

"What is it with these little orange bastards?" he remarked.

He then dropped it into his mouth and swilled it down with large gulp of beer.

"What on earth are you doing?" I exclaimed.

"Finding something out," he replied.

He stood up, downed the rest of his beer and slung on his jacket. "I'm going back to the flat now. I'll see you in four days."

"Sherlock, you'll be dead in three."

"Four days," he repeated.

Holmes disappeared along Baker Street and I fully expected that to be the last time I would see him alive.

I couldn't begin to imagine what Holmes thought he would achieve from this ridiculous experiment. To me, it was perfect folly. I was convinced that before Holmes' four day moratorium was over, we would have another victim. Surely he would be better employed hunting down the killer.

Four of the longest days later, I borrowed the spare key from Martha and crept cautiously into the flat. I made my way up the stairs to find Holmes sat cross-legged on the settee, his feet resting on a short stool. He looked up briefly from his laptop to greet me. "Hiya, Doc. Has it been four days already?"

"Yes. Are you okay?"

"Fine," he said dismissively. "Has Lestrade found out anything on how those girls might have come into contact with the pills?"

"He has a few ideas," I replied, "but nothing firm. All the girls seem to have drunk or eaten in a number of public places. So there are a number of possibilities."

"Even the actress?"

"Yeah, she was a fan of 12 Harland Place in Norton."

"I've heard of that place. They do nice steaks."

"Sherlock," I interrupted, "how, why?"

"How, why, what?"

"How come you're still alive?"

"Easy really. I just closed down the area of my mind the pills were trying to bend. I reckon if you got pissed enough they wouldn't work at all. All that work they put into developing an antidote and a bottle of Blue Sapphire would've done the trick. They just needed to get the rats rat-arsed.

"It's possible that all of Ralphie King's mates were drugged on that night. Ralphie copped it, poor cow, because she was the only one not drinking. Just goes to show. They should put a warning on soft drinks. I tell you what, I've done my last shift as a designated driver. Did Stanley have wine with her meal?"

"I don't know. Probably not. She drove to the restaurant."

"And I bet you a pound to a penny Gia was teetotal. This must be confusing the hell out of whoever's doing this. They must be wondering why some of their victims are waking up with nothing more than a half-decent hangover."

5

It wasn't long before we got to test Holmes' theory. Lestrade was called to James Cook Hospital where one of the registrars was behaving strangely. Picking us up from Albert Road on the way, Lestrade greeted us as we jumped in the back of his car. "Where the fuck have you been?" he snarled.

"On me holidays," replied Holmes.

We arrived at the hospital to find Simone Merivale barricaded into her office. Through the window in her door, we could see her coiled up in the foetal position on the floor.

Holmes tapped on the glass. "Doctor Merivale, we've booked this room for a meeting."

Immediately, a zombified Merivale climbed to her feet and started to clear the wreckage from in front of her door.

"I don't believe that," said one of the assembled medical staff. "We've been trying to get her out of there for the last three hours."

"Do you have any alcohol?" asked Holmes.

"This is a hospital, not a nightclub," commented one of the senior consultants.

"Surgical spirit, ethanol, anything," snapped Holmes.

"I have a bottle of tequila in my desk drawer," said a matronly nurse to the confused surprise of the rest of the group. "I won it in the raffle," she protested.

"Brilliant, can you bring it, please, with a couple of glasses or cups or something?"

The nurse returned just as the path into the room had been cleared. Holmes thanked the nurse and took the bottle of Jose Cuervo Especial Gold from her. Holding it up to his face to study the label for a while, he then mumbled, "Sometimes it ends in debauchery. Sometimes it ends in tequila."

He paused a few moments before placing two plastic cups the nurse had also supplied over the neck of the bottle and making his way into the office, closing the door behind him. Taking Merivale by the hand, he sat her down on the carpet. Loosening the top of the bottle with his teeth, he poured two decent-sized measures.

At first miming the action he then downed the drink. Merivale followed. He refilled the glasses and they went again. Five or six goes and maybe forty-five minutes later the bottle was empty. Merivale's head slumped sideways onto Holmes' shoulder and he nodded that it was okay for us to enter.

"What shall we do now?" I asked.

"Get a kebab," responded an inebriated Holmes.

The next morning, we met up with Lestrade at the Baker Street Kitchen. As Holmes downed copious amounts of milkless tea, he relayed a story. Doctor Merivale had been involved in a tragic event a while back, he said. I did have a vague recollection of the case myself, however Holmes' memory of the events was archival.

A few years ago when Merivale was still a junior doctor, she administered an injection to a newborn baby. It wasn't within her role to undertake such a task, but the nurse who should have attended was caught up with another patient. Unfortunately, Merivale miscalculated the dose by a factor of ten and the baby was brain damaged and died.

It could and probably should have been the end of her, however given the mistake was made with the best of intentions, the tribunal showed leniency. She was barred from paediatrics, but allowed to practice in other areas, initially under close supervision. Being as determined as she was, the terrible tragedy transpired to be no more than a hiccup in her accelerating career.

"Don't you see?" exclaimed Holmes.

"See what?" I replied.

"We have a potential motive," he responded.

"Maybe for the attempt on Merivale, but that doesn't explain the other three murders."

"Where's the best place to hide a needle?"

"In a haystack?" asked Lestrade.

"No. In a pile of needles. Look," continued Holmes, "I might be miles offside here, I'm talking Bernie Slaven, but the first three murders might just be noise to mask the real target. If Merivale had copped it from a brain bending drug, it would have been poetic licence."

"Poetic justice," I corrected.

"Yeah, that as well. We need to find out where the MacGregors are now."

"MacGregor?" queried Lestrade. "There was an Alice MacGregor on the staff list Openshaw gave me for Belasis Pharmaceuticals."

Holmes sat back in his chair with a knowing raise of the eyebrows.

"That's enough for me," said Lestrade. "I'm bringing them in."

"No," said Holmes. "Let me talk to them. If it's not them, it gives the killer a way out."

"Sorry, Sherlock, we've had three, nearly four murders. I can't let the MacGregors kill again. There's fifty of those little orange bombshells out there."

"Will they kill again?" I asked. "If Merivale is their true victim then won't they stop now, or at least double back and try to finish the job?"

"Maybe not," sighed Holmes. "If it's them, they would want to bookend it. Make sure the attempt on Merivale doesn't stand out. Come on, Lestrade. Let them run. Just keep a bead on them. This is a win-win situation. Don't play for a fucking draw. If it is them, we can catch them in the act, if not, then we haven't given the real killer the thought to go to ground. Don't turn this into a bigger clusterfuck than it already is."

6

Lestrade questioned the MacGregors for three days. Sometimes alone, sometimes with the slightly-built female detective we had not yet been introduced to. In the absence of a name, Holmes had taken to calling her boneface, razor cheeks or the laughing skull. It was interesting to see how animosity could grow between two people who had not once interacted.

I couldn't imagine a more normal couple than Alec and Alice MacGregor. Nor could I begin to fantasise that they were the serial killers of three innocent young women. Alice worked as a specialist cleaner at Belasis Pharmaceuticals and Alec, a semi-retired fitter who had struggled to hold down a job since the death of his child, had seemingly one vice. He stole away occasionally to the Tees estuary to watch the storm petrels migrating across the windswept slag of South Gare.

Lestrade rounded on this solitary endeavour immediately, seeing it as something odd, a protrusion he could use to cleave into MacGregor's character. I don't think he could have been more wrong. That bleak Teesside coastline was where he found solace. The cold, stripping rain was the only distraction he had available to him.

Both Lestrade and his commanding officer, Superintendent Spaulding, invited Holmes into several of the sessions with the MacGregors, but on every occasion he declined. From the vantage point of Interview Suite Two's observation area, we watched Lestrade goad and harry that poor couple. To their ultimate credit, they were steadfast, their story unwavering. They had nothing to do with the theft of the drugs nor the deaths of those three girls, never mind the attempt on Merivale's life. There was clearly no love lost for Merivale, but they saw no prize in revenge. "How would killing someone else's child help mine?" commented Mrs MacGregor on more than one occasion. The problem for the MacGregors was their alibi. At the times the pills would have been administered, they were with no one but each other. They kept themselves to themselves and to Lestrade that represented an admission of guilt.

Over recent weeks, I had seen the relationship between Holmes and Lestrade build. In those few days, that was pretty much undone. There were times when Holmes stood with his back to the glass, not bearing to watch the cruelty being seeded just a few feet away. Arms folded, he stood motionless in soporific detachment.

On one occasion towards end of the assault, Lestrade stormed out of the interview room to come crashing in through the door of the observation area. "Come on, Holmes, what am I not seeing?"

"That they might not 'ave fucking done it, you daft tit," growled Holmes.

I was convinced they could come to blows, as were the nearby police officers who, to a man, shaped to intervene.

The absolution of the MacGregors came via yet another death. Alana Cosgrave, a stable girl from Neasham near Darlington, was found hanged in her lodgings. We never visited the scene, however it was clear from the crazy ramblings of her suicide note and its references to beetles crawling into her mouth and ears, that she was in some distress when she took her life.

Holmes approached the MacGregors as they left the police station. I was out of earshot, however from the observable body language it appeared that Holmes was offering an apology.

Later, after we had gathered in Lestrade's incident room, the tension between Holmes and the inspector was palpable. It was Holmes who broke a short uncomfortable silence. "The locations these victims are turning up in are quite spread out. Don't serial killers tend to operate in a localised area?"

"Usually," I responded.

"How old was Cosgrave?" asked Holmes.

"Twenty-seven," replied one of the uniformed female officers.

"Twenty-seven," sighed Holmes. "I'm sure that isn't a thing."

Holmes' drift into thought was diverted by the entrance of Doctor Pondicherry. "We have the lab results back on those stomach contents."

"Ralphie King?" I asked.

"Yes," said Pondicherry, "and the other victims. It seems the lab speeds up a bit when news of a killer on the streets is spread across the antisocial media."

"You're calling them all 'victims'," said Holmes. "Does that mean the drug was found in all the samples?"

"Yes, well, all except Cosgrave. The lab isn't quite that fast. The odd thing is the variation across the samples. It appears that the drugs taken by each victim were not from the same batch. The active ingredient, this neurokineodroxaline substance, is paired with something else. Something organic which we don't recognise. The relative proportions of the two components differ across the victims."

"Uniformly?" asked Holmes.

"Pretty much," responded Pondicherry.

"Do you mind if I take a look?"

"Of course not," she replied, handing him the file she was carrying.

"Neckera Rangiferina, Dead Man's Moss."

"I'm impressed," exclaimed the doctor.

"I can be more impressive than that. Why don't you nip round to 22 Baker Street, Flat 1B one night. Wednesdays are a good time to catch me in."

Pondicherry responded with a look of indignation.

"Dead Man's Moss won't work as a regulating agent," continued Holmes. "By the time you got enough of it in there, you'd be knocked out. It probably would work as an antidote." He gave Pondicherry a long stare. "Interesting," he whispered.

"Are we saying that the pills these girls were given weren't the ones taken in the robbery?" asked Lestrade.

"I'm not saying anything," he responded.

The pursuance of the three-pint puzzle adjourned to the Twisted Lip. Holmes was distant and ignorant of his surroundings. It wasn't unusual for his mind to be elsewhere, this was what he called his processing state, however on this occasion his vacancy appeared tinged with disappointment.

"What can anyone have against twenty-seven year olds?" I asked.

"Maybe our man was on an eighteen to thirty holiday and was the only one who didn't get a shag. Here's the thing," said Holmes, "these killings are not intended, they're just consequences."

"What do you mean? Consequences of what?"

"The drugs are being tested. That's why the ingredients vary. Someone is trying to find the right level of inhibitor to use. They don't realise it's never gonna work."

"That would explain the narrow age group," I added.

"It might," muttered a thoughtful Holmes. "I think we need a visit to Belasis Pharmaceuticals."

"Should we get Lestrade?"

"No, fuck him."

7

We arrived at Belasis Pharmaceuticals to be greeted by the receptionist Sally Monteith. Miss Monteith's appearance aligned well with the pristine surroundings of the building in which she worked. Perhaps no older than her mid-twenties, she was dressed in a sharp white blouse, a tight-fitting navy blue skirt, with her dark brown hair immaculately dressed in tight buns either side of her head. Her pale skin was contrasted with a deep red lipstick that was the only thing not in keeping with the business-like image she otherwise presented.

As often happened in the presence of an attractive woman, Holmes' personality transformed. "Hello, Miss Monteith," he said, holding out his hand and maintaining her grasp long past the time period that is probably deemed appropriate. "Could we speak with Mister Openshaw, please?"

"I'm afraid he's not in today. We've not seen him for a few days. We're getting quite worried. It's really not like him. He's usually here seven days a week," she said, extracting herself from his grip with a nervous smile.

"Really," said Holmes. "I'll see if I can track him down for you. How about Alastair Bruce? Is he in?"

"He's not in today either."

"Ah, that's a shame. It's him I really needed to see."

"Actually, he usually visits his parents in Norton on a Wednesday. He should be there after about seven. You could catch up with him there."

She scribbled down an address and handed it to Holmes, who for the whole time had her fixed in his stare.

"Thank you, you've been very helpful." His attempt at seduction was pitiful.

"I think I'm in there," he said as we left the building.

"Yeah, probably," I responded.

"What? You don't think so."

"No."

"She was turning Japanese."

"What do you mean?"

"She had a nip on."

"I think that was just the draft from the door. Besides she's too young for you."

"Nah, divide by two and add seven. Sorted."

"You'd be pushing it."

"Cheeky get."

Jack and Kitty, Bruce's parents, were a lovely couple, short on stature but long on conviviality.

"It's some friends of Alastair's, Kitty," announced Mr Bruce as he led us into a well-looked-after sitting room. "I'm afraid Alastair's not here at the minute. He likes to pop up to the Highland Lad on a Wednesday for the quiz."

"Right," remarked Holmes, "is he in a team?"

"No, he does it on his own. He doesn't need any help. He used to work over in America, you know."

We were about to make our excuses when Kitty rattled in with a tray full of china tea cups and saucers.

"Would you like some tea, boys?" she said, placing the tray down on the table in front of us.

When she returned to the kitchen, Mr Bruce leant over and whispered to us, "The wife has a touch of the Alzheimer's. If she offers you a biscuit, it's best if you say yes. Otherwise she'll just keep asking. Just put it in front of you to remind her."

Just as Jack had predicted, Kitty re-entered the room, placed the decorative teapot on the table, and asked us if we would like a biscuit.

"Oooh," she said, "I bought some chocolate digestives the other day. I know how you boys like biscuits. I'll go and get them."

She returned with some Rich Tea.

I found it quite funny, sitting there with Holmes sipping tea from the most delicate of china cups. My stifling of a smirk prompted Holmes to gesticulate a 'what?'. I just dismissed his query with a shake of my head.

As we sat there, Mrs Bruce dropped to her knees and started searching around the carpet.

"What are you looking for, dear?" asked Mr Bruce.

"Some marbles. I saw them here earlier. I was going to give them to the boys."

"Aw, have you lost your marbles?" sighed Mr Bruce.

I had to remove myself from the moment to prevent myself from exploding with laughter. Holmes admonished me with a concerned glare.

We finished our tea and Mr Bruce showed us to the door.

"Many thanks for your hospitality," said Holmes, with me adding a confirmatory nod.

"Our pleasure, lad," responded Mr Bruce. "We don't get many visitors, since Kitty, well, you know."

Holmes and I shook his hand.

As we made our way up to the Highland Laddie, I was rebuked by Holmes.

"I can't believe you," he said, "a member of the medical profession, a psychologist, making fun of that poor woman's condition."

"Oh, come on," I defended. "I wasn't making fun of her. It was his unfortunate choice of phrase."

"Well, I'm disgusted," he retorted.

The Wednesday night quiz was in full flow when we entered. 'The Laddie' is actually a really nice pub. Spacious and airy with a minimalist, contemporary decor, it avoided the garish stain-camouflaging carpet and argumentative wallpaper patterns of similar establishments.

Alastair Bruce was sitting on his own on a bar stool by a high table near the far wall.

"Hello, Alastair. Fancy seeing you here," said Holmes as he took a seat at his table.

"Drinks?" I volunteered.

Bruce shook his head.

"A Blonde, please," requested Holmes.

While I was at the bar, I quizzed the barmaid who served me. I asked her if she recognised Bruce and she said she did and he was there most Wednesdays. She also confirmed he was there for the quiz the previous week. The night that Ralphie King, Miss Merryweather and their friends had visited. Without me prompting, she told me that Ralphie and her friends had actually sat at Bruce's table and joined him in that week's quiz.

"Were you here last week?" I asked as I rejoined them at the table.

"I was," replied Bruce. "I'm here most weeks. I like doing the quiz."

"Did you see the girl who died?"

"I don't think so."

"The barmaid just told me you entered the quiz with her and her friends."

"Ah yes," replied a nervous Bruce. "I remember now. They were quite annoying. All lipstick and glitter. Was that last week?"

"Where were you at the times of the other attacks?"

"I don't know," came the frustrated response. "At home probably."

"Alone?"

"Well, yes. I live alone.

"For all of them?"

"Yes, all four," snapped Bruce. "What can I do, invite someone around every evening in case I need an alibi for some random crime?"

Holmes dipped his brow and flashed Bruce a thoughtful stare.

"I think we should go, Doc. Let Alastair concentrate on the quiz."

"Why you did stop me?" I protested as we made our way through the village along Norton High Street. "We didn't even finish our beer."

"Because I'd seen enough. It's him. He shouldn't know about all the victims. Cosgrave won't have hit the news yet and we kept Davies' connection secret. Well done, Doc, you've cracked it. It was inspired asking that barmaid. There's not much sober people miss in a room full of drunks. There's also a couple of other things that won't do him any favours in court. It's a bit disappointing, isn't it?"

"What, that his research will come to nothing?"

"No, that the smartest bloke on Teesside turns out to be a bit of a wrong un."

"How can we make sure, Sherlock? It doesn't seem enough to me."

"We could get him to dance."

"Metaphorically, you mean? Harass him into making a mistake?"

"No, I mean really. Guilty feet don't have any rhythm. Apparently."

I'm not really sure what was worse. The joke or the circumstances around which he was telling it.

We flagged a cab and made our way back to the Twisted Lip. Positioned behind our more familiar tipple of Engineer's Thumb, Holmes elaborated on his thinking. Bruce had returned from America when his mother's Alzheimer's became unmanageable.

Being the dutiful son, he visited his parents every week, however he couldn't bear to see his mother in the condition she was in. He therefore spent most of the evening in the Highland Laddie.

His work at Belasis Pharmaceuticals promised a cure for his mother. This perhaps was his real reason for leaving Yale. He was however frustrated on Openshaw's policy on animal testing as it slowed progress. Each week, his poor mother lost more of her mind and he wasn't closing in on a cure fast enough. That's when he decided to source some more suitable guinea pigs in the form of Ralphie King et al. Although the test subjects were a lot younger than his mother, he reasoned the significant factor was that they were female. It was the desperation driven by the sand grains falling too rapidly through the hourglass that drove his misplaced faith in Neckera Rangiferina, Dead Man's Moss. He was banking on this being the inhibitor he had been searching for, abandoning the scientific due diligence he was renowned for in the process.

"So what were the other things you mentioned you'd spotted earlier?" I asked.

"The equipment," said Holmes. "When the lab got done over, all the good stuff, the stuff he'd pulled together himself, wasn't touched. The only things that got bust were things you could probably buy in Dixons."

"And the other thing?"

"Yeah, well, I kind of engineered that. I kept having the stomach contents sent to Belasis for analysis in the hope that they would assume the police weren't testing them as well. That worked better than I'd hoped actually. It's not only the criminal that needs to cover his tracks. Ah, speaking of tracks. The break in was executed from the outside, but planned from within, by someone who knew no windows had been left unlocked. Even a crap thief would have tried a few before breaking one."

I smiled in frustration. As always, it was so simple. How had I not noticed those things. Especially the computer kit. I'd seen enough of his method to spot at least something.

My concern now was that Bruce knew we were on to him and might take flight.

Holmes dismissed this. "Nah, he's got himself down as a smart arse. He doesn't think he's gonna get caught. Especially by two raggy-arsed scroats like us."

"Raggy what? Sorry!"

"Sorry, one raggy-arsed scroat and a posh bloke who looks a bit like Will Self."

"I don't look like Will Self."

"Yeah, you're an absolute spit. Oh, actually I think I mean Will Smith."

"Will Smith? The black Hollywood actor?"

"No, the fella from Redcar who used to sell crabsticks down our local. The Fish Prince of South Gare."

Whereas I was concerned about Bruce absconding, and the comparison of my aesthetic to a roaming fishmonger, Holmes' concerns were elsewhere. He reasoned that there was more to John Openshaw's disappearance than a period of absence without leave. He said he'd be very surprised if Openshaw turned up alive.

Holmes' prophecy was confirmed the next day when the Evening Gazette reported a story of a man found floating in the River Tees. The news article suggested that local businessman John Openshaw had probably succumbed to an accident, however given the recent deaths relating to drugs produced by his company there was some reasonable conjecture that his death may have been suicide.

Doctor Pondicherry pulled back the cover to reveal the still face of our client.

"Stomach contents?" questioned Holmes.

"Lab," responded Pondicherry.

"Well, he wasn't twenty-seven," exhaled Holmes. "If he was, he had a fucking tough paper round. We're talking Grangetown. Either that or a glass collecting gig at Henry Afrika's."

Both areas of questionable health and safety.

"At least his death hasn't been a total waste," continued Holmes. "There's a couple of conclusions we can draw from this. One, we're not getting fucking paid. Two, we definitely know who our man is."

"Who?" asked Pondicherry.

"Alastair Bruce," I responded. "But how does Openshaw's death make Bruce more definite?"

"Because Openshaw was the only other candidate. He's kind of ruled himself out now."

"Does DI Lestrade know this?" asked Pondicherry.

"Not yet," replied Holmes. "I've been managing down his information. He has a tendency to bang like a boghouse door. Come on, Doc, let's go and give Bruce a tickle. He lives up in Wolviston."

9

It had been a long time since I'd been to Wolviston. It's a pleasant little village that once delivered a couple of Britain in Bloom awards. I'd not been there for some time and it was a shame. I do like a typical English village with a church, duck pond and local pub. The pub in this case being the Wellington Inn, referred to locally as 'the Welly'.

Bruce lived in a place of newer construction called Drearcliffe House. It was a detached property of four or perhaps even five bedrooms and was far too big for single occupancy. Bruce clearly had money.

We walked up the gravel drive to be greeted by Bruce at the door. "Come on in, lads," he said. "I've been expecting you. Oooh, that makes me sound like a Bond villain."

He was oddly jovial given the circumstances.

"I assume from our chat the other night you've rumbled me as the 'Orange Pill Killer'. You know I never meant to kill those girls."

"Yeah," said Holmes. "The sad thing is they all died for no reason. Dead Man's Moss was never going to work."

"Yes, I've drawn that conclusion myself. Never mind, I'll find something else."

"Not where you're going," I interjected.

"And where am I going, Doctor Watson?"

"Prison. For a very long time."

"No, I'm not. Sorry have I missed something here? Are you two goons the police?"

"No," said Holmes. "We're gonna citizen's arrest you."

"Is that even a thing anymore?"

"I think so. But it doesn't matter anyway cos there's two of us. You're coming with us back to Middlesbrough where Detective Inspector Lestrade's gonna roger you senseless."

"The thing is, Sherlock, I've planned for just this scenario and dropped another one of my little pills into someone else's decaf skinny latte. Of course, I will tell you whose decaf skinny latte, but not a moment before I get off my business class flight to Cuba."

Holmes' face contorted as he bit into his bottom lip to consider his next step.

"One of these you mean," he said, presenting an orange pill between his index finger and thumb.

"Look after that," said Bruce. "It'll save a lot of lives one day."

"This one's going to save a life today," said Holmes. With that, he threw the pill at Bruce. By some miracle, it flew straight into his mouth, causing him to cough and bork as he tried to regurgitate it.

"You know what you need," said Holmes as he rattled a plastic bottle of grey tablets. "A few of these of these. Dead Man's Moss. Neckera something fucking or other. These act as the antidote you couldn't be arsed to develop."

Bruce lurched towards Holmes only for Holmes to push him in the chest.

"A-ar," exclaimed Holmes. "You've not finished telling me about this decaf skinny latte yet. I think it takes about an hour before your brain starts melting. It seems to work a lot faster in men. But you know that, don't you, from the one you slipped John Openshaw before you flung him in the Tees. What did he do to you? Did he draw the conclusion that the Doc here and me have too?"

"Holmes, you can't do this. My mind is unique. Without me, there will never be a cure."

"Yes, I fucking can, I'm not the fucking police. I don't care about what some psychotic twat thinks he can or can't do at the minute. I'm more bothered about this young girl you're in the process of killing."

Bruce twitched in desperation.

"Can you feel anything yet? With a brain like yours, it might be a bit quicker. Actually, I think I can hear the little grey cells fizzling out. How many fingers am I holding up?" he said, whilst showing Bruce a V sign.

"Okay, okay," screamed Bruce. "She's called Joanne Simpson. She's a barmaid working in a pub called the Ship Inn in Saltburn."

"You've poisoned a barmaid?" exclaimed Holmes. "Do you not know what a vital service they provide?" Holmes held out his hand. "I'm gonna need your car keys."

Bruce rummaged frantically in his pockets before pulling out a single key and throwing it to Holmes. In return, Holmes threw Bruce the bottle of pills.

"There you go. Take three and call me in the morning."

As we made to leave, Holmes turned back. "How come you picked on twenty-seven year olds?"

"Twenty-seven year olds? What are you talking about?"

"I fucking knew it," he exclaimed.

Bruce's Fiat 500 wasn't the ideal vehicle for a mercy dash. However having previously experienced Holmes' driving, I was somewhat relieved at the limited speed it was capable of achieving.

As we rushed along the A19, Holmes asked me to ring Lestrade and get him over to Bruce's place. There was no rush he said, as Bruce would be asleep for at least the next day and a half. He also asked me to ask him where Joanne lived.

"Shit, she might not even be in Saltburn. What the fuck's this?" he said, jabbing his fingers at the radio. "Radio fucking Four?"

My call with Lestrade confirmed that Joanne actually lived in a room above the Ship Inn.

"Excellent," said Holmes. "This might actually work out alright."

My comfort in the little Fiat diminished as we hit the Monte Carlo-like bends in the bank that leads down to Saltburn seafront. I was sure we were going to tip over and roll down the cliff onto the beach.

We reached the pub and abandoned the car in the middle of the road before running in. A bemused barman recoiled as we dashed to the bar.

"Joanne Simpson, where is she?" shouted Holmes.

"In her room. Sorry, who, who are you?"

"I'm Sherlock fucking Holmes. You need to take us to her. She's in danger."

The confused young barman led us up some stairs and to a heavy wooden door painted blue. "Are you there, Joanne?" he said as he knocked on the door.

"Out the way," said Holmes, pushing him aside.

Holmes tried the handle and the door opened to reveal a slight blonde girl curled up on the floor in her underwear. She looked back at us with confused yearning.

"Hello, Joanne. My name is Sherlock. My friend here's a doctor. He's come to give you some medicine." He handed me a bottle of the pills before moving to the small sink to fill a glass.

"How many?" I asked.

Holmes looked at her. "Two maybe," he responded.

Joanne obediently took the pills, swallowing them with a small sip of the water.

"You're going to be fine now," reassured Holmes. "You just need to sleep for a while."

He picked her up and laid her on the bed, taking a blanket that was laid folded at the foot and placing it over her. "Dream a little dream for me," he whispered.

He looked at me and nodded. There was no need for words.

10

The news across the headlines the next day was sensational. To my mind, the most memorable being 'Sherlock Holmes Catches Mad Scientist'. Memory fails but that may have been the selection of the Northern Echo.

Most of the newspapers dedicated six or seven pages to the story including biographies of both the poor girls who lost their lives, and the villain of the piece, Professor Alastair Bruce, who was yet to regain consciousness and consequently yet to be charged for the murders. The word 'allegedly' was peppered through the various accounts to the point of monotony.

The facts on the case itself, and how we'd concluded on Bruce were however achingly thin. As was the mention of my contribution to the case, which I felt pivotal. It was obvious that Sherlock Holmes cast a shadow that would be hard to escape.

If I'm honest with you, I wasn't overly bothered. My reward came with the opportunity to observe the method of that strange creature at such close quarters.

The neglect of my mention was however insignificant compared with the scathing assessment of Detective Inspector Lestrade and his colleagues. Littered with the word 'incompetence' and its various synonyms, there was a weight of opinion that the protagonists provided by the police in this sorry affair should be relieved of their duties. Both Lestrade and, his superior, Superintendent Spaulding were mentioned by name.

I wondered what this might do to the recently re-fractured relationship between Holmes and Lestrade.

If Lestrade wished for a career in the police force beyond the next couple of weeks, he needed an ally in Holmes. Although Holmes didn't have an equitable reliance, a relationship with the police was useful in that it facilitated access to areas that wouldn't otherwise be available. The dynamic across the next story would be interesting.

On the evening of the day we sent Professor Alastair Bruce down the river, we partied 'like it was nineteen ninety-eight'. Mary, Martha, Holmes and myself spent most of the evening in the Baker Street Tavern before moving on to Sticky Fingers. Given the Tavern's approximation to the Twisted Lip and it being just a few doors along Baker Street from it, it was odd that Holmes and I added little to its footfall. Apparently we, like the characters in our various episodes, were creatures of some habit. Breakfast in the Baker Street Kitchen, a liquid lunch in the Twisted Lip and pub food in the Irish bar on Bedford Street for dinner. Holmes referred to this as 'tea'.

On this occasion, we'd opted for the Baker Street Tavern in order to give Mary a change of scene. That said, even though she did work long shifts in her capacity as bar manager, Holmes and I probably spent a similar amount of time in there to her. Like the Twisted Lip, the Baker Street Tavern was a micropub converted from an old terraced residence. Varied second-hand furniture and decoration provided it a bohemian feel that complemented the real ale and craft beer it purveyed. I'm not really sure what the difference is between craft beer and real ale, but I still have a taste for the paler variants of either.

The Rolling Stone-themed Sticky Fingers was a revelation to us forty-somethings. I was expecting it to be loud and conversation-denying, but for a good proportion of our visit the music was provided by two well-dressed youths playing an acoustic set featuring tunes some of which I actually recognised.

Mary and I slept late the following morning. I recovered my awareness to find numerous missed calls and voicemails from Jordan Dale, my contact at the Evening Gazette. He was desperate for my account of the recent events. That evening I sat down to pen 'The Case of the Fifty Orange Pills'.

DEATH IN THE TWISTED LIP

1

As we sat in the Baker Street Kitchen that morning, the commotion building in Baker Street was soon apparent.

"Shall we go and see what is happening?" I asked, as the third or fourth police car rounded the corner, to head in a direction against the one-way street.

"No," said Holmes, "we're only halfway down this pot of tea."

"It looks serious," I observed.

"So is wasting bloody good tea. They seem to have hit my requirement for a four minute forty-five mash pretty much spot on this morning."

"They have," I responded. "Cathryn has bought herself a stopwatch. You better leave a tip today."

"A tip?" he protested. "What, for doing her job? Nobody gives me a bloody tip for doing my job."

"You don't have a job."

"I do. I'm a consulting detective for Cleveland Police. Don't you remember Superintendent Spaulding saying I was 'instrumental' in the conviction of Charlie McCarthy? He's now doing ten to fifteen with sod all chance of parole this side of a couple of World Cups."

"You've never even been paid, and I'd rather not talk about that."

"What, the World Cup? I don't blame you. We're never going to get anywhere with the lack of movement upfront they showed against the Czechs. You know, I've applied for that England job forty-seven times and the wankers have only replied twice. Although I'm pretty sure it's me who got McClaren the sack. That's probably why the git never gave me me umbrella back."

"No," I glowered. "I was referring to the wrongful incarceration of Charlie McCarthy."

"You're a touchy bugger, you, aren't you?" he sighed.

"Hang on," I said, "that brolly was yours?"

"Yeah," said Holmes, "he nipped into the Irish Bar one night when it was pissing down. He pitched in with the quiz actually. It was his answers on the sport round that fucked it up for us. Back then, the poor bugger couldn't buy a win."

"Come on, Sherlock," I said, diverting the conversation from his surreal meandering to the events unfolding just a short distance from where we were sitting, "let's go and see what's happening."

"No," he snapped. "This tea's fantastic. Top up?"

At that point, our looming argument was curtailed by a phone call from Mary. In some state, she pleaded with me to get down to the Twisted Lip as soon as I could. Not caring whether Holmes followed or not, I leapt to her call.

Holmes and I stepped down Baker Street and into the midst of chaos. More police vehicles than I could count littered the scene, each parked where its journey had concluded. Police personnel of various forms and rank milled around frenetically, with no apparent objective.

In the middle of the melee stood the formidable figure of Detective Inspector Lestrade, directing the seemingly undirectable.

"I was wondering if you'd show up," the inspector called as we slipped under the scene of crime tape. Your 'different perspective' never spotted this one, did it? There's a dead body in there, about ten doors from where you live."

Holmes appeared oblivious. "Upstairs?" he asked Lestrade.

"Yeah, how did you know that?"

"All the SOCOs peering out of the window at WPC Vernon."

"They don't call women police officers that any more, Sherlock," I said.

"What?"

"WPC"

"Why not?"

"It's not PC."

"What do they call them?"

"PC."

Holmes returned a confused dismissal.

"Mind if we have a look?" I asked, reasoning that given the currently fractious relationship between Holmes and Lestrade, the request would more likely be granted if it came from me. Lestrade grimaced in resistance, causing Holmes to look away and exhale a bored sigh of inevitable rejection. I'm sure it was against every wish and instinct for Lestrade to grant my request, however within the ensuing chaos we both knew Holmes was the best chance of an accelerated conclusion to the matter in hand. Lestrade bit through his frustration and gestured to one of the scene of crime officers to join us.

"Get these lads kitted out, can yer?" he requested.

Even though I'd brokered the deal, I was still expecting to be excluded from it. That I was implicitly included provided me a sense of achievement. I assumed Lestrade would concede to Holmes' assistance, but fully expected myself to be left kicking around in the street. Last kid to be selected for the team scenario avoided, we made our way into the Twisted Lip dressed in ill-fitting paper overalls, shoe socks and latex gloves.

As we entered the bar, I told everyone to stop. I looked around to examine the scene. I hadn't actually noticed anything and, in honesty, I was feigning to over-accentuate my participation. Holmes just looked at me with confused embarrassment.

"It's okay,' I said. "It's nothing."

Holmes never mouthed the words "for fuck's sake" but I could tell he was thinking them.

We made our way up the steep, creaking old stairs to be confronted by the most heinous scene I had been subjected to to that date. The victim, an overweight, balding man in his mid to late fifties was arranged spread eagled on the floor. Large nails, driven through his wrists and his ankles pinned him in position. His death mask was one of sheer terror.

"That's Dave Arrowsmith," said Holmes.

"My god, it is," I realised.

"You know him?" asked Lestrade.

"Yes," muttered Holmes. "He's a local landlord. He looks, looked, after a few office spaces and industrial units."

The pathologist, Doctor Shreya Pondicherry, stooped over the body, her activity unaffected by our arrival. "He's been dead between six and ten hours," she said without breaking from her examination.

"There's not much blood," I observed.

"No," replied Doctor Pondicherry, "the nails were driven in post-mortem."

"If the nails were put in after he died, then why the look of terror on his face?"

"My best guess at this stage is he was tortured. There are definite signs of trauma to various areas of the body. It looks like he took quite a beating. As far as I can establish, the perpetrator went too far and his heart gave out."

"It's not everyone who can torture a man to death and then layout the body and drive nails into it," I commented. "Whoever did this is affected by some quite severe psychosis."

Holmes gave me a long thoughtful look and nodded agreement.

"Was he killed here?" asked Lestrade.

"He was a big unit to lump up them stairs if he wasn't," muttered Holmes. He then moved away from the body to take a seat at the far end of the room. Sitting close to still, his eyes sweeping the room in a staccato motion, his only significant movement was an occasional twitch of the neck to readjust his view.

On the curtailment of his familiar survey, he leaned back in his chair to look up and stare at the ceiling.

After a couple of minutes, I joined him, taking an adjacent seat. "What do you want to do?" I asked.

"I need to check one thing," he replied.

Walking over to where Doctor Pondicherry was still examining the body, he stepped over as if it were but a minor inconvenience. He then dropped to his knees, crooking his neck in order for his eye to look across the floorboards. After a short while, he jumped up and sprang to his feet.

Floating around the room, he examined the various styles of chairs of differing sizes, tapping some with his latex-gloved fingers before honing in on one in particular. He picked up the chair and returned to the area of the floor he had previously been examining. Placing it gently on the floor, he said, "He was sat on this when he died. There's fresh scratches in the floorboards that only this chair could have made. He must have been strapped to this chair as he struggled."

He then returned to his knees to view the chair legs at close proximity. "Kev," he said, looking up to address a tall, thin and greying scene of crime officer, "do you have some tweezers I could borrow?"

Holmes took the implement and used them to collect something from one of the chair legs. "Rope strand," he said, "blue, polypropylene, the type they use to lash down tarpaulins."

"A lorry driver then?" I asked.

"Maybe," he mumbled, "but they usually go for prostitutes not landlords." There was a trace of humour in his tone that suggested he wasn't serious.

He carefully handed the tweezers and their contents to the SOCO, before stepping back to glance quickly around the room, tapping his temple with his finger as he did so. His face wore a mask of concern cut with disappointment.

"Let's get out of here," he said. "It's depressing."

Holmes and I made our way out of the building and along Baker Street to take station away from the activity.

"Who on earth would want to torture and kill a local landlord?" I asked.

"It's a good question, Doc, possibly the one we should try to answer first, but there's another one. Why here? Whoever did this could have done it anywhere. Why did the get pick our local?"

Holmes turned away in frustration and stepped up the street before returning to address me.

"Did you ever play over the fields when you were a kid? Can you remember seeing dead crows pinned to the fences? They used to say the farmers were trying to scare off the other birds. I never believed that. It was a message between people. Why would a crow care about another dead crow? This feels like that. This is a message, but from who to who?"

2

The horrible murder of Davy Arrowsmith occurred not long after what I subsequently chronicled in the Evening Gazette as 'The Case of the Fifty Orange Pills'.

One of the consequences of my ill-fitting prose, which wasn't edited nearly as much as I'd expected, or indeed hoped, was the emergence of Holmes as a local celebrity.

Jordan Dale, my contact at the Gazette, was hungry for a follow up article and had offered to double the fee I'd been paid for my previous article. The publication of my second foray into print, after 'The Case of the Valley Drive Mystery', had led to a spike in the paper's circulation and the editor along with the paper's advertisers were keen to capitalise on this. There was also talk of syndication of my articles across national newspapers including the Sunday Times. The wild idea of a novel was even floated. The problem was that until the unfortunate demise of Davy Arrowsmith, I had nothing else to write about. A frustrated Jordan even suggested I should make something up at one point.

Holmes himself was a fan of my musings. It was somewhat out of character, however he did cut out and piece together my first publication, in order that he could frame and hang it in the prime position above the fireplace in Flat 1B, 22 Baker Street. For a short while, the powered down digital photo frame, which normally took pride of place, took a side seat. Latterly I began to suspect that his creation was not there to proclaim his contribution to the case, but rather to serve as a reminder to me of the erroneous conclusions I had allowed drawn. Either way as Holmesmania grew, so reduced his level of comfort and the article was soon relegated to a position propped against a wall, obscured behind a tottering stack of books.

Then came the event horizon. The point of no return. The renaming of the Baker Street Tavern in his honour. If I were to be cynical, I would suggest the canny landlord of the Tav was trying to blag a ride on the Holmesmania bandwagon, however Mister Pearce assured us this was nothing more than his best way to show thanks to Holmes for what he'd done to protect the youth of the town. Holmes' efforts to remove those evil orange pills from the streets and out of harm's way, said Pearce, showed what an ordinary man could do for his community. It may have been Pearce's clumsy labelling of Holmes as 'ordinary' that seeded the friction between the pair.

Personally I found the thought of a pub called Sherlock's hilarious, more so given how the very suggestion made Holmes squirm. Pearce however was determined to arrange a renaming ceremony in which poor Holmes was to be marched out to pull a cord and reveal the rebranded pub in all its regalia.

It got to the point where Holmes and I couldn't move along Baker Street without Pearce rushing out and chasing us on our journey.

"Mister Holmes, Doctor Watson," he would call. "The sign's coming next week. I only need half an hour of your time."

Holmes' responses varied between a "fuck off" and, on some occasions when he was in a slightly better mood, a "fuck off".

Then one afternoon Holmes seceded. "Okay Michael, if you promise to shut the fuck up, and never speak to me again, I'll do it."

"Brilliant," smiled a victorious Mr Pearce.

"Remember. You'll never speak to me again. Except when you're serving me and Doctor Watson a minimum of five free pints a week."

"Deal," he replied with little time for consideration.

Given recent events, my preference would have been cancellation of the renaming ceremony, however there was a feeling in many quarters that we should try and maintain an air of normality. Not that the renaming of a business after a local unemployed man was particularly normal.

I didn't knock for Holmes on the afternoon of the event. On seeing the throng outside the pub, I decided to lean on the wall of the street opposite Number Twenty-Two in order to capture Holmes' face as the realisation dawned.

As Mary and I stood in wait, his voice sounded from beside us. "Shall we do this?"

How he crept up on the both of us like that is beyond me.

"Hello, hello everyone," he said as we pushed our way to the front of the crowd that included Detective Inspector Lestrade, Superintendent Spaulding and Councillor Raaz, the Mayor of Middlesbrough no less.

Pearce, in his best suit and boots, handed Holmes a cord and asked him to say a few words.

"I name this pub Sherlock's. May God bless her and all who drink in her." With that, he pulled on the cord, and the large red cloth covering the frontage of the pub fell to the floor revealing its all-new livery.

As the applause subsided, a question rang out from the crowd. "Mister Holmes. Paul Williams of the Evening Gazette. What does it feel like to be honoured in this way?"

"Very humbling. I'd like to thank Mister Pearce for the time and investment he's put into creating all this."

"Ian Bullock, Licensed Victuallers Magazine. Will you be drinking in Sherlock's?"

"I may pop my head around the door occasionally. I don't actually drink anymore."

"Really?"

"I don't actually drink any less either."

The crowd murmured with only some identifying his attempt at humour.

"Steve Heighton, Herald and Post. Do you think Cleveland Police would have brought Alistair Bruce to justice if it weren't for your help?"

"I have the utmost confidence in Detective Inspector Lestrade and his colleagues. But if there are ways in which I can assist them, I am very happy to do so."

"Tony Wilkinson, Northern Echo. Do you have a message for the people of the region?"

"Yeah," said Holmes, "don't believe in Batman."

The members of the assembled crowd looked at each other confused before rumbling into applause and muted laughter. Holmes took that as an opportunity to slip away back along Baker Street to his flat.

I reasoned he would come to regret that quip.

As we followed him up the street, I offered Mary a proposal. "Why don't you rename your pub in my honour? 'Doctor Watson's', 'Doctor Watson's Emporium'."

"Yeah," said Mary, "that's not gonna happen."

3

Following the distraction of Holmes' celebrity obligations, we resumed our search for Davy Arrowsmith's killer, said resumption occurring at the doorstep of Arrowsmith's widow.

The home of the Arrowsmiths was a cosy mid-terrace, typical of many properties close to Middlesbrough town centre. Their street, although a distance from Baker Street, consisted of houses of the same pre-war era and red brick construction.

We had actually visited the house on a previous occasion during the unsuccessful investigation of a reality television show, called the Goldfish Bowl, which apparently disappeared overnight. This show was purportedly filmed in a building for which Davy Arrowsmith was the landlord. On that occasion, the intransigent

Mr Arrowsmith had refused our crossing of the threshold.

Holmes tapped on the door and we were greeted by Mrs Arrowsmith, a small homely lady dressed in a smart patterned dress protected by a worn, but spotlessly clean, pinafore. I somehow recognised her but it escaped me from where. I assumed she must have worked in one of the shops in town.

"Hello, Missus Arrowsmith. I'm Sherlock Holmes. I was a friend of David's. D'you mind if we come in?"

"He never mentioned you and no one ever calls him 'David'."

"Yeah, we used to meet up for a beer occasionally."

"He was teetotal."

"He was a good man."

"He was a twat," she sneered, "but I miss him. I don't know what I'm going to do without him." Her lip started to quiver and her eyes shaped into a squint as tears began to roll down her face.

Holmes stepped into the doorway and wrapped his arms around her. "You're going to get through it. That's what people around here do. They bounce back. No matter what's thrown at them, they bounce right back. Doctor, can you please get Missus Arrowsmith a cup of tea? With plenty of sugar."

We sat in the compact sitting room, each of us cradling a china cup of tea.

"Missus Arrowsmith," said Holmes.

"Joan," she insisted.

"Joan, do you mind if I ask you a few questions about Davy?"

"The police have already been here, son. An Inspector Facade was here for over half an hour this morning."

"I'm sure they have. But I've never thought the coppers around here very good. They kind of start with speeding motorists and end with sorting out punch ups in the Lord Raglan. Most of which they start."

"Sherlock Holmes?" she uttered. "I know you. You've been in the Gazette. You're Batman."

"Na, na, na, na, nana, nana," smiled Holmes.

"Was Mister Arrowsmith in any trouble at all?" I asked.

"I don't think so," she answered.

"If he was, you can tell us. We're not the police. All we're interested in is catching whoever did this."

"Sorry, pet, he never told me about his business. The only time I'd get to know if there was ever owt wrong was when he got a strop on. He'd get in some hellish moods."

"What was he like recently?"

"Fine, he seemed happy," she said, her voice starting to crack. "Would you like some corned beef panackelty, boys? There's some in the oven. I can soon warm it up for you."

"It's okay," said Holmes, "we've only just eaten."

Mrs Arrowsmith gave us a quizzical look.

"I'm sorry, lads," she continued, "I cooked and cleaned, he worked and paid the bills, and we went for a fortnight in Tenerifee a couple of times a year. I don't know what he got up to at work, but he wasn't a bad lad. He's never been in any trouble."

She finally succumbed towards the end of the sentence and slipped into tears. In response, Holmes moved across the room and put his arm around her. He gently rocked her and put the side of his head on the top of hers.

"Oh dear," she quivered, "who's gonna tell Pat. He's his best mate. He'll be devastated, the poor lad."

"You could have had some of the old girl's panackelty," I said as we wandered across town to Baker Street.

"I fucking hate corned beef panackelty. You should never cook something that's already been cooked. Especially if it ends up tasting shit."

"What about refried beans? I quite like them on the side of a chilli."

"No, they're fucking horrible as well."

"I'm not sure if she'll cope," I remarked.

"She'll cope," responded Holmes. "It's an instinct bred into her. We all stare down a barrel, only the gun changes. She'll do alright. Better than we would have done if we'd eaten any of that fucking panackelty."

"It's a bit odd that a bloke who didn't drink ended up in a pub dead," I commented.

"There's a lot that doesn't make sense," exhaled Holmes.

4

I spent most of the next day with Mary. Conscious that I'd not been giving her the support the circumstances deserved, I cleared my appointments and took her for lunch at the Purple Pig, an excellent little restaurant on Linthorpe Road, not far from Baker Street.

Mary, as always, was understanding. The most important thing she said was for me to help Holmes find the killer. If anything, her selflessness made me feel worse. I was also a little put out that she saw me as nothing more than Holmes' helper.

In the evening, after dropping Mary at her sister's, I climbed the stairs to Flat 1B to find Holmes laid full length on the settee.

"You're not gonna catch Arrowsmith's killer lying there," I said.

"I'm not sure I want to," replied Holmes.

"What d'you mean?"

"For every inaction, there's an equal and opposite inaction. It's Newton's fourth law of some bollocks or other."

"I'm still not getting you, Sherlock."

"Don't you see, Doc? Every since we started dicking around with all this shit, it's got worse. There was never this type of crime round here before we started taking an interest. It's like Missus flaming Marple. As soon as she shuffles up, you better run like fuck because as sure as hell some poor sod gets his head stoved in with a handy piece of lead piping. It's gotta be her doing all the murders. I'm not too sure about that fucking Poirot either. The little French twat. If we do nothing, perhaps it will just stop. Go back to being how it was. Car theft, the odd bag of weed and the occasional drunken punch up."

"And that's just you," I remarked.

"Ha, nice one," chirped Holmes.

"By the way, Poirot's Belgian."

"Yeah, I know. He manages to mention that in every episode."

"Are you serious, Sherlock?"

"Yup."

"So you've just been lying there all day?"

"Pretty much."

He swivelled round and sat up to face me.

"Don't you see? That message. Nailing poor old Davy out like a crow might have been for our benefit."

"Yeah," I replied, "but I've done some research. Those crows are nailed out by gamekeepers to demonstrate their work to the farmer. Who would we be in that analogy?"

"Good point, mate. It's not like we're recruiting, is it? Besides you get no time off and the pension scheme's bollocks. So who's the farmer? Maybe we should start there."

"It's as good a place as any," I responded.

"I don't know," sighed Holmes. "Yesterday we thought the Lip was the key thing. I don't know where to start but I don't think it's from here. Let's just sack it off and let Lestrade deal with it."

"We can't do that. We're part of this now."

"That's exactly my point and I'm tired. So fucking tired."

I wasn't going to allow his retreat. "Right, Arrowsmith wasn't just killed, he was tortured to death. Was he tortured as some sort of retribution or was the killer after something?"

"After something," replied Holmes. "The wounds were all round his body. The killer was trying different things. They wanted a different result from what they were getting."

"So what was the thing and why wouldn't Davy give it up?"

"There's no way of knowing that. There's no data."

"Then speculate," I shouted. "What did Davy have that no one else did?"

"You mean, guess?"

"No, I mean speculate. What is the balance of probability?"

"I can't imagine that Davy would have anything worth killing for."

"So it's something he didn't have," I said, unsure where I was leading this.

"That could be it," said a muted Holmes. "He wouldn't give him what he wanted, because he couldn't. He didn't have it to give. No matter how bad the torture got, he couldn't get him to stop."

"The torturer clearly didn't think that."

"Maybe not. But then he had less of a stake in the transaction."

"But he's now a murderer?"

"I expect he already was. There's one thing I am certain about."

"What's that?"

"I need a beer."

With the Twisted Lip out of action, we relocated to the paint-scented Sherlock's bar. Holmes scowled disdain as we crossed the door. If his mood was uncertain when we entered, that was clarified a pint and a half of Ragworth Blonde in, when Detective Inspector Lestrade made an appearance.

"What have you got, lad?" asked Lestrade.

"Fuck all," sneered Holmes.

Given all we did have was conjecture, he wasn't far from the truth.

"Why don't you just grab some random couple off the street, I dunno maybe someone mourning the death of child, and beat the holy fuck out of them?" said Holmes.

"Look, Sherlock, there's a murderer out there. A particularly sadistic bastard. We need to put our differences aside."

"No," came a low volume response. "I'm always gonna be different to you. And d'you know what? I think it's about time you omni-skilled twats put a shift in."

Lestrade gave a long, frustrated look accentuated with a threatening nod, before leaving. It was apparent that the once manageable relationship between Holmes and Lestrade had been strained to the break. This was due to a recent event where Lestrade, on Holmes' careless suggestion, had dragged a couple from their home and subjected them to a particularly callous interrogation. I was left with the feeling that Holmes was annoyed by his own contribution to this incident, and he was reflecting his anger back on Lestrade.

"That could have gone better," I said on Lestrade's exit. "I think you might have upset him."

"Yeah, I'll file that under 'couldn't give a shit'."

"I assume you are to keep counsel on this one."

"Yep, I don't want to put any thoughts into Lestrade's head."

"Mmm, no. They might be lonely."

"Good, lad," laughed Holmes. "You know, maybe we do have something to do with this. Maybe everything and nothing."

"I'm not sure I understand you."

"No. I'm not sure I do either. But why the Lip? Why was Davy there? That's our place. I've never seen Davy in there. Why would anyone make that the venue?"

5

We arranged to convene the next morning in Hud Couture on Baker Street. I arrived early to find Martha running through her morning preparations. Since the incident at the Twisted Lip, Martha had been keeping an eye on Mary so I asked her how she felt she was coping. Martha reassured me that, given the circumstances, she was bearing up quite well. She had actually been talking about getting permission to reopen the Twisted Lip. This was not something that Mary had spoken to me about and I assumed she had avoided this discussion to circumvent any barriers my concerns would put before her.

One of the few serious conversations I ever had with Martha was soon curtailed when Holmes crashed in with Mary.

"Get the kettle on, Marth, Mary needs a cup of tea."

"I can put the kettle on but you used the last of the tea bags yesterday."

"Ah, no worries," said Holmes, "I'll go and get a pot of four forty-five from the Kitchen." Without waiting for a reaction, he slipped out the door and along Baker Street.

"John," said Mary as the door clicked shut, "I'm thinking of speaking to the police about reopening the pub."

"I'm not sure about that, Mary. Wouldn't it be better if you left it a few weeks?"

"I'm sick of kicking round. I'd rather just get on with it."

I wasn't sure, but knew that the best person to judge this was Mary herself. I trusted in her for everything else and found it difficult to see how I could contest her view.

Not long after he had left, Holmes kicked back through the door with a largish object wrapped in a tea towel. He placed the object on the counter and unwrapped the tea towel to reveal a large blue and white striped ceramic teapot full of steaming tea.

"Where's the cups, Marth?" he asked gleefully.

"They're in the back," she said. "But there's a little problem, we have no milk."

"There's no such thing as a little problem," he responded jovially. "It's the solution that varies in size. I already have a pint-sized solution for this one." He then pulled a glass bottle of milk from his jacket pocket.

"Sherlock," I said, "Mary's thinking about reopening the Lip."

"Nice one, I'm gasping for a few pints of Digit. Me grey cells think me throat's been cut."

"Do you not think it would be better to leave it a few weeks?"

"Why? Davy will still be dead. And it will still be the scene of a gruesome murder."

"How delicately put, Sherlock," I remarked. "Have you ever thought of a career in clinical psychology?"

"Nah, it's too indoors for me. Actually it's probably better to open sooner. All them sickos coming to see the murder scene will drive the profits up. Mary, can you stick a reserved sign on my table?"

"Well, that settles it then," I responded. "We can have a reopening party."

"That's a bit insensitive, Doc," scowled Holmes in mock derision.

After draining the capacious teapot, Holmes and I set off to "see a man about a hound". Holmes raced along Baker Street, apparently energised by his copious tea intake.

"Where are we off to?" I panted, struggling to maintain his pace.

"To see Pat Wright," he replied.

"Who?"

"Davy's mate, Pat."

Our yomp took us to a grassed area just off Grange Road, behind the Middlesbrough Institute of Modern Art. Holmes strode across the grass to a man exercising a small whippet. At least I think it was small, I'm not sure how big whippets should be. Dressed in a donkey jacket, very similar to Holmes', that appeared to be slung over nothing more than a white vest, the man had a startling resemblance to Arrowsmith.

"Bloody hell, it's Batman and Robin," said the man as we approached.

"Patrick Wright?" asked Holmes.

"Aye, son."

"Joan Arrowsmith told us you and her husband Davy were mates."

"Aye like, Davy was me best mate," he replied with a sternness in his voice that suggested he was masking his true mood.

"If you don't mind me saying," I remarked, "you and Davy are the double of each other."

"Aye, he was a good looking lad, like."

"Do you mind if we ask you a few questions?" asked Holmes.

"Why would I mind?"

"Did Davy have any enemies, anyone with a grudge against him?"

"Someone who might have killed him, you mean?"

"Yeah, I do mean that."

"If I knew that, I'd have done the bastard by now."

"Sorry," sighed Holmes, "I'm struggling to know where to go with this."

"Look, lad, I'll tell you where I'd be looking. A while back, Davy made a lot of money renting out a shitty room above a shop in town. He'd never saw that sort of money before, and he saw nowt like that since. Where there's brass, there's muck."

"The Goldfish Bowl", I recounted.

"Aye, that was it. He said something about that. I used to call him a jammy get, but the money's not much good to him now, is it?"

"None at all," I replied.

"Thank you, Mister Wright," said Holmes, "you've been very helpful."

We both shook Wright's hand and made our way back across the field to Grange Road. As we hit the pavement, Holmes side-glanced a look of faux indignation.

"What?" I protested.

"If this capper gets solved by a bloke who can't even be arsed to put a shirt on, I'll never forgive you."

"Me?" I recoiled. "You never thought of it either."

"I can't think of flaming everything."

The Goldfish Bowl was a reality television show central to one of the early cases Holmes and I had investigated. A group of local youths taking part in the show had approached us when, over the course of one night, it disappeared into the ether. We visited the room in which the show was supposedly being recorded and couldn't find a trace of the show ever being there. That was when we first met Davy Arrowsmith, the landlord of the building the room was in.

We had several theories as to why anyone would go to the trouble to create and then delete a television show, the most compelling being that it was a charade to cover up the robbery of a local bank. Ourselves along with Detective Inspector Lestrade approached the bank with this theory only for them to perform extensive checks and conclude their systems were safe.

In the end, we figured the motive, for this otherwise pointless charade, belonged to the shadowy protagonist of a previous incident. Through me, Holmes had been engaged by two Americans named Smith and Jones wishing to utilise his unique computing talents. Masquerading as FBI agents, they had tricked us into locating a salacious media file which they said had the power to unseat governments both sides of the Atlantic. The file in question ultimately turned up in the possession of Irene Adler, otherwise known as 'the woman'. At the last moment, as a longing-looking Irene was driven away by Agents Smith and Jones, Holmes realised we'd been duped and that a likely consequence would be Irene's death.

A terrifying chase ensued, culminating in the rescue of Irene, the destruction of the file, and the death of the two Americans.

The late Smith and Jones however were no more than foot soldiers. Someone or something, a person or an organisation had employed them to recover that file. When they failed, the focus shifted to us, specifically Sherlock Holmes. The Goldfish Bowl appeared to have been created for our benefit by a mysterious adversary wishing to put us under examination.

The nefarious nemesis theory was to gain credence on a later occasion when we journeyed to Sheffield to track down Martha's estranged husband, Lance Corporal Paul Hudson. To curtail a story I'd really rather not recall in detail, Hudson, while stationed with the Army in Afghanistan had been approached by Smith and Jones. Their intention was to recruit him into the same organisation in which they worked. When it became apparent to Hudson that this organisation was an evil and rather deadly criminal establishment, he recoiled. He escalated the approach of Smith and Jones to his superiors, the outcome being that he was placed in a witness protection programme. The cover story created by the authorities involved Hudson walking to his death in the Afghan desert.

It transpired that Hudson had been singled out because of his association with Holmes. His first assignment was to be the location of the media file that Smith and Jones ultimately came to Middlesbrough to retrieve. The ham-fisted approach of the sausage-fingered Smith and Jones did unveil a clue as to the identity of their employer who they referenced as 'the Professor'.

Pat Wright had a point. Arrowsmith was involved in a transaction with this shadowy character. He had come closer to the Professor than anybody alive at that point. Although his interaction was actually conducted via an email address and a holding company in the Cayman Islands that ultimately disappeared from the face of the Earth, his killer wasn't perhaps to know this.

It made perfect sense. Arrowsmiths' torturer wanted information about our mysterious Professor. Poor Davy couldn't tell him what he didn't know, and this was taken to be good old Teesside intransigence. The interrogation shifted up a couple of gears and in the process Davy's heart gave out.

6

Although we had the semblance of a motive for Arrowsmith's murder, the identity of a suspect remained firmly in the abstract. Given that the killer must have overpowered Arrowsmith, we assumed them to be male. The heinous nature of the crime told us the killer was psychotic. We also reasoned he was looking, for whatever reason, to connect with the Professor. Other than that we had nothing. Given the newly strained relationship between Holmes and Detective Inspector Lestrade of Cleveland Police, we were unlikely to glean anything from the local police force. That was somewhat of a shame given that their forensic examination combined with Holmes' unique perspective may have borne out results.

We sat in Sherlock's, a paralysis of conflicting thoughts muting any discussion. The more idler of my notions caused me to wonder if the Ragworth Blonde served in Sherlock's was too poor a substitute for the elixir of the Engineer's Thumb we once enjoyed a few doors up. It was Holmes who disturbed the prevailing silence with a thoughtful whisper.

"'When we were children, did we chase a snake into the cane fields?'"

I waited for whatever was coming.

"We can't chase him. We don't know where to look. So we need to smoke him out."

"Yes, but how?" I asked.

"By making him think we have what he's after. That we know all about this Professor gadgie."

"And how do we do that?"

"Not 'we', Doc, you. You need to write one of your little stories for the Gazette, and in it suggest we know a little more about the Professor than we actually do."

"Okay," I said, enthusiastic with the approach, "I'll write a story in which we track down the evil Professor X only for him to outsmart us and evade our capture."

"Whoa," said Holmes, "we don't want to make ourselves look like complete twats. Scratch 'outsmart', add something else. Well, just do what you do really, but include something about us knowing who the wanker is."

That evening I set about writing 'The Case of the Goldfish Bowl'. To blend fact with fiction did seem a corruption of my burgeoning literary career, however given the circumstances, this seemed a minor peccadillo that I could fix in a subsequent article.

I caught up with Holmes the next morning in the Baker Street Kitchen. He took the print of my article and leafed through it whilst simultaneously consuming yolk-sodden toast soldiers.

In this version of events, Holmes and I had tracked down Professor X and foiled his attempt of bank robbery at the very last moment. Given this was my first foray into fiction, I did accentuate the contribution of my character somewhat, but felt this justified given I was the author and consequently the de facto owner of the dramatic license.

The story culminated in a chase on foot through Middlesbrough and to the Transporter Bridge where Professor X evaded our grasp by leaping from the river bank and capturing the cradle of the bridge as it made its way across the river. The Professor, who had only just made the jump, clambered over the cradle's gate and waved back at us smiling. Taunted by this, Holmes backed up to attempt the now larger jump himself. If it were not for my intervention, it was certain he would have plunged into the Tees and to his death.

Holmes laughed and smiled throughout the story, which I took as a good sign. When he had finished reading, he placed the manuscript on the table and laughed.

"Bloody hell, Doc, it's a nice little pot-boiler you have there, but it's nothing like your other stories. This Watson character's a piece of work, isn't he? I think you need to tone down the drama a few notches or twelve. Make it more like what you did before."

Somewhat crestfallen, my face dropped.

"It's a good story, Doc, it's just not very realistic," he laughed. "You also need to point it at me a bit more. Turn down the fader on Doctor Watson super sleuth and put the spotlight on me. I need to appear singularly unique."

"I'll take me out altogether, shall I?" I snapped.

"Look," laughed Holmes, "it's only a story. Do you wanna be the bait? Mary's not gonna be happy if it's you who's the next one nailed to the floor of the Lip."

He had a point. I gathered up the papers and without speaking made my way home. Holmes smiled and shook his head as I passed the window.

The rewrite took me the rest of the morning and into the afternoon. Once I was happy that the tone and pace was consistent with my previous work, and that I was little more than the narrator of the piece, I printed out my work and made my way over to Baker Street.

Knocking on the door of Number Twenty-Two to no reply, I looked around the door of the boutique to find Holmes enjoying a cup of tea with Martha.

"Hey look, it's Jules Verne," mocked Holmes as I entered.

Holmes took the printout from me and read it from his position leaning against the shop counter. With none of the merriment of his earlier review, he read through the new pages in silence, occasionally nodding and taking sips from his tea, without ever diverting his focus to locate his cup on the counter beside him.

In this next rendition, we tracked the Professor to his home, a large house in an undefined village in the Teesside locale. A fight ensued between Holmes and the Professor and, although Holmes was triumphant, he was left with a dilemma. He could shoot the Professor using a weapon he'd disarmed from him during the struggle, or he could turn him over to the police. Unsure of the evidence against the Professor, Holmes favoured the latter.

But that was not the dilemma. The Professor ranked high in a sprawling organised crime cartel. Holmes had to let him walk free or suffer the retribution of his partners in crime. Said retribution included harm to us, our friends, our family, and 'the occasional school or hospital perhaps'. Holmes fixed the Professor with a long dead-eyed stare before stooping to place the gun on the floor in front of them. "You take care," said Holmes as he left the room. "We don't want you having an accident. Teesside can be a dangerous place when it wants to be."

The bit I thought most clever was that the article served as a warning to the Professor. The people of Teesside were now aware of him and it was therefore in his interest to stay away.

"It's very good," commented Holmes, "but it's also still no good."

"Oh come on," I protested.

"The story's fine, very much like the last one. It's just too explicit. We need to make him think we're hiding something. It's about suggestion, not statement. People leak information. We need to do something similar. You know like the way a cheating husband will casually mention the name of the woman he's screwing to his wife, 'Charlotte said something funny at work today.' 'Are you having an affair?' 'No way, she's ginger!' That kind of thing. You also need to weave in a bit of ambiguity. Get him intrigued. Don't tell him I know where this Professor bloke is, but suggest there's a strong possibility I might. You need to write between the lines."

"What d'you mean? Some sort of subliminal message?"

"Yeah, that's it. Even the words you select should suggest a subtext. They need to add texture."

"I'll have a go," I said, "but it all sounds a bit above me."

"Nah, Doc, you're a natural. You don't always shed light, but you shine like a star."

I hacked the story to bits that night. It is a lot harder than you might imagine to 'write between the lines'. The result was a piece which told a similar story to the previous one but with holes left for the reader to fill. That was my attempt at ambiguity. Had I left these gaps for the sake of brevity, or was there something I deliberately wasn't saying?

Being unsure of my output, I chose not to waste any more paper on it. Instead I slung my laptop under my elbow and made my way to the Baker Street Kitchen. Arriving just as it opened, I ordered a pot of tea and flicked open the laptop to give my work a last minute proof.

Holmes rolled up forty to forty-five minutes later. He placed his usual order of three soft-boiled eggs, four pieces of toast and a pot of tea at the counter, before taking a seat at my table. On his gesture, I slid over the laptop.

"You need a new computer," he said. "Hang on a bit."

With a few keyboard strokes, he opened a black window and started writing illegible commands to it in white text. After no more than a few minutes, he popped the window closed. "There you go," he said, "I've tuned her for you."

Taking a cup from my teapot in the absence of his own, he toggled back to my story and started to work his way through it intently. He read in absolute silence, transfixed to the point where he ignored the arrival of his breakfast. On the completion of his review, he sat back in his chair, exhaling through his nostrils as he travelled. He then noticed his cooling breakfast with an element of pleasant surprise.

"Perfect," he said thoughtfully, his mind already focused on what was to happen next. "You get that into the Gazette and I'll dig out me Hong Kong Book of Kung Fu. You haven't got a claw hammer, have yer?"

7

'The Case of the Goldfish Bowl' was published in the Evening Gazette the following Thursday. Having read it first online, I made my way into town to pick up a few hard copies from one of the street sellers.

I remember an odd feeling that I was being watched. I glanced round but saw nothing of particular concern barring an old vagrant huddled in a doorway. I was sure I'd seen him there before.

The next thing I was aware of was a thud from behind at the base of my neck. As I fought the sickly feeling that was depriving me of my consciousness, I was steadied by an individual. Through my unfocused view, I could still recognise the outline of the vagrant I'd seen earlier. I looked down to my chest to see that the hand steadying me was grasping a blade. By this point, I was operating on nothing more than instinct. My instinct and the knife told me to go where I was led. I remember a glass door, some wooden stairs, which were a struggle to climb although aided, and not much else.

I came to in the upstairs room of the Twisted Lip strapped to a chair. My instinct was to struggle, however the ties that bound both my hands and legs gave up little. In my mind's eye, I saw Davy Arrowsmith in exactly the same predicament.

The fog cleared from my eyes to reveal my assailant. Tall, blond and military in frame, he strode around on the exposed floorboards. He still wore the clothes of a vagrant, which lacked harmony with his physique. Oddly, the main thing that struck me was his smell. His smell was soaped and perfumed, and opposed to the aroma you would expect to emanate from a tramp and his garb.

"Doctor Watson, good afternoon," he said. "I thought you weren't joining me for a moment there. Colonel Sebastian Moran at your service, sir. I have a few questions for you. You're not going anywhere, are you?"

I sat silent not knowing how to respond as he looked me up and down to emphasise my predicament.

"Seemingly not," he remarked.

He then walked over to one of the tables, the floorboards creaking under his foot. He picked something from the table that sounded metallic in nature as he rolled it into his grasp.

I was horrified when I saw the four six-inch nails, similar to those used to pin Arrowsmith, a few feet from my face. To reinforce his intention, he rubbed the heads of the nails across my cheek.

"You know, Doctor, my line of work is such a lonely road. I thought after twenty-five years in the army, I'd enjoy going freelance, but I do miss the camaraderie. Don't get me wrong, I still enjoy the killing, but it's not as much fun when you can't have a beer and a laugh about it afterwards."

I chose to remain silent, reasoning that the longer he rambled on the more chance there would be of someone discovering us. With the Twisted Lip closed for business, my plight seemed desperate. Sooner or later, Mary or Holmes would notice my absence but that might take hours. I could only have minutes.

"Of course, Doctor, you must know what it's like for career military men like me to leave their work and their comrades behind. Can you see where I left my hammer?"

"Stop killing, then," I interjected, feeling I needed to somehow divert the path of oncoming events.

"Sorry?" came the puzzled response.

"It's generally accepted that when you go through a major change in your life, it's better to leave as much of the old situation behind as you can."

"Really?" replied Moran, pausing to think. "You know, normally I would believe you, but given your current situation I'm reasoning your therapy maybe a little biased. Thanks for the advice though, I will consider it."

He turned to walk away from me before spinning back around. "Mmm, nope. I've considered it and it's a no. Killing is the only pleasure I have left in life. It's ironic really, but killing is the only thing I have to remind me I'm still alive."

"You're suffering from a post traumatic stress disorder. You can be treated. I could treat you."

"No, Doctor, I've always enjoyed killing. That's why I signed up. I think it stems from my childhood when I used to off the neighbours' cats with my air rifle."

"What are you going to do?" I asked, figuring that I needed to switch from my current tack which appeared to be heightening my predicament.

"That's up to you," he replied. "If you tell me what I need to know, I might not nail you to the floor. FYI that's not a metaphor. I intend to use these nails. Now, where did I put that hammer?"

"I'll tell you whatever you want."

"Excellent. This Professor X chappie, where can I find him?"

"I swear I honestly don't know."

"Ah, that's a shame. That's more or less what the last chap said. This is getting a bit dull now."

"He didn't know either."

"But your article in the Gazette said you did. It stopped only just short of giving me his postcode."

"It was written for you. To make you think we knew who he was." By now honesty was the only remaining policy. "It was designed to draw you out into the open."

"Really, really? Well, that is clever."

"Why do you need to contact him anyway?" I asked, again trying to tack against the prevailing wind.

"Oooh, you're like Jeremy Paxman, aren't you? Oh yes!" he exclaimed. "This is one of them scenarios, isn't it? You know, where cos you're gonna die, I tell you everything. Actually you are going to die and so I'm not overly bothered what you know. You see, Doctor, being a career criminal, especially when you're as talented as I am, can be a very lonely existence. All these brilliant things that I do and I can't tell a soul about them. It could drive you insane.

"Then there's the ideas. Oh, those wonderful ideas. But the really good ones, the magnificent ones, are generally more than a one man job. Can you see my problem, Doctor? I can't scale. I did have a career plan. I was in discussions with two chaps I bumped into over in Bastion. Unfortunately, they were involved in a bit of a car accident. Not far from here actually. Hence the need for me to go direct to the organist, and for you to tell me how to get in touch with him."

"I don't know who or where he is. That's the truth."

"I don't believe you," he sang, before driving his fist into my ribs.

With the breath driven out of me, I struggled to respond. "Why would I lie?" I wheezed.

"I don't know, you're the psychologist," he retorted before swinging the back of his knuckle across my chin. As I sputtered on the blood seeping from my mouth, Moran stepped up and down in front of me. He could only have been considering his next blow.

"You know," he said, "I thought this Professor X, as you call him, was supposed to be ubiquitous, eyes and ears everywhere. The all-seeing eye. I was sure I was being surveilled and that pulling you would be enough to encourage an audience with the great man. That's disappointing. I hope it's you and not me he doesn't give a shit about."

"Maybe he's just running a bit late," I retorted, in some pain.

"Ha ha," he exclaimed, "I seem to have had the same plan yourself and Holmes had. You know, entice the quarry into the open." With that, he drove his heavy-booted foot into my shin.

As I squirmed in pain, determined not to cry out, I heard the steps of someone slowly making their way up the staircase.

"This could be him now," said Moran. "Oh dear, this is hardly the attire for a job interview."

I looked up with some relief to see the figure of Holmes emerging up the stairs.

"Aright," he said. "I think I'm your huckleberry."

"Sherlock, he's got a knife," I warned.

"But I prefer to use my hammer," added Moran. "Ah, here it is. It was in my pocket all the time. Actually this isn't my pocket. I need to point out these aren't my clothes, they're just a disguise. Do you have a weapon, Sherlock?"

"Just this," replied Holmes, tapping his temple with his forefinger.

"So much for you being the bait," I grimaced, still reeling from the pain occupying the length of my body.

"Yeah, that was always going to be you," responded Holmes. "A military man was never going to stage a full-frontal assault."

"Military man?" I exclaimed, feeling I'd somehow been left out of the picture.

"Sorry," continued Holmes, "who but a trained killer would be so desensitised to suffering and death. It was always going to be you he pulled, and he was always going to bring you here."

"So if you knew all this what took you so long getting here?"

"I was finishing my tea," said Holmes nonchalantly. "Four minutes, forty-five seconds exactly. Bang on again."

"Sherlock!" I protested disconsolately.

"It was good tea," came the retort.

"Excuse me, gentlemen," interrupted Moran. "Any chance we could we return to the case in point here?"

"Yes," responded Holmes. "How rude, Doctor."

"We haven't even been introduced," added Moran. "Colonel Sebastian Moran, at your service."

"Supreme Commander Sherlock Holmes," came the mocking response. "Shall I start the twatting now, then?" he whispered, his face fixed in a deadly stare.

Moran feigned confusion. "I have a weapon, a hammer, and you just have a head, that I'm going to hit with the hammer."

"No yer not," said Holmes, grabbing a chair and, in a single action, crashing it into Moran's side. Moran, swept by the blow, collapsed over a table, flattening the table and dropping his hammer as he went. The hammer skidded across the floor to rest directly under the chair I was sitting on.

Holmes looked at the remnants of the chair to see only the back and two rear legs remained. Dismissing its usefulness, he flung the woodwork at his opponent. Moran, still prone on the floor, rolled to avoid it, returning to his feet in the process. Holmes who had by now selected another chair, squared off to Moran, who in response grabbed a chair of his own.

The two opposed each other like mirrored lion tamers, each feinting to provoke an action out of the other. Holmes, who to this point had been the constant aggressor, lurched forward, entangling the legs of his chair into the one held by Moran. The two grappled as two stags in the rutting season. Given their respective statures, Holmes competed well, his balance compensating for Moran's greater upper body strength.

As they manoeuvred around the floor, their feet sliding and stamping as each resisted the other's force, they moved closer and closer to where I was sitting, immobilised by my ties. As they approached, the thought flashed through my mind that I could flip onto my side to avoid their advance. Reasoning that this would leave me more exposed, I decided against that course of action.

Just as I'd feared, their struggle took them exactly in my direction, until the point where they stood either side of me. I had to crick my neck to avoid the bridge of the chairs overhead. Mid-struggle, Holmes looked down at me, winked and snapped a brief grin. On the opposite side of the equation, I could hear the action of Moran's foot apparently trying to dislocate the hammer from below me.

I held my breath as the two edged slowly across me, only resuming respiration when they reached what I considered to be a comfortable distance. My respite was short-lived. Holmes, seeking to break the deadlock, flicked his wrists unhooking himself enough to make a swing into Moran's flank. Moran, although unbalanced, was aware enough to pivot and block. The blow however caused him to sprawl across the room, his momentum arrested by the collapse of another table.

Holmes, looking to take advantage, rushed him only for Moran to evade and trip the oncoming Holmes. Holmes crashed to the floor, tumbling through the legs of another two tables before coming to a rest. They both jumped up and scrambled to re-arm before resuming their earlier face-off.

With both of them panting heavily and showing signs of the struggle, they edged slowly round, each valuing the lull in hostilities.

"You're quite an adversary," breathed Moran.

"You're not," sneered Holmes, only for Moran to laugh in response.

Moran sharply crossed his wrists, propelling his chair in the direction of Holmes. Holmes swung like a batsman driving for the boundary. On contact, the two chairs shattered, scattering wooden shrapnel across the bar. Mid-action, Moran turned on his heels and made off back down the stairs.

Holmes spent a fraction of a second surveying the resulting carnage. Other than the chair I was strapped to, not a single stick of furniture remained intact.

"I won't mention this to Mary if you don't. Anyway, back in a bit," he said before clattering down the stairs in pursuit.

"Sherlock," I called, "take the hammer."

As the dust settled both literally and figuratively, I was concerned for Sherlock's welfare. He'd more than held his own in the tussle with Moran, but in different circumstances there was every possibility he would not fare so well. Moran after all was both a trained soldier and a sadistic killer.

My immediate predicament however concerned the few lengths of polypropylene rope that bound my wrists and ankles. With my options limited, I started to cry for help, my hope being that the door to the bar had been left open and my calls would be audible from the street.

It wasn't actually that long before I was discovered, my saviours coming in the form of two sisters of pensionable age named Norma and Valerie.

They cautiously made their way up the stairs to be confronted by the aftermath of the battle. Surprisingly unperturbed by the scene of devastation, they began an interrogation.

"What the hell's going on here, like?" asked Norma.

"It's a long story," I sighed. "Can you try and untie me, please?"

They both looked at me suspiciously.

"Be careful, Norma, he looks like a wrong un," warned Valerie.

"Okay," I said, "don't untie me, but please go and find me someone who will, the police, anyone."

After a short period of negotiation, Norma left to locate assistance, that coming in the form of a community police officer. While she did, Valerie stood guard, a chair leg as a makeshift weapon. Even then my release wasn't straightforward and it took a call to Lestrade before my bonds were released.

I limped the short distance along Baker Street to Hud Couture to find Martha at work behind the counter. With my distress apparent from both my movement and the coagulated blood on my face, Martha broke off with concern.

"What the hell's happened to you?" she said, coming close to inspect my wounds.

"We found Arrowsmith's killer," I replied.

"I can see you have," she said. "Where's Sherlock?"

"He's gone after him."

Her whole body relaxed in despair, her mouth wide as her mind cycled through the possibilities.

"It's okay," I consoled, "he can handle himself."

"He thinks he can," came the concerned response.

I laid the hammer and rope I'd carried back from the Twisted Lip on the counter. On seeing this, Martha's confusion and concern elevated.

"He'll be fine," I said, my reassurances doing little to allay her concerns.

A while later Holmes staggered into the boutique looking like he'd finished outside the medals in a face kicking contest.

Martha gasped at the sight, pulling a chair from behind the counter for him to rest upon.

"My god," she exclaimed before running into the back for a first aid kit. Her attention noticeably more intimate than she had afforded me earlier, she dabbed antiseptic on the various cuts and bruises that ruined his face.

"You should have seen the other bloke," said Holmes, wincing through the application of Martha's treatment.

"Really?" I queried.

"Yeah," said Holmes, "not a mark on him."

I only have Holmes' account of the intervening events, however I can tell you that in all the time I knew him I never once found him prone to exaggeration or false witness. If anything the converse was true and his tendency would be to underplay.

Holmes had chased Moran down Linthorpe Road at what he described as "top speed". When they reached the Central Park restaurant, Moran swung into Albert Park. Soon after, as they reached the Brian Clough statue, Moran slowed up and turned to face Holmes. Maintaining his momentum, Holmes had clattered into him. In his words, it was "like hitting a brick shithouse's big brother". With every breath knocked from him, Holmes lay prostrate on the grass.

Moran, who had fared a lot better in the transaction, rose to his feet and started raining kicks into Holmes' head and body, occasionally stooping to supplement a round-armed fist. The more Holmes tried to recover, the more savage the beating become. In the end, his only option was to stay still.

On the cessation of the violence, Moran delivered one final consolation kick and left a prone and motionless Holmes for dead. Holmes, drawing on the dregs of his strength, rolled over to lie on his back and looked up to the statue of Clough, shadowing over him in the sun. "Sorry, Brian," he'd mouthed.

Holmes gave a brief laugh, grimacing in pain as he did. "I'm sure Brian looked down on me and replied, 'That's Mister Clough to you, son'."

"We'll never find him now," I said. "All we have is this hammer and some old rope."

"It's new rope," coughed Holmes, "and I think you're right. He won't like being exposed. He'll go to ground."

"You're not thinking of carrying on this madness, are you?" interjected Martha.

"Am I bollocks," said Holmes. "I've found the killer, it's up to Lestrade to catch the twat."

"We've found the killer," I interrupted, pointing at my less impressive wounds.

"We've found the killer," chimed Holmes, laughing, spluttering blood and wincing in fractured harmony.

Lestrade arrived at the boutique with little compassion for our respective injuries.

"What the fuck have you two been up to?" he asked.

"We walked into a car door," retorted Holmes.

"How many times?" replied Lestrade.

"We found Arrowsmith's killer," I said, trying to drive us to the point.

"Oh aye, a bit handy, is he?"

"Very," I continued. "He's ex-military. Colonel Sebastian Moran."

"Never heard of him. Where is he now?"

"We lost him," I responded. "He got away."

"Amateurs," snipped Lestrade. "Leave it with me."

It soon became obvious that we needed the machine that Lestrade commanded nearly as much as he needed the method provided by Holmes. Within hours, he had Sebastian Moran's picture splattered across newspaper websites and the bulletins of the local television news. Shortly afterwards, the story came to national attention.

The centrepiece of the campaign was a live television news conference. Lestrade gave Holmes and I little choice but to be involved. It was standard stuff really. We sat behind a long table, Lestrade central with Holmes and I to one side, whilst Superintendent Spaulding and a couple of other police officers sat at the other. Posted behind us were several large photographs of Sebastian Moran.

Lestrade's rhetoric was much like you will have heard before. He warned the public to be extra vigilant and, under no circumstances, to approach Moran, who he described as extremely dangerous. As he did so, he paused as if to make reference to the injuries visible on Holmes and myself.

The Q and A that followed was largely inane and pointless. The only memorable interaction related to a question pointed at Holmes by one of the assembled journalists.

"Do you have anything to say, Mister Holmes?" she asked.

"Yeah, he knows where I drink," was the response.

I pulled Holmes up as we filed away under the chatter of camera shutter noise. "What was all that about?" I asked. "Are you wanting round three?"

"No," protested Holmes. "I was meaning a man's drinking place should be sacred."

I was unconvinced.

I left the room with the feeling that the capture of Sebastian Moran would not be possible without the considerable assistance of the people of the Republic of Teesside. He was a soldier. Camouflage was his thing. We needed every set of eyes available.

Mary reopened the Twisted Lip that night with little ceremony. After a brief examination of the devastation upstairs, the police concluded that there was little more to be gleaned in the way of evidence useful in the search for Moran.

As we sat reminiscing with the familiar mistress of a pint of Engineer's Thumb, Lestrade entered.

"Ah, Inspector La La," said Holmes, "I was wondering when you'd shuffle up. Where are the rest of the Teletubbies?"

I actually welcomed the return of Holmes' childish goading. After a period of hostility between the two, it felt like normal service was resuming.

Lestrade didn't respond other than to join us, placing the hammer and rope I collected earlier on the table in front of us. Both were now sheathed in evidence bags.

"So this appears to be all we have in the way of evidence," he commented. "A hammer and a few pieces of old rope."

"It's new rope," said Holmes.

"You pointed that out earlier," I said. "What difference does it make?"

"Not much, except it will have been bought recently."

"They must sell hundreds of miles of that stuff," said Lestrade.

"Yeah, but you don't buy a hammer everyday. I remember me dad coming home with one. It hung in the shed for years. That one is brand new. I'd be looking for a little hardware shop somewhere south of here that's recently sold a hammer and some rope to the same bloke."

"South?" queried Lestrade.

"That's the direction he legged it in. He's not from round here so he probably won't know the area. There's every chance he ran through the only part of town he was familiar with."

"This all makes perfect sense, Sherlock," I said, "but how will knowing where he shopped help us find him? I don't think he'll be making a repeat purchase."

"No," agreed Holmes, "but it will give the inspector and his boys an area to focus their search on. If you find the shop, draw a line between here and there, you'll find where he was staying somewhere along it, probably on the far side of the shop. He might even still be there."

Lestrade nodded in agreement.

"Actually that's interesting," continued Holmes. "Where could he stay that doesn't leave a trail. You can buy hardware with cash but a room generally needs some form of identification."

"Perhaps he's just broken into somewhere," I suggested. "He had no problem breaking into this place."

"Maybe," said Holmes, "but he smelled too clean to be squatting in some foisty old gaff. He has the use of a shower and was sleeping in laundered bed linen."

His eyes scanned the air. "His clothes," he said in almost a whisper. "They were the perfect camouflage when he was crouched in a doorway waiting to jump out on Arrowsmith and the Doc, but in other locations he would stick out like a sore thumb. He'd look out of place in a street of houses. We're looking for some sort of hostel or a Dexy's Midnight Runners gig."

"And you think he could still be around here?" asked Lestrade.

"Impossible to know," said Holmes. "It depends on what he has decided to do given the heat he's generated: withdraw or dig in."

The next day, Lestrade's men located a hardware store, the owner of which recalled selling a claw hammer, some polypropylene rope and a bag of six-inch nails to a man answering to Moran's description.

A short distance to the south, they identified Saint Martin's, a rundown church that offered refuge to ex-servicemen struggling with their luck. It was the perfect hiding place for Moran. He would be more than comfortable exchanging war stories with the staff and the rest of the clientele. Any tweaks required to his back-story for the sake of anonymity would be minimal.

Armed police took station in adjacent buildings and provided surveillance on the comings and goings whilst they awaited orders. A man of similar build and gait to Moran was observed leaving and returning, however Lestrade decided against taking the shot. That was the arrogance of Moran. Even with the whole of Teesside on the look out for him, he still had the effrontery to nip down the shops for a box of cigarettes.

At two in the morning, the church was stormed. Moran, who was armed with a semi-automatic pistol, unleashed a few shots but in the face of an inevitable conclusion, he surrendered without further resistance.

Our reunion with Sebastian Moran came at his pre-trial hearing. Although the damage Moran had inflicted on Holmes' person had done little to subside, the remodelling of Moran's features by Lestrade and his men was factors worse. It was clearly a much bigger car door that he'd come into contact with.

One of the magistrates referenced Moran's state before the proceedings officially commenced. "This prisoner seems to be in some distress?"

"Yes, Your Worship," replied Lestrade, "the prisoner did sustain some minor injuries in his attempts to resist arrest."

"He must have put up quite some resistance," commented the magistrate.

"It was significant, Your Worship."

"The prosecution are to be presenting a written confession?"

"I believe so, sir."

"Given his state, this may well have to be excluded."

"Oh, for fuck's sake," said Holmes, slightly louder than he perhaps intended.

"And who are you?" asked the magistrate, annoyed by the interjection.

"Sherlock Holmes."

"Ah yes, our local vigilante."

"Consulting detective."

"Mister Holmes, you will be quiet or I will hold you in contempt."

"You haven't started yet," sniped Holmes to the elevation of the magistrate's annoyance.

Despite the exclusion of the confession, the evidence against Moran was compelling and it was no more than a formality that the case was passed up to the Crown Court. Given the seriousness of the offences, which included abduction, grievous bodily harm, possession of a firearm, torture and murder, bail was not forthcoming. He was remanded in Holme House prison until his trial.

As he was led away, Moran gave Holmes a menacing stare. Holmes smiled confidently back at him and pursed him a kiss, flicking his eyebrows in the same action.

9

Holmes rarely made much of his achievements, except in jest. If anything, he played them down. There was occasionally a faint aura of self-actualisation, and this was perhaps the one thing that suggested he might actually be human. The bizarre thing was this seemed to occur on the most trivial of outcomes.

The arrest of Sebastian Moran was, to my mind, a major success. He had conjured it up from nothing and that a psychotic menace such as Moran no longer stalked the streets was a result for all.

Holmes appeared freakishly unmoved by the outcome. He curried no reward, personal or otherwise, from the capture of Arrowsmith's killer. His prevailing mood seemed to me to be one of distraction.

Our celebration in the Twisted Lip was muted.

"Are you okay, Sherlock?" I asked.

"Yeah, fine, Doc," he responded.

"That was quite a result you pulled together there."

"Don't play down your part in it all," he smiled.

The session was fading to its conclusion when Lestrade stepped in. "That turned out quite well," he said as he scraped back a chair to join us.

"It doesn't feel like that," said Holmes. "I've been battered from arsehole to breakfast."

"You'll heal," he responded, "and don't worry, we gave him plenty back."

"Yeah, I noticed that," sighed Holmes. "Shame it made such a cow's arse of the confession."

"Ah, don't worry about that. Anyway, I just thought I'd pop my head round. I can't sit and chat, Missus L has got something in the oven."

Holmes turned to me on Lestrade's exit. "On a scale of one to twat, he's a twat." He then sighed. "I've got to bail, Doc, I'm absolutely knackered."

We turned out of the pub to see Lestrade striding down the street. He had almost travelled the distance to his car, parked a hundred or so yards away. Holmes twitched, his jaw dropping before he sprung to sprint after him. He caught up to Lestrade just as he was pressing his fob to open the door. Holmes collided with him, sending them both skidding along the pavement. In the same instant, Lestrade's car exploded in flames, showering metal and glass as far as the spot where I was stood rooted.

They were dead. They had to be. I ran down the street to where they were laid and pulled on Holmes' jacket, rolling him from his position on top of Lestrade. He stared back at me, eyes and mouth wide open.

"Fuck," he gasped.

Rolling onto his back, he staggered to his feet with some assistance from myself. He stabilised before returning to where Lestrade was lying motionless. Pressing two sooty fingers into the side of the inspector's neck, he looked to me with some concern.

"Call an ambulance, John. The good news is he's alive," he said before appending, "Just like the bad news then," in a mutter.

As I dialled, Holmes returned his attention to Lestrade. "Come on, you fucker, wake up! It doesn't end like this. Come on!" he called, his voice escalating to a shout.

Holmes sat on the pavement next to Lestrade, his hand on his shoulder until the ambulance arrived. When it did, he assisted the paramedics in easing Lestrade onto the stretcher and then with its transit into the van. His hand followed the backdoor as the medic closed it from within.

Holmes stood motionless watching as the ambulance trundled down Baker Street. As it turned into Albert Road, the blue lights flashed, the siren hailed and Holmes slumped back down to the road. He looked up at me, sat with his wrists on his arched knees. "What the fuck's going on, Doc?"

He then turned his attention to his coat which was shredded and singed from the explosion. "Bollocks," he muttered, "my jacket's buggered."

He lay back on the asphalt, his eyes scanning the early evening sky as if in search of an explanation.

NOT THE END...

Holmes will return in
Holmes Volume 2: The Blue Debacle, due out 2016.

THE IRREGULARS

Many thanks to all the poor souls who suffered early drafts of these stories. Your feedback and encouragement was and will always be very much appreciated.

Caroline Berry
Claire Bradshaw
Garry Brazier
Steve Bolton
Ian Bullock
Laura Cousins
Andy Flesher
David Forrest
Nick Hannah
Allison Hatchell
Mark Heard
Steve Heighton
Kirsti Hyne
Matt Holmes
Helen Jarosz
Anthony Jones
Matt Lancashire
Andy Leivers
Anita Leversidge
Chris Lofthouse
Julie Lofthouse
Damian Lord
John Lupton

Robert L Marcum
Stuart McCallum
Tim Milson
John Nicholson
Simon Peacock
Cathryn Pearce
Michael Pearce
Michael Richardson
Kevin Rigley
Julie Simpson
Andrew Stevenson
Michael Stevenson
Michael Streets
Gary Tennant
Roy Tomlinson
Joanne Vernon Cook
Richard Walker
Jon Wall
Mark Webber
Paul Williams
Tony Wilkinson
Andrew Wilson
Tom Wharton